"It's okay," Amanda heard him say. **"You're out."**

"I..."

"You're bleeding," he said suddenly, sharply.

She realized it hadn't been rainwater she'd felt dripping down her face. And then Adam was touching her cheek. It was so cold out, or she was in shock because just that touch felt almost unbearably warm. Hot, even. It sent a jolt through her that brought her back to her senses.

"The car," she moaned, hating that she was leaning on him but unable to quite find her footing. Even as she looked, the rain was dousing the flames, yet she could see how badly the car was damaged.

Adam was looking at Amanda's head now, gently pushing her hair back to inspect. "Look at me." She didn't want to look at him, not him. "Amanda, look at me. Forget who I am for a moment. You hit your head and I need to see your eyes."

She looked up then. Odd. She didn't remember his eyes being that dark. They were the same color as the sky, gray, stormy.

And worried.

That was sweet. She almost smiled. Then she remembered who he was.

* * *

Be sure to check out the rest of the books in this miniseries.

Cutter's Code: A clever and mysterious canine helps a group of secret operatives crack the case

* * *

If you're on Twitter, tell us what you think of Harlequin Romantic Suspense! #harlequinromsuspense

Dear Reader,

When writing a long (this is book eleven!) series like Cutter's Code, there are always secondary characters that stick in your mind. Characters who, when you finish the book, make you think, "Hmm. Maybe someday..."

Amanda Bonner was one of those. A fatal shooting brought her into the life of Quinn Foxworth years ago, even before his own life was turned around by Hayley Cole and her dog, Cutter. And I always intended to go back and see how she was doing after the night that fractured her life. When I did, I discovered that a lot more had happened that night than I'd ever realized.

So now that clever canine Cutter has made it clear she has a problem, the Foxworth Foundation, and perhaps only the Foxworth Foundation—and Cutter—can help her. And it brings back into her life the very man she has blamed all this time for the shooting that destroyed her world.

I hope you enjoy the read as much as I enjoyed bringing some happiness to two lost souls.

Justine

OPERATION
SECOND CHANCE

Justine Davis

HARLEQUIN

ROMANTIC
SUSPENSE

Recycling programs for this product may not exist in your area.

ISBN-13: 978-1-335-62654-7

Operation Second Chance

Copyright © 2020 by Janice Davis Smith

This edition published by arrangement with Harlequin Books S.A.

For questions and comments about the quality of this book, please contact us at CustomerService@Harlequin.com.

Harlequin Enterprises ULC
22 Adelaide St. West, 40th Floor
Toronto, Ontario M5H 4E3, Canada
www.Harlequin.com

Printed in U.S.A.

Justine Davis lives on Puget Sound in Washington State, watching big ships and the occasional submarine go by and sharing the neighborhood with assorted wildlife, including a pair of bald eagles, deer, a bear or two, and a tailless raccoon. In the few hours when she's not planning, plotting or writing her next book, her favorite things are photography, knitting her way through a huge yarn stash and driving her restored 1967 Corvette roadster—top down, of course.

Connect with Justine on her website, justinedavis.com, at Twitter.com/justine_d_davis or on Facebook at Facebook.com/justinedaredavis.

Visit the Author Profile page at Harlequin.com, or justinedavis.com, for more titles.

For Molly.

We rescued her after she ran away from her old home. It was always a point of pride that she never wanted to run away from us. She was meant to be mine, but she was really my dad's best friend. My brother's, too.

For sixteen years (I can't believe it!) we were greeted by the rapid thump of her tail when we walked through the door. My dad and I taught her to howl on command—we'd sit on the floor in front of the couch and howl together. She loved tennis balls, chasing after birds and the extra ice that slipped out of the ice maker.

She had the softest golden fur, freckles on her nose and big trusting eyes. I'm convinced I'll never meet another like her, and I'm okay with that—she deserves to be irreplaceable. The joy she brought to our home cannot be measured; I am lucky to have known a spirit like hers.

We love you, Hooch.

—Shannon, Brandon and Dad

This is the latest in a series of dedications from readers who have shared the pain of the loss of a beloved dog. Since I personally knew Molly (and my dog still looks for her every time we visit) I truly understand the pain of missing that tail that, even when she had the shakes and could no longer see or hear well, never stopped wagging. There's a lesson for all of us in that, I think.

Chapter 1

It took every bit of determination Amanda Bonner had in her to walk across that grassy stretch once more. She knew the way so well it didn't matter that it was still dark, sunrise not coming until seven thirty this time of year in the Northwest. In fact, she was surprised there wasn't a path worn by her feet, so many times had she been here.

Amanda wished she could make the change, move from mourning her father's death with visits to this quiet cemetery on that grim anniversary to celebrating that he had lived and loved her by visiting on his birthday instead. But it had been five years, and she felt no closer to being able to do that.

She'd reached it, that cold, metallic rectangle set in the grass. The small flag that was always there was slightly crooked, and she straightened it with the same reverence her father would have shown. The grave site was tidy, well kept, but the department saw to that. Cops took care of their own, even, or perhaps especially when one of them had gone down in the line of duty. They all knew they could be next.

Amanda stared down at the marker. She couldn't see the letters in the darkness, but she didn't need to. Her father's name, and the dates of his birth and death, separated by that line, that short, featureless line that was a pitiful stand-in for the years between, for all the joy and pain, for a life.

In her mind she heard his voice, so clearly, at the funeral of the mother who had been gone for so long now. "It's the hyphen, Mandy," he'd said, using the nickname she'd hated, but now would give anything to hear again. "It's not the dates that matter, it's the hyphen. It stands for everything in between. The life you live. Do it right."

He'd done it right. He'd been her hero, and in the end a hero to many more. He'd died doing what he'd sworn to do, protect and serve. He'd saved lives. Not to mention the countless other lives he'd touched, people he'd helped simply by doing his job.

She knelt beside the grave marker, reaching out to touch it. The metal was cold, not at all comforting, but she did it anyway, tracing the letters, avoiding the numbers.

Her throat tightened, and she had to swallow hard, then again, then a third time. She shivered. Despite her determination her eyes filled. She fought it. She was twenty-eight years old, damn it, her father had been dead for five years, and she should be in control of this by now.

She felt no presence, no warmth, no sensation of closeness. She hadn't expected to. She wasn't even sure why she kept coming; wherever her father was, if anywhere, it wasn't here. But it was the only physical place she had, so she came.

She put the blanket she carried down on the grass,

then sat on it, facing the mountains to the east. She pulled her knees up and wrapped her arms around them, huddling against the December predawn chill as she waited for the sunrise.

Adam Kirk fumbled with the strip of fabric at his neck. It was one of the things he hadn't yet found the solution to, the intricate motions of knotting a tie at his throat one-handed, and with his nondominant hand. But he would. Someday.

His cell phone chirped a reminder that he was supposed to leave in ten minutes. With a sigh he surrendered. He pulled off the blue tie and held it in front of him; following his sister Natalie's suggestion that he simply tie it before he put it on. He managed it there, where he could use both hands. He slipped the noose—his father's word for it—over his head, under the collar of the crisp white shirt, and by pressing the tail end against his chest with his right hand, tightened it neatly with the other.

"You don't have to go, you know."

He glanced at the mirror, saw his sister's face from where she was standing in the doorway of his room. Nat's brow was furrowed with worry. She'd grown up well. She would never make a mess of her life the way he had.

"Yes, I do," he answered quietly.

"From what you've told me of him, he wouldn't expect you to."

"It's not his expectations I'm dealing with."

Nat sighed. "You've got an outsize sense of responsibility, bro."

He felt the knot in his gut that had been there since he'd gotten up at 4:00 a.m. tighten another notch. "I am responsible."

"Stop it. You are not."

He didn't answer. There was nothing more to say. He knew what he knew. And the simple fact was that a good, good man, and a good cop, was dead because of him. That five years had passed didn't change that.

"Please be careful, Adam. It's such a long drive."

"Mmm."

"You'll be back tomorrow, right? Before the snow hits?"

She sounded anxious. He knew it was because the snow that was forecast for the Palouse would likely dump on the Cascade Mountains—which he had to traverse—first.

"Should be," he said.

"If it's too bad—"

"Nat, stop." He turned to look at her. "I love you, but stop."

He pulled on his heavy jacket in deference to the temperature, which at this hour sat a good five degrees below freezing. If he was lucky, he'd be there before eleven. He had an appointment tomorrow morning, then he'd hit the road back, hopefully beating the near-blizzard they were predicting.

"I started your truck." He turned to look at her, surprised. She only shrugged. "It'll be all nice and warm. And I packed you a lunch. Coffee's in the thermos."

For a moment he just stared at the young woman who had once been that little girl who had tagged after him like one of the ranch dogs. Then he hugged her, rather fiercely.

"Hey. I'm the big brother, I'm supposed to look out for you."

"You always have. I'm just paying a little back." She pulled back slightly and looked up at him. "Will you do one thing for me?"

"If I can."

"Promise me you'll think—at least think—about making this the last time?"

He actually had thought of it. Five years seemed... significant somehow. But when did responsibility like this—and guilt—ever end?

You know when. Never.

He kissed her forehead, and headed out into the cold. And he didn't make that promise.

The bright winter sun arrowed down from the mountains and through the trees. It was incredibly quiet, as it seemed it should be here in this place. Quinn Foxworth looked out across the sea of green, the tidy, regimented lines of markers. He'd been in places like this too often. And he hated it every time. Even before he'd been old enough to understand what death and forever really meant, he'd hated it.

"I love you for this, you know. That you remember, and honor."

Hayley's voice was gentle, her hand soft around his. As always, his heart sped up at the sound of her voice, at her touch. He wondered if he could find the words to tell her how much stronger she made him. How much her quiet understanding meant to him. He would try, later. But right now he'd spotted the small figure huddled by a gravestone halfway down the row.

"She's here."

"Do you want some time alone with her?"

He looked at his wife. Smiled at her. "She'll want to see you as much as me."

"I doubt that, but thank you. Still, I think I'll hold back a little. Give you a moment. Here, take these." She handed him the bouquet of flowers she'd made him stop to pick up on their way here.

Quinn nodded, and gave her hand a squeeze. Then he walked toward the grave and the young woman beside it. She'd obviously been there awhile. From what he knew of this yearly ritual, probably since before the sun rose, never mind the cold. It was warmer now, at least in the sunlight, and she'd shed the heavy coat that now lay beside her on the blanket she was sitting on.

She didn't seem to notice him as he approached, and he was unsurprised to see the dampness on her cheeks. He knew as well as anyone that grief like this never went away, it only changed.

"Doesn't seem possible it's been five years, does it?" he said softly.

Amanda's head snapped around, and when she saw him she leaped to her feet. "Quinn!"

She ran to him and enveloped him in a hug. He hugged her back. "I won't ask how you are today, because I can guess."

She looked up at him. "I know you can. But I'm okay the rest of the time, truly. It's just today that's so hard."

He nodded. "I know. It always will be, to some extent. But your work's going well."

She had become what she called a victim advocate shortly after her father's death. She had told Quinn about her choice that first year, when they had happened to meet here on this same day. "I felt so helpless, and I had so much help from Dad's friends, and you, making decisions, thinking clearly for me when I couldn't. I can't imagine how anyone without that kind of support system survives something like this. So I want to be that system, for people who don't have anyone else."

That had been enough for him to contact Charlie and suggest the Foxworth Foundation help out.

"It is," she answered now. "Thanks to Foxworth and Dad's insurance. You may get to stop supporting us someday."

"We'll support you as long as necessary, and probably after that, too," Quinn said. "Not sorry you turned down that lucrative job offer?"

Amanda smiled. "No. Working for the city council would have been close to my worst nightmare, although it was nice of Ms. Harris to offer." She looked up at him intently. "What about you? You're all right? No…lingering aftereffects?"

"I'm fine." It was true; he felt nothing more than an occasional tightness from the bullet he'd taken in the moment before he'd grabbed her dying father's sidearm and taken down the man who'd come out of the shadows and shot them both. Well, and some extreme pleasure when Hayley lingered over the scar above his hip before she journeyed farther south…

She looked around, saying, "Is Hayley with you?" and snapping him out of that pleasant reverie. And then she spotted his wife several yards away and waved at her. "She's so sweet. No wonder you're crazy about her."

"That I am," Quinn said with a grin, still feeling the heat his last thought had brought on.

Hayley nodded to Amanda, and began to slowly walk toward them as Quinn bent to place the spray of flowers beside the headstone.

"She looks as happy as she did at the wedding," Amanda said. "And so do you."

"I am. And I hope she is."

"Thank you both for coming," Amanda said. "It means so much to me."

"Five years felt like it should be marked, somehow," Quinn said.

"I—"

She stopped abruptly, and Quinn saw her looking past him. Instinctively, he turned. Spotted the man approaching them from the east.

"Adam," he said softly. "He must have felt the same way."

"I do not care what Adam Kirk feels, about anything, ever," Amanda said tightly. "And I'll be leaving now."

Quinn's head snapped back around. There had been nothing short of venom in her voice. It was so unlike her he frowned.

"You still blame him?" he asked.

She frowned. "Of course I do. It was his fault. He could have stopped it, and he didn't."

"Amanda, he couldn't—"

"My father died because he was sloppy. Because he made an assumption. He admits it himself." Her voice rose slightly. "And I hate him."

"Believe me," came a low voice from behind them, "I know. And you're not alone."

Quinn turned again, and this time Adam Kirk was close enough for him to see his eyes. And there was a look in them he recognized all too well. They used to call it battlefield guilt.

Survivor's guilt.

Chapter 2

Both of them. Adam swore to himself over his lousy timing. Quinn Foxworth and Amanda. He would have turned around and come back later if Amanda hadn't spotted him. But running would only prove her right. Although why that mattered when he already knew she was right, he wasn't sure.

And so now here he was, about to be face-to-face with the two people who knew the complete truth. The man who, when he'd thought he was innocently stopping for a cup of coffee had ended up doing what Adam should have done that night, and the woman whose life had been forever changed by his mistake.

He made a sharp movement with his right arm, trying to force it. As always, it replied with a jab of pain and a refusal to bend any farther. But the pain was what he'd needed, and he had a grip on his roiling emotions again. Enough that he could at least face Quinn, who was looking at him assessingly, and with a recognition beyond that of realizing who he was.

"Adam," he said quietly.

"Mr. Foxworth." He said it respectfully, although he doubted it would make any difference to this man. He glanced at Amanda, who was glaring at him with such hostility he wondered how he was still on his feet. "I'll... wait," he said, and turned away from her without saying anything more. He walked a few feet to his right, belatedly realizing someone was there. A woman. But no one he knew.

"Adam."

He stopped, blinking, as the woman called him by name. "I...don't know you, do I?"

"We've never met, no. I'm Hayley, Quinn's wife."

"Oh." He didn't remember Quinn having been married before.

"Almost a year now," she said, as if she'd heard his thought. "We met a little over two years ago when he kidnapped me and my dog."

Adam blinked. "He what?"

"It's a long and, if I do say so myself, entertaining story. But not something you want to hear just now, I'm guessing."

"No, Mrs. Foxworth. I need to get...out of Amanda's sight. If I'd realized she was here, I would have waited until she was gone."

"Hayley, please. And I understand. She does seem a bit...angry."

He let out a sour chuckle. "Angry isn't the half of it."

"She still blames you?" At his look she nodded. "Quinn told me the story. And," she added, "he said it wasn't anyone's fault. And more, that you probably saved his life, after he was shot."

"He's more generous than he should be," he said flatly.

"I certainly wouldn't argue that, although not in the sense you mean."

"Amanda's father died because I didn't check carefully enough before I went inside the store. He had an accomplice still outside who killed Greg. Nothing can change that."

He had never forgotten anything about that day, no matter how much he would like to. And even if his mind had cooperated his right arm, the elbow shattered by a gunshot, wouldn't. The limit on its range of motion reminded him multiple times a day, and every time the weather changed he was even more sharply reminded for the time it took the old injury to adjust.

The bottom line was that everything Amanda Bonner had screamed at him that day in the hospital was true.

"I understood you were cleared of culpability by the official investigation," Hayley said.

He held her gaze then. "In large part because of your husband's deposition. Like I said, more generous than he should be."

He turned to go, but she spoke again, and he couldn't walk away without being more rude than he wanted to be to Quinn Foxworth's wife.

"You're living over on the dry side, Quinn said."

He was a little surprised Quinn knew that, but then realized his cutting and running for home had probably been common knowledge.

"Yes. My family's got a ranch outside Palouse, on the Palouse."

She smiled at his phrasing. "That's quite a drive to here. Do you do it often?"

"Once a year," he said flatly, pointedly.

"On this day," she said softly, and it wasn't a question. "Tell me, does the trip bring you any absolution, in your mind?"

His gaze sharpened as he stared at her. Then he nearly laughed at himself. He should have known Quinn would marry a sharp, smart, perceptive woman. "No. Not an iota."

"No one demands as much penance from us as we do from ourselves."

"No amount could make up for Amanda losing her father."

"No. Nothing can."

Something that had come into her voice made him say, "You know, don't you?"

She nodded. "My father was also a police officer. Killed in the line of duty when I was sixteen."

His eyes closed and he let out a weary sigh. "I'm sorry."

"Unlike with some who say that but know nothing about it, I believe you."

That made his eyes snap open. "I—"

He broke off as something moved on the edge of his vision. He looked that way. It was a dog, heading toward them at a run.

"Uh-oh," Hayley said. "That dog I mentioned? He's really smart. As in open the truck hatch smart."

"He's yours?"

"Uh-huh. And," she added as the animal rapidly covered the ground between them, "he's apparently on a mission. Quinn?"

She called out the last, and her husband turned to look. But instead of being upset or worried that the dog was loose, he looked only interested.

Adam watched as the animal slowed to a trot now that most of the distance separating him from his people was covered. He looked like he'd be about knee-high to him, and his coloring was rather distinctive, mostly black over his head and shoulders and a sort of russet tan from there back to a very full, plumy tail. He greeted Hayley with a quick swipe of his tongue over her fingers, and she stroked his head. But then she, as Quinn was doing, just waited.

The dog stopped in front of Adam, sat and looked up. The animal's gaze was so intense it was a bit unsettling. He wasn't sure if he should try to pet the dog or not, but then a wet nose nudged his hand. His right hand. He gave the animal a tentative stroke. The dog leaned into it, in a way that somehow eased the turmoil in his mind, and unknotted his gut. He stared at the animal, a little stunned at how much better he felt. Even his elbow, aching a bit in the December chill, felt better.

"Meet Cutter," Hayley said softly. "The four-footed member of the Foxworth team."

"And perhaps the most indispensable."

Quinn's voice came from behind him; apparently he'd come over to see what was up with the dog. Thankfully, for Adam, Amanda had remained where she was.

"He's…" He couldn't think of a word.

"Yes, he is," Hayley said. "Amazing, isn't it?"

"Does he always have this effect on people?"

"Unless you're one of the bad guys," Quinn said. "Then you'd likely have lost that hand by now."

"And in case you're wondering," Hayley added, "he's an excellent judge of character."

"Among other things," Quinn said, with a glance at his wife that had so much love—and heat—in it that it made Adam lower his gaze.

The dog got to his feet again, gave Quinn the same swift lick of greeting he had Hayley, and then trotted off toward Amanda. Adam couldn't resist watching. The dog sat at her feet much as he had before but, apparently familiar with him, Amanda didn't hesitate to bend and stroke his head. He leaned into her in the same way he had Adam, and he could see by her expression it was having the same calming effect.

But then the dog did something odd. He stood, turned, sat again, this time with his back to Amanda, and stared at Quinn and Hayley. Then he came back to Adam, sat in the same way and did the same stare.

"Well, well," Quinn said with interest.

"Indeed," said Hayley, with a glance from him to Amanda and back again.

Adam had no idea what all that was about. He glanced at Amanda, and she seemed just as puzzled.

"So tell me," Hayley said, "before her father's death, how did you and Amanda get along?"

Adam blinked. What on earth had made her ask that? He wished she hadn't. Because it brought back all those memories. Of the first day he'd met his partner's daughter, who had not at all been the girl he'd sort of expected but a lovely young woman. The kind who would have turned his head anywhere. But then he'd always had a weak spot for redheads, and her long, silky fall of hair had that burnished autumn-leaves color that always caught his eye.

And when she had smiled at him up from under thick, gold-tipped lashes, her eyes that vivid, heart-stopping green, he'd thought, for a moment, there might be something...

But now all he knew for sure was that she hated him. And she had every right.

Chapter 3

Amanda still couldn't believe he was here.

Adam Kirk. The man who had been her father's partner that night, who should have had his back. Yes, he'd still been a rookie, but nearly off probation, and even he had said if he'd been quicker to realize what was happening, his partner might still be alive. And yes, he'd been shot himself, but only in the arm, while Quinn had been shot in the torso and still had managed to grab her father's weapon and take the shooter down.

And on top of that, he was a quitter. He'd left the department after the killer's trial, left town after that, and never come back. She had no respect for that, she who had been raised by the man buried here, who had taught her to never quit on anything she really wanted.

She stared at Adam across the distance between them, her jaw tight. She hadn't seen him since the trial, and hadn't spoken to him since the day she'd blown up at him in the hospital. She refused to feel bad about that, even now. He'd been there with only his arm bandaged while her father was down in the morgue. He'd had it coming, every bit of it. And he knew it. He'd never said a word back, he'd just refused to meet her eyes and taken it, so she knew he knew it.

She wished she could have hung on to that odd sort of calm that had come over her when Cutter, the Foxworths' dog, had come to her. She didn't like feeling this angry. And sometimes she wondered if her lingering anger had something to do with the fact that when she'd first met her father's new partner, she'd practically drooled. Dark hair and gray eyes that made her question her usual preference for blue. That tall, lean body, that way of walking that wasn't quite swagger, and made sense when she'd learned he'd grown up on a ranch. Which also made him the cowboy of her more girlish dreams, an image that had been sealed in her mind the day he'd shown up at the police-sponsored booth at the fair in Puyallup in a black cowboy hat.

And suddenly she was back to that day, looking up at him, wanting to make him smile so she could see that dimple in his right cheek flash. So she'd teased him that he was a police officer, he should be wearing a white hat now.

White hats get dirty too easily, Mandy.

She had allowed him the use of the nickname, a sign of her instant attraction she supposed. Of course she'd retracted that permission, furiously, that night in the hospital when she'd told him exactly what she thought of him.

But now, as she looked at him across her father's grave, she remembered his words as if they'd been a warning. He didn't wear a white hat because he didn't really deserve the appellation, the symbol. He didn't wear a white hat because he knew he'd dirty it.

She was startled when Quinn and Hayley—and Cutter—seemed to be leading Adam back toward her. The dog, in fact, was nudging at him from behind, just as a herding dog would a stray.

Quinn hadn't blamed Adam for what had happened that night, even though he had been hurt much worse. She had been puzzled at first, since it was so obvious, but realized she was looking at it like someone who had grown up around cops all her life. And rule number one was, you always have your partner's back.

Adam had not had her father's back.

"Took you five years to decide you cared enough to show?" The words broke from her before she thought. She didn't want to have a fight here, over her father's final resting place.

Adam's head came up then. And her first idiotic thought was that his eyes were a darker gray than she remembered. "I've been here every year," he said quietly.

He had? Or was he just saying that?

"I've run into him here twice," Quinn said, as if he'd heard her doubts.

A long moment of silence spun out, seemingly magnified by the peaceful setting.

"I didn't know your father," Hayley finally said, her voice soft. "But from what I've heard and read, he would not want his beloved daughter to spend the rest of her life angry."

"I'm not. Most of the time."

Her gaze flicked to Adam in time to see him wince. It gave her no pleasure to have hit home. And, as on that day in the hospital, he said nothing.

"Amanda, it wasn't his fault," Quinn began, but somewhat to her surprise, Adam cut him off.

"It was. And she knows it as well as I do. I deserve every bit of what she feels about me. I was his partner, and I didn't have his back." He shifted his gaze to Amanda. "I'm sorry I disturbed you. I didn't see you in time, or I would have waited."

He walked past her then and stopped next to her father's headstone. He bowed his head and closed his eyes, and she found herself wondering what he was thinking. Then he straightened, stared at the stone for a moment. And lifted his right hand toward his forehead as if about to make a formal salute. But he stopped short.

Like he did in everything.

And then, silently, without another look at her, he walked away.

Adam wanted nothing more than to get back in his truck and head home. If he hadn't had that appointment in the morning he would have. But the orthopedist had been adamant about this final checkup. He supposed he had some city paperwork to sign off on or something. Otherwise Adam didn't see the point. His arm was as good as it was ever going to get, at least as it was now, he knew that. The only thing they'd been able to offer for the existing joint was a seemingly endless stream of surgeries that might or might not help. He'd already had six, carried around enough plating and screws to set off metal detectors, and adding another surgical scar wasn't high on his list of things to accomplish. Eventually, he might go for the elbow replacement surgery they'd been pushing. But for now, he'd had enough of hospitals, doctors and, most of all, scalpels.

The only thing he liked less was this urge he felt to run. Again.

And so he didn't. He instead made himself drive to the center of their old beat, found a parking place in front of the hardware store, got out and began to walk. It had changed a bit in five years. He passed the bakery, where Greg had often stopped not for the cliché of doughnuts, but for a particular cinnamon roll treat his daughter loved. They had still lived together, their relationship close, tight, since Greg's wife had died when their daughter was barely five.

He remembered the first time it had hit him that Amanda was an orphan now. And the fact that she was an adult didn't make that any less true, especially as close as they'd been. He had tried to imagine what it must feel like, what he would feel like, what it would have been like if he hadn't had his folks, if they hadn't been there to see him through the worst of his physical recovery. He couldn't.

He passed the pet supply store, thankful not to see any sad-eyed, hopeful puppies that made him want to buy them all just to get them out of there. They'd given that up apparently—thankfully—because the window was instead full of treats and leashes and collars and some sweaters the ranch dogs would tear to bits rather than be caught wearing.

As he got closer, he realized his fists were clenched and his neck was tight. He tried to relax them, but it lasted only another three steps. Because then he was on the corner, looking across the narrow side street to the convenience store. Set back from the road enough for one small row of parking spaces, the 24/7 operation had always been on their patrol list. The owner at the time had been a Sikh, a badass guy whose grandfather had fought with the Allies in Italy in World War II, a fact Adam had learned during one of Greg's impromptu history lessons given in this very store, to the delight of the owner who pronounced his account accurate. That man and his entire family had come to Greg's funeral.

Adam had heard they'd sold the store soon after, not wishing to stay where this man they had considered an honored friend had died. He didn't know who owned it now, and it didn't really matter. The only thing that mattered was what had happened here.

The first thing he noticed was that they'd resurfaced the parking area. That didn't matter either; he still knew exactly where Greg had gone down. He himself had been inside, but the instant when he'd gotten to the doorway after the sound of shots was acid-etched into his brain. His partner down, blood already pooling beneath him, and the stranger a couple of feet away, also bleeding, but who had somehow managed to roll over, grab Greg's weapon from his limp hand and fire three rounds into the darkness at the side of the store.

Quinn Foxworth, doing the job he should have done. All because he'd believed the night cashier when she'd told Dispatch the robber had just run out the door and up the street. That Greg had told him to go on in while he checked the area didn't matter either; he should have had his back.

Shoulda, coulda, woulda.

The old refrain rang in his head now as he once more faced the fact that what he should have done, could have done, would have done were all pointless and useless now. He'd done what he'd done, he hadn't done what he didn't, and the end result never changed; one of the finest men he'd ever known was dead. His adoring daughter's life would never, ever be the same.

And he had no right to complain just because his wouldn't, either.

He turned on his heel and walked back the way he'd come. He didn't know what he'd hoped to accomplish by coming here. He only knew that what he had accomplished was to make his already grim mood even darker.

Chapter 4

The Foxworth dog was amazingly polite, Amanda thought as she refilled Quinn's coffee mug.

When they'd first come in, she'd only been thinking she'd like to get to know Hayley better, which was why she'd asked them to come back to the house with her. She'd glanced out into the living room while she made the coffee and had seen Quinn standing in front of her father's official department photograph on the wall, looking lost in thought.

Hayley had taken a seat on the sofa, with Cutter sitting politely at her feet. She'd never had a dog, although she'd always liked them. It wouldn't have been fair to the animal when she'd been away at school so much and her father had worked odd shifts.

When they were all seated around the low coffee table, Cutter got to his feet and came to her. He sat in front of her, watching her with that same steady regard he had at the cemetery. Instinctively, she reached out to stroke his head. And there it was again, that same feeling of…calm. Soothing, that's what it was. The dog's thick, plumed tail wagged slightly, and that only added to the feeling. She decided she could forgive him for being upset that Adam had left; he must be one of those dogs that just loved people. Maybe that's what caused the feeling of tension easing.

"Amazing, isn't it?" Hayley said. Amanda looked up to see Quinn's wife smiling.

"Yes," she said.

"You should see him when he makes visits as a therapy dog."

"I'll bet he's really good at that."

"He is. Took almost no training at all. They said it's instinctive with some dogs."

Amanda stroked the dog's head again, then impulsively leaned down and planted a kiss between his ears.

"Oh, now you've done it," Quinn said with a chuckle. "He's going to make himself at home."

"He's welcome to," she said, meaning it since clearly the dog had excellent manners.

But she was a little surprised when Cutter got to his feet and began to wander, not idly as if curious, but… almost intently, as if he were looking for something.

"Are you glad you moved back here?" Quinn asked.

She knew he meant the house; she'd had her own place for a couple of years, but had moved back here immediately after that night. And she knew she owed this man above all others honesty. "Yes and no. It both comforts me because he feels close, and hurts because he's gone. Although it would be worse if it was actually in the city where he worked." As if they could have afforded that, even if they'd wanted it. She sighed. "People keep telling me to move, but…"

"Everybody walks this path at their own pace," Hayley said gently, and Amanda remembered her own mother had died several months before she'd met Quinn. "And you may reach a point where staying does you more harm than good, but only you can decide when that is."

"Just be honest with yourself," Quinn advised. "If it hurts too much to go, stay. If it hurts too much to stay, go."

"That's my husband, ever logical," Hayley said with a loving smile.

"If I only knew the answer to either of those," Amanda said wryly.

"Leave for a while, then, and see how it feels," Quinn suggested. "Go somewhere for the rest of the winter. Be a snowbird for a bit."

"I've thought about that," she admitted.

"So do I," Hayley said, "whenever I go south to visit my brother. Which we'll be doing in a few days." A broad smile curved her mouth. "He's getting married."

"Congratulations to him," Amanda said, meaning it; she had nothing but good feelings about the Foxworths and anyone connected to them. "I was—"

A sharp bark cut off her words. Cutter had disappeared, and the bark had come from the back of the house. She instinctively looked at Quinn. For translation, she supposed.

"Hmm. That's interesting," was all he said, but he got up and headed toward the sound.

Amanda followed. She was a bit apprehensive and more than a little startled when she realized the dog had gone into what she now called—or tried to—the library, but which had also always been her father's office. His desk was here, and the laptop she'd spent so much time poring over immediately after his death. The bookshelves along one wall were full; her father had grudgingly used an e-reader for some things, but print had always been his first choice. She had also kept her own books there, mostly from before her own e-reader days, which she had taken to much more thoroughly than he had.

That's because I'm old, Mandy.

He'd been half joking, but it still wrenched at her. Because he would never get old now. She'd heard someone say once that you never really understood what forever meant until you lost someone you loved. She hadn't gotten it then. She did now.

Cutter was nosing at the bottom shelf, which held her childhood favorites, including a magical series she to this day went back and read now and then. And she had been very tempted lately, as this grim anniversary had neared, to begin anew with book one, hoping to find some escape in the much-loved story.

She gave a start when the dog pawed at the middle book; she didn't want it damaged. The books had all been gifts from her father, who had amusedly gone with her to the midnight release parties at the bookstore that was now, sadly, half the size it had once been. But she saw that Cutter was being very gentle about it, in fact he was more patting the book than pawing at it. Then he stopped, that paw atop the book, and looked up at Quinn.

"What have you got there, boy?" Quinn asked as he crouched down. He pulled out the volume the dog had been touching, the middle—and longest—book of the series. The moment he did Cutter sat. Quinn straightened, looked at the dust jacket of the hardcover. "Yours, I assume?"

"Yes." She quickly explained about the books and their meaning to her, and the connection with her father.

Quinn gave her a steady look. "You ever go back and read these again?"

She colored slightly. They were children's books after all. Supposedly. But she'd always found worth in them, even now. "Yes. I do."

Quinn glanced around the room then. Nodded toward the desk in the opposite corner. "Your dad used this room as an office?"

"Yes," she said, her brow furrowing now, wondering what that had to do with anything. Wondering even more what Quinn was finding so significant. "What is it? Does he smell something on that book?" She managed a faint smile. "I admit I tended to eat when I was reading them, because I couldn't put them down for dinner."

"You're not the only one." Hayley's quiet voice came from beside her. "I remember reading those to my mom when she was sick. It was the only thing that gave her any enjoyment when it got really bad."

Amanda smiled, and grabbed Hayley's hand to squeeze it.

"Let's see if we can find out what's got him intrigued," Quinn said.

Amanda appreciated how carefully he held the book, and it made her think he had probably done the same with his own father's things one day in the past. She knew the basics of how Quinn and his sister had founded the Fox-worth Foundation, in memory of their parents who had been killed in the terrorist bombing of an airliner when they had been just children. And that the foundation's mission had been born out of their fury and frustration that the perpetrator had been released after a backroom political deal.

Yes, Quinn had had to deal with this kind of pain much younger than she had, and the knowledge of that had only increased her respect for the man. And the proof of his utter happiness with Hayley—and Hayley's own joy, after losing her father just as she had, and her mother's long illness and death—now gave her some hope for her own future. Someday.

She watched as he flipped the pages of the volume, her mind straying into the story it held. But then, about halfway through, he stopped. And then he looked down at his dog.

"Found it, boy," he said softly. The dog's tail thumped against the wood floor. "Good thinking," he murmured then. "It wouldn't fall out in a quick search, or be seen by someone just riffling pages..."

"What?" Amanda asked, almost breathlessly.

Quinn looked up at her then. "Your father knew you read these periodically, right?"

"Yes, he did. It always made him smile because it was part of...us."

Quinn nodded. "And so he knew exactly where to hide—" he held the book out for her to see "—this, so you would eventually find it."

And in a small hole, carefully cut into about a half inch thickness of the book's pages near the binding—not disturbing a word of the text, she noticed—something was nestled, secured by a single layer of clear tape.

A flash drive.

A cold chill rippled down her spine. The memory formed as clear as if her father were here before her right now. It had been one of the few times when he used her full name, and that alone had gotten her attention.

If anything bad ever happens, Amanda, remember where you always found comfort, in those stories.

She'd thought he meant things like losing her mother's ring, or getting a bad grade. But now…

"Oh, my God," she whispered. "He told me. I didn't realize it until just this moment, because I didn't understand, but he told me where to look…if anything happened to him."

Quinn's arm came around her, steadied her. "Then let's see what he wanted you to find."

Chapter 5

Adam spent a mostly sleepless night in the small motel near the University of Washington Medical Center where his appointment was. The appointment was fairly quick, although he'd had to wait nearly an hour. The results were what he'd expected. The only thing left to try for real improvement was the joint replacement. Major surgery and a lot of rehab. Again.

As he walked back to his truck after his usual "I'll think about it," to the doctor, he was already planning his departure. Or escape. He'd go back across the floating bridge and hit the 405, take it down to Interstate 90, and then he'd be headed home. The weather looked like it would hold until he got well over the Snoqualmie Pass, so it should be clear sailing.

He stopped to pay his bill since the place didn't run to video checkout, and told the clerk he'd be leaving within the hour. The place did run to a coffeepot in the room—

this was Seattle after all—and he started a fresh pot while he changed back into jeans and packed his other clothes and what little else he'd unpacked. He preheated the thermos with some hot water, then refilled it with coffee that should get him home even after the few hours' sleep he'd managed. Then he poured what was left into the now empty cup from this morning, grabbed up his duffel bag and the thermos and headed for the truck, pulling the door closed behind him.

He had just put his bag on the seat and the cup in the holder when his cell rang. A faint smile flitted across his mouth; Natalie, no doubt, making sure he was getting on the road. He pulled the phone out and glanced at the screen. Frowned at the unfamiliar number that wasn't in his contacts. But he knew the area code was for the other side of the Sound, so he answered.

"Adam? Quinn Foxworth. Are you still in town?"

His brow furrowed with curiosity. What would Quinn want with him, after yesterday? Why did he even have his number? "Yeah. I was just getting ready to leave."

"Glad I caught you, then. Can you delay going back?"

"Ask the snow heading for the Cascades. Why?"

"Amanda is here, at Foxworth. And we need your help."

He went very still. There wasn't a single thing he could think of that Amanda Bonner would need—or want—his help with.

"My…help?"

"With something she found. It could be nothing, or it could be important. Can you get here?"

"Does she know you're calling me?"

"She knows."

"And she agreed to it?"

"Yes." There was a pause before Quinn said wryly, "Not happily, I admit, but she agreed."

"She must be desperate."

"We all are, at this point."

And just how was he supposed to say no to that? He had no idea what they thought he could do, but for Amanda to agree to contacting him, desperate must be the word.

He sucked in a deep breath, and said, "All right."

Adam didn't know what he'd been expecting, but the building hidden in the trees wasn't it. He wasn't even sure he had the right place, no matter how much his map program insisted. He wasn't familiar with this side of the Sound. The ferry ride had been pleasant and had given him a chance to grab a quick lunch from the galley aboard—the famous clam chowder had been one thing he'd missed from over here on the rainy side. But once on the other side of the Sound he'd had to focus on finding his way. Especially since it had started to rain as he was getting off the ferry.

There was no sign, nothing except the street number on a post out on the road. He'd made the turn and followed the winding drive until he caught a glimpse of the square green three-story building that almost blended into the evergreens that surrounded it.

When he got closer, he glimpsed through the trees a small parking area, and a second warehouse-looking building to one side. And in between the buildings was a…helipad?

He frowned, slowing down even more. What exactly was the Foxworth Foundation? One of the few people he'd stayed in touch with at the department had told him

Quinn had some kind of a charitable organization, but that was all he knew.

He approached cautiously. Thought he heard something. This was a mild winter day by Palouse standards, so he rolled down the window to listen. And heard the sharp but muffled bark of a dog. Quinn and Hayley's Cutter? Or a strange guard dog who would be looking to take a bite out of him?

And then he slammed on the brakes. There wasn't a jolt because he'd been going so slow, but he felt exactly as if there had been. Because as he'd made that last turn and come into the clearing the buildings sat in, he could also see the entire parking area. And sitting there, instantly recognizable to him, was a very familiar car. Greg's precious classic Camaro. The vivid blue, racy little coupe brought back a flood of memories. And Adam had to fight down the inner ache.

Amanda was driving her father's beloved car. She'd kept it. And not just that, it looked as pristine as it had always been when Greg Bonner had been driving it. It was a classic, he'd said, and he worked to keep it in tiptop shape. Adam remembered when that had segued into a lecture about treating your weapons the same way. A dirty, neglected gun might fire most of the time, but the one time it didn't was likely going to be the time you needed it most.

Of course, that's assuming your partner had your back and so gave you time to fire at all.

His fingers curled tightly. And he moved his left hand and slammed his right elbow with a fist. The answering pain gave him the edge he needed to get back under control.

He'd just parked his truck, a safe distance from the taunting blue car, when a door in the building slowly opened. The moment it was wide enough a dog slipped through and headed for him full tilt. He recognized the ground-eating run as well as the coloring.

No one came out behind the dog. He wondered who had opened the door and just let him out. Maybe the now pouring rain had stopped them. He got out of the truck cautiously. True, the dog had met him yesterday, and seemed friendly enough, but this was clearly his own turf and he might be feeling a bit more protective.

Cutter came to a halt before him, then reached out with his nose and nudged his hand in greeting. The right hand again, Adam noted, even though his left was closer to the animal. Was it simply that more people were right-handed and he knew it, or did the dog somehow know that that arm was damaged? He himself certainly did right now, and he wished he hadn't been quite so energetic with that punch.

Cutter gave him a soft *whuff,* then turned back the way he'd come. He went a few steps, then stopped and looked back at Adam. The invitation—order?—couldn't have been clearer.

"Lead on, dog," he muttered, and started after him.

The moment he saw Adam was going to follow, Cutter trotted toward the door he'd come out of, seeming heedless of the rain. But if he was the herding breed Adam was guessing he was, being out in weather would hardly be a deterrent.

When they got close enough, Adam saw a square metal pad beside the door. This one didn't have the wheelchair logo, but he guessed it was an access pad. Even as he thought it Cutter rose up on his hind legs and batted a front paw at it. The door began to swing open, and Adam wondered if that was why it was there, to give the dog free rein. Hayley had said he was very smart. And if he managed to open a vehicle hatch, he supposed something like this was child's—or dog's—play.

He hesitated while holding the door. Not because it was a strange place and it felt odd just going in, because Cutter had made it quite clear he was if not welcome, at least expected. No, he hesitated because he had the strangest feeling that stepping through that door was going to change everything. That being face-to-face with Amanda again was going to shatter what he'd gained by going home and spending long days riding the Palouse. He hadn't found absolution there, for it wasn't to be found, but he had achieved a rather fragile peace. And she was the one person most capable of shattering it.

Cutter's head came back out the door, as if to ask why he wasn't already inside.

"You'd better come in," Quinn's voice called from inside. "He won't give up until you do."

Adam looked down into Cutter's dark eyes. There were the gold flecks he'd noticed yesterday, giving the dog's stare a depth he wasn't used to seeing in an animal. But he read the truth of Quinn's words in the intensity of that gaze.

He stepped inside. And was startled. Because the bottom floor of this rather industrial-looking building was anything but. Instead it looked like the massive great room of a home, with comfortable seating of four chairs and a sofa in a square around a thick rug laid out before a gas fireplace that was burning merrily, no doubt supplying the warmth he could already feel. At the back on the left was a small but efficient-looking kitchen, on the right was a door open just enough to see it was a bathroom, and another door beside it that was closed.

He noticed all this as if he was taking inventory. And he knew it was to avoid looking at the three people seated in front of that fire. Quinn and Hayley in the armchairs on one side, and in one of the chairs on the other side, the one closest to the fire… Amanda. He didn't have to look to verify it was her, he could feel it.

He noted he was on a tile floor, and there was a long row of hooks on the wall, so he guessed this was essentially a mudroom to shed wet things. His jacket definitely qualified, so he pulled it off and hung it on one of the hooks. There was a mat to dry his feet, so he used that, as well. Noticed also a stack of towels in a basket by a bench where he guessed you could sit and take off boots and shoes if they were wet enough. He didn't think his were from just that walk from his truck.

Cutter sat next to the basket, just watching him.

The dog. It hit him suddenly the towels were there for the dog. He should have realized sooner, his mom kept a couple by the back door for the same reason.

"Want me to dry him off?" he asked across the room.

"Have at it," Hayley answered. "I'd appreciate it. He's been so crazy all day he's driving us mad."

She sounded approving, and he wondered crazily if he'd passed some sort of test. Both she and Quinn were watching him. But Amanda—he risked a glance now—was staring determinedly at the fire. Frowning. It didn't take a genius to see that he'd been right about her not really wanting him here.

Still not looking at any of them, he picked up one of the towels. The moment he did Cutter stood up and stepped toward him. This was the routine, he guessed, and the clever dog knew it. He stood patiently as Adam ran the towel over his coat first, then each leg and paw. It wasn't the easiest of chores done mostly one-handed, but he got it done all right. And the dog himself signaled when it was done by backing away.

Adam hung the now damp towel on one of the hooks. Cutter was again doing the "follow me" routine. So he did, even as he wished himself somewhere, anywhere else than in the same room with Amanda.

He headed for the end of the sofa farthest from her. But Cutter kept getting in his way, leaving only one path open to him, and again he was put in mind of the dogs back home, chivying cattle or horses until they went where they were supposed to.

"Dog," he muttered. Cutter looked up at him innocently but refused to move so that he could get to any seat except the chair next to Amanda. Right next to her. Arms touching close. He could step over the dog, but something about the way the animal was looking at him…

He surrendered, figuring at least this way he was looking across to Hayley and Quinn. Who were, he now noticed, watching their dog with interest, but with no apparent desire to call him off. Instead they exchanged a glance that seemed significant, even if he had no idea what the significance was.

Amanda kept staring at the fire. He almost spoke to her, to tell her he understood she didn't want him here, but stopped himself. There was nothing to gain there—it was obvious to all here how she felt. Well, except maybe Cutter, who didn't seem to have gotten the message.

He waited. Silence spun out in the room. And suddenly he felt very stubborn. They'd called him here, he certainly wouldn't be here if they hadn't, so it was up to them to start…whatever this was.

He joined Amanda in staring at the fire. Silently. And figured this was as close as they would ever come to being in accord.

Chapter 6

Amanda wasn't happy. She hadn't wanted him here but had to admit the logic of Quinn's point. And so she had agreed to the call, still half hoping he wouldn't answer or would refuse to come. He surely had to know he wouldn't be welcomed. By her, at least. She didn't know about Quinn; the man was more than capable of hiding his feelings behind that cool exterior.

At the very least Adam could have sat somewhere else. Even if Cutter did keep getting in the way, he was only a dog after all. He could have stepped over him or something. Then again, where he was it was easier for her to avoid looking at him. She could just keep her eyes on Quinn and Hayley, or the fire. So maybe the dog had done her a favor.

Even as she thought it Cutter, who had taken up a position on the floor in front of them both even though the space between their feet and the big, heavy coffee table was a bit cramped for him, gave a short woof. It sounded just about like she felt, wanting to get on with it.

"Point taken," Quinn said, sounding amused. He leaned forward and picked up the laptop from the table. The laptop where they had now plugged in the flash drive Cutter had found. She still had no idea how, and Quinn and Hayley merely shrugged and said they'd given up trying to figure out how the dog knew what he knew.

"We—or rather Cutter—found this flash drive hidden in Greg and Amanda's office. Very well hidden. In a place where only Amanda would have likely found it, eventually."

Quinn hit a couple of keys, and the flat screen above the fireplace came to life. He hit a couple more, and the now familiar image appeared. She looked away, unable to bear looking at the familiar handwriting.

"Recognize this?" Quinn asked.

Adam studied the image for a moment, his brow furrowed. And now Amanda couldn't resist looking at him, when he was safely focused on the screen. He looked... older. Not just the five years it had chronologically been, but as if he'd aged two for every one. Not that he wasn't still a good—okay, great—looking guy, but the time had left its mark. At least on the boyishly handsome face she remembered.

And had fallen for at first sight, fool that you are.

He unexpectedly glanced her way then, and she flushed as he caught her looking at him. Her gaze darted away, even as she tried not to, knowing it was a guilty reaction. She wanted to simply stare him down, showing he didn't just mean nothing to her, but that she loathed his very presence.

"I... It's Greg's," Adam said. "But you must already know that."

"Yes," Hayley said, her tone quiet. "Amanda told us. And how he hated typing."

Adam nodded. "He was old school. Said the process was different, mentally, between typing and handwriting."

"There's truth in that," Hayley agreed. "They've done studies."

Again he nodded. "So he'd write things and then take photos of the pages to have a digital record."

"Must have gone over well on police reports," Quinn said.

"I did those, mostly. I was pretty fast at it."

"Do you recognize this, specifically?" Quinn asked.

Amanda found herself holding her breath as he looked back at the projected page. She hadn't realized until that moment how much she hoped he could make sense of the jumble of seemingly unconnected words and letters and numbers.

"I don't think so, but I can't be sure. That's Greg's code, though."

"Code?"

Amanda couldn't stop herself from asking. Adam started to look toward her, then stopped. And she saw suddenly he didn't like this any more than she did. It gave her a little jolt, to realize she had never, ever considered or cared about his feelings back then, other than to hope he was as miserable as he deserved to be. And her earlier thought about how much older he looked than the young-faced rookie she'd remembered came back to her, and she could only conclude that her hope had come true. Somehow it made her feel worse rather than better.

"He had this personal code he used when he wanted whatever it was kept private."

"You mean secret?" Quinn asked.

Adam nodded. "Usually it was just hunches, speculation, things he couldn't be sure of or prove. He didn't want to send anyone off on a wild hair he had no proof of."

"Our tech expert was able to break the encryption on the file and open it, but he hasn't been able to decode the document itself. And because it's in handwriting, an algorithm for the computer to work on it would be iffy at best."

Adam nodded. "One of the other reasons he did it this way. He had a healthy skepticism about putting everything digital."

"He's not alone there," Quinn said, rather grimly.

Cutter, restless again, got to his feet and started to pace. Which she understood, since she felt the same way, as if she were hovering on the precipice, and one breath of air would send her over.

Quinn went on. "Amanda called some of her father's friends still at the department. None of them could make sense of this, either."

"They couldn't, unless they knew how Greg set up the code."

"Do you?" It burst from her, again against her vow to remain completely silent while he was here. But this was too important.

"Yes." He stopped.

"Don't play games, Adam Kirk," she snapped. "This file was last saved the day he died. It could be important."

He finally looked at her then. And she saw the shadows that darkened his eyes. Shadows that were familiar, for she'd seen them often enough in the mirror. She saw the muscles in his jaw tighten, then release. Then he looked back at Quinn.

"It's a double alphabet code."

Quinn glanced at the screen. "What about the numbers?" he asked, obviously knowing what Adam had meant by that.

"They were to work with his foundation alphabet, because it had repeating letters."

"So he numbered them," Quinn said in understanding. "A one through five, N one through five, and so on."

Adam nodded.

"Could someone please explain to the non-secret agent in the room?" Amanda said, trying to keep her frustration out of her voice. She knew she was touchy about this, and Adam should get some credit for at least coming when he was asked. Shouldn't he?

Quinn answered her. "Double alphabet. One, the real one. The second, the encoding one, can be anything. The simplest—and oldest—is the real one in reverse order, but you can use anything as long as you have twenty-six letters."

"But how does it work?" Hayley asked, and Amanda threw her a grateful glance, glad she wasn't the only one lost.

"You just write out the two, then substitute the encoding alphabet letters—or in this case also some numbered letters—for the real alphabet," Quinn explained.

"Or if you're like Greg," Adam said with a sad smile, "you do it from memory. I swear, he could read his encoded stuff like it was straight English."

Amanda's breath caught. It had always amazed her, her father's memory. *Brain's a steel trap for trivia, Mandy*, he had always warned her when they had watched a quiz show on television when she was a kid. Somehow that Adam knew that unsettled her. As if he had shared something personal she had thought of as her own. Childish, but sometimes she just slipped back into being a girl who really missed her dad.

"But we're still at the starting block without his encoding alphabet," Quinn said.

Adam sucked in a deep breath Amanda could hear. Then he let it out slowly. "I know that, too."

Amanda stared at him. And suddenly another memory, one pushed out of her mind long ago, crashed back. *He's a good man. I trust him completely.*

Apparently it was true, if he'd trusted him with the key to his code. Her father hadn't made many mistakes about who he trusted. Only one, that she knew of. And he was sitting right here, studying his hands.

"I get he probably swore you to secrecy," Quinn said, "but under the circumstances…"

Adam looked up then. But not at Quinn. At her. And then, slowly, he said, "It's Amanda Catherine Bonner Aspen."

Amanda nearly gasped aloud. Quinn looked at her. "Your full name and a significant location?"

She nodded a little numbly, even as she felt her cheeks heat. Her full name and where she had been conceived, on her parents' first anniversary trip.

And one look at Adam's face told her he knew the exact significance of that location. Her father had told him. Probably in that joking way guys had, about getting lucky that night or some such. Her father had been ever decorous around her, but he'd been every inch a man, and she'd heard enough of him with other friends to guess at this.

Belatedly—very, very belatedly—it struck her that Adam and her father had likely shared that kind of relationship, with the kind of joking that made women mostly roll their eyes. The kind that explained why he knew exactly what Aspen meant in the context of her life.

And she had no idea how that made her feel.

Chapter 7

Adam paced the room, occasionally stopping to look out the expansive windows. They'd moved upstairs to what was apparently the office space of Foxworth, contrasting with the homey setting below. It was a large room with a meeting table, some cubicles and cabinets along the side, and an impressive computer station on the back wall. The opposite wall was almost all window, looking out on the clearing the building sat in, across an expanse of meadow to a stand of thick trees with now bare maples stark against evergreens and a couple of madronas.

Those evergreens and the stylish, red-barked madronas were also among the few things he missed about this side of the mountains, where he'd also left behind the shattered remnants of his life's dream.

He turned away from the window and resumed his pacing, glancing at the computer station where another of the Foxworth personnel, a guy Quinn had introduced as Liam Burnett, their local tech expert as opposed to the guy in St. Louis, had arrived and was looking at the file on the flash drive. Cutter, who had been restlessly pacing and refusing to settle, greeted him with delight, so obviously there was a big connection there.

"Hey, partner," Liam had said, bending to scratch behind the dog's right ear, which made the animal wiggle in delight. "Ria says Hi, and you'd better come over for some cookies soon."

Cutter gave a short little woof that sounded for all the world like "Yep!" Adam spent a lot of time with dogs on the ranch, but he'd never seen one quite as communicative as this one.

Liam went back to studying the file, then gave a slow shake of his head. "Sorry, boss," he said to Quinn. "It's not likely any character recognition program would be able to translate this accurately."

Adam thought he heard a trace of a drawl in the man's voice, and wondered where he was originally from. Texas, maybe; they had a hand on the ranch from Tyler, and he sounded like Liam.

"Cursive's very tricky in the first place," Liam explained further, "since even the same letters can be shaped differently. Add in that there are too many spots where the size of the letters and numbers change to fit what space he had left, and the pages they're written on were unlined and so the rows of text aren't always straight, and it's impossible."

"So in this, at least, the human eye and brain has it all over the electronic one," Hayley said.

Liam grinned. "Yes. Hard though that is for me to admit."

He sent the photographed images to the printer as he set up a decoding grid with the double alphabet laid out for each of them. They would be doing this the old-fashioned way. There were twenty-five pages of notes on the drive, so they each took five and settled in at the table to translate, letter by letter, dating each page with the date on the original.

Even Cutter seemed to realize this required concentration and quiet, because he padded over to first look out the window, then plopped onto a comfy-looking dog bed beneath the glass and settled in to wait.

Adam had to shift things a bit, to get to the angle he needed to write—thankfully no one seemed to notice the rather odd positioning—but he still finished first. Maybe because he had a better idea of what he was looking at, more familiarity with his partner's phrasing. He recognized place names quickly, and thought maybe he'd absorbed more of Greg's code than he'd realized. He sat there reading through the decoded pages he held, frowning a little. When Liam handed him his pages he only nodded and started reading those, too. Quinn, Hayley and Amanda finished moments later, and they all slid their pages across the table to him. He was already putting them in date order before he realized what they'd apparently all tacitly decided, that he was the one to read all this and figure out what it meant.

For a moment the thought of trying to make sense of all this seemed beyond daunting. But he owed it to Greg to at least try. And so he read. Made a couple of notes. And read. More notes. The room stayed silent, and in a moment when his mind strayed he had a vision of them all watching him, holding their breath. It made him want to hurry, but he forced himself to go at it methodically, as Greg always had. He'd been nothing if not thorough. Which told Adam the answer was here, somewhere, he just had to find it.

When he finished reading the last page he sat staring at it. In part trying to process everything, but also because he knew the moment he put down this last page they'd all be waiting for him to explain everything. And he could, some of it. What he couldn't give them was the biggest, most important piece.

Finally, he gave in and set down the page. And although every part of him told him not to, the first person he looked at was Amanda. He wondered how she felt, having her name and that place laid out before them all, knowing that this above all was what her father had valued so much to make it the key to all of this.

She met his gaze, waiting silently. And in this moment, this precious moment, there was less of the anger there, even less hatred in her eyes. Because he might be able to give her something, some final piece of her father?

It was a moment before he could manage to speak.

"I…remember some of this. Four of these interviews I was there for. But the notes he made here don't seem to have much to do with what we did those interviews for. Or with each other, for that matter. The other three I don't know about. Judging by the times on them, they were done either after hours or when I was on another assignment, so I wouldn't have been there."

"Another assignment?" Quinn asked.

He was glad of the reason to look away from Amanda. "I was still pretty new, so they would stick me in other divisions for a week or so at a time so I'd know where they were coming from."

Quinn nodded.

"And you remember when those times were?" It was Amanda, and it would be beyond rude not to look at her, even if he was wondering if there was an accusation in the question.

"I remember all of it," he said flatly. "Every day." *And it haunts me every night.*

"After hours?" Hayley asked then. "Did he do that often?"

"If he had his teeth into something," Adam explained. "He was the most dedicated cop I ever saw." He looked back at the pages stacked in front of him. "And he had his teeth into this."

"The question is," Quinn said, "what exactly is 'this'?"

"It looks like a long list of various meetings or gatherings of the criminal element," Adam said, with a gesture at the pile, "that aren't connected to anything specific. Except..."

"Pix," Quinn said.

Adam's gaze shot back to Quinn's face. And he saw in the man's eyes what he'd forgotten for a moment, that Quinn Foxworth had been a soldier, a fighter, long before he'd become...a champion against injustice, or for lost causes or whatever he was now.

"Yes. It occurs in nearly every reference. If there's anything that tied it together, in Greg's mind at least, it was that."

"What is pix?" Amanda asked.

"I wish I knew," he said. "Greg obviously thought he was onto something big."

"Is there any chance he would have used the actual letters for this one thing, instead of the code? Should we be looking at Btp, instead of Pix?" Liam asked.

Adam shook his head. "If he wanted it secret, he'd never risk something someone could just guess." He looked back at the pages yet again. "The way it's used, in context with the rest and capitalized, it seems like it has to be a name."

"Agreed," Quinn said. "Question is, thing or person?"

"I would have thought person," Hayley said, "but I suppose it could be a place."

"An organization, maybe?" Amanda put in.

"Could be," Quinn said. He looked at Adam. "Any common thread in the cases you remember here?"

"Not that I can think of right now. I'd have to see the case files to really remember."

Quinn nodded. "I'll see what we can do about that."

Adam opened his mouth to say it was unlikely they could get the full files, then remembered who he was talking to. Quinn Foxworth was remembered and remembered well at the department, and he could probably get whatever he darned well pleased. He, on the other hand, would likely get the door shut in his face, no matter what the official investigation had concluded.

"It has to be important," Amanda said quietly. "He never would have hidden it like that if it wasn't."

"Agreed," Quinn said.

"Where exactly did he hide it?" Adam asked. "He didn't freeze it in an ice cube, did he?"

Amanda's head snapped up. "He told you about that?"

He couldn't stop his smile. "Yeah. He was pretty proud of that one."

For the barest instant, he thought she almost smiled back. "He should have been. It took me nearly two weeks." She glanced at Quinn, who raised one eyebrow at her. "I got a speeding ticket. Dad took away my car key and hid it. Said it was somewhere in the house, and I could drive again when I found it. Took me nearly two weeks. I looked in the freezer, but I never thought to look actually *in* an ice cube. I just remember wondering why he had an old-fashioned ice cube tray in there when we had an ice maker."

This was the most normal she had sounded since he'd

gotten here. Not that there wasn't the undertone of sadness when she spoke of her father, but she didn't sound miserable. Just full of her love for the man who had practically raised her on his own. And it was that that made him speak again.

"Did he ever tell you how proud he was of you, that you didn't drop his name trying to get out of it?"

"He told me I did the right thing," she said. "That it wasn't something to be proud of, it was just what a good person did."

"Well, he was proud," Adam said. "But then, he was always proud of you."

"And I him," she said, and a tiny bit of that old snap had crept back into her voice.

He vowed he would stay in speak-only-when-spoken-to mode from here on. And keep his gaze away from the woman who kept drawing it without even trying.

"We'll dig into this a bit," Quinn said. "I'd like to know how this is all connected, and why it was so important that he hid it so carefully." He glanced at Adam. "Taped in a small square cut out of just enough pages near the spine of one of Amanda's favorite books."

Adam immediately did what he'd vowed not to do and looked at Amanda. "The wizard books," he said. Her eyes widened slightly. He lowered his gaze. "He told me once one of his best memories of when you were a kid was reading those with you."

There was a long moment of silence, during which he stared at the stack of pages, before she spoke. Her voice was quiet, and held a stronger note of that sadness. "Thank you for telling me that. It's one of my best memories of him, too."

The way she said it eased him, at least she wasn't mad at him again. He wondered how she would feel if he told her just how much of her Greg had shared with him. Her dreams, her fears, his worry because of this or that, and the fears any father of a daughter had, amplified geometrically by being a cop and too often dealing with the worst of the worst out there.

You've done your best, Greg. She's fit, she's strong, you've taught her to fight, she's smart and she pays attention.

But if she crosses paths with the wrong guy, it may not be enough.

If she crosses paths with the wrong guy, there's a good chance he's going to be the one running away screaming.

"You were the light of his life," Adam said softly. "He never stopped talking about you. Or worrying about you."

"And I never stopped worrying about him," she answered. And then, with acerbity back in her voice she added, "For all the good that did."

And so the truce seemed over. And Adam tried to tell himself he should be glad it had happened at all, even if it hadn't lasted.

Chapter 8

Now that Foxworth had clearly taken over…whatever this was, Adam was pondering what to do. He should have been well on his way home by now, probably through the pass and halfway there. He opened the weather app on his phone, since they somehow had a strong signal even out here. Better than at home anyway. Which was just as well, kept him from buying fancy, expensive phones. They had decent internet at the house and barn, but out on the Palouse, good luck with any kind of connection.

The storm that was still pouring rain on them here was already dumping snow in the mountains. The camera at Snoqualmie showed a near whiteout. Right now they were letting people through with snow tires, but from the look of it they'd be requiring chains soon. And the thought of wrestling chains onto his truck mostly one-handed was enough to make him groan inwardly.

Stop the pity party, Kirk.

"Thinking about tackling that?"

Hayley's voice from behind him snapped him out of his thoughts.

"More thinking about not tackling it," he admitted.

"Wise decision, I think."

Hayley came around the chair, sat in the one next to it and handed him a cup of coffee. Adam took it gratefully. They'd moved back downstairs when they'd reached the point of rehashing the same ground again and again and accomplishing nothing. Until they knew who or what Pix referred to, they were at a loss.

"You're going to keep digging into this?" he asked.

Hayley nodded. "If only for Amanda's sake. Because he was obviously working on it when he was killed, it's important to her."

Adam glanced toward the small kitchen, where Amanda was with Quinn, apparently putting together some kind of lunch.

"He's been looking out for her ever since, hasn't he?"

"Yes." She smiled. "My husband is hardwired that way."

"So it wasn't just…what happened to his parents?"

"That only solidified it, I think. Gave him direction, and determination."

"He told me he wanted an organization that wasn't hamstrung by regulations or politics, like cops are."

Hayley nodded. "He wanted to be able to focus on helping, whatever it took."

"Admirable," Adam said. "I wish I could help more."

Hayley gave him a quizzical look. "We still wouldn't have a clue if you hadn't come to help."

"Doesn't seem like much."

"You're pretty hard on yourself," Hayley said, leaning back in her chair and taking a sip from her own mug.

He didn't think so, but it seemed rude to protest what was clearly meant as a kindly observation, so he only shrugged.

"I presume you meant to beat that today?" she asked, nodding toward the snowy image.

"Yeah." He grimaced. "I'd better call home."

"You need a place to stay tonight?"

"I can go back to the motel by U-Dub," he said.

"That's where you were last night?"

He nodded. "Doctor's appointment this morning," he said absently, focused on calling up his contact list; Nat would be outside, prepping in case this storm still had snow left when it got to them, so he'd try her cell first. She wouldn't be happy, but neither was he, leaving her and their folks with all the work.

"Still, huh?"

It took him a moment to remember what he'd said, and when he did he wished he hadn't. "Still trying to sell me on more surgery," he said, hoping she'd let it go.

"Would it help?"

"They say yes."

"You don't believe them?"

He put down the phone; Quinn's wife was nothing if not persistent. But she was so kind it was impossible to dodge without being bad-mannered about it. "It's more that I'm really, really tired of them cutting on me." Which was true, but also a dodge, because they'd also told him he would end up with more function and much less pain, and he wasn't certain he deserved that.

"That," Hayley said, "is totally understandable." Then, unexpectedly she said, "Why don't you stay here tonight?"

He blinked. "Here?"

She gestured toward the back of the room. "There's a

comfortable bedroom back there, and a bathroom with a shower. And there's food in the kitchen—you can help yourself."

It was too much, for how little he'd done. "I...thank you. That's really nice of you, but I think I'll head back over and be that much closer in the morning, or whenever this lets up and I can get through."

"Your choice," she said, "just know it's an option."

He nodded. "Thanks again." He hesitated, then thought it would be easier to ask her than Quinn, and said, "Would you let me know? If you find out anything?"

"Of course," she said easily.

When he got up to leave, Hayley gave him a hug, Quinn shook his hand and Amanda, rather stiffly, said simply, "Goodbye."

She had her purse over her shoulder and her keys in her hand, so he gathered she was leaving, too. But she was hesitating, so he guessed she wanted to say something to the Foxworths without him hanging around. Oddly, it was Cutter who protested his departure the most energetically, almost blocking the door and looking from him to Amanda and back, his gaze intense, as if he were trying to communicate something. He whined slightly, and it had such a worried sound Adam almost laughed at the dog. But something about this animal made laughing at him seem...inappropriate, if not foolish.

It was Hayley who called him back to her, also oddly by saying to the dog, "Not yet."

When he was back in the truck, he remembered he was going to need gas. Might as well do it now in the hopes of an early start home in the morning. Or maybe he should just start home now, and hope they had the pass plowed by the time he got there. Not that it would do much good if it was still coming down that fast and thick, but he'd feel better.

Until you got stuck up there and had to tough it out in freezing temps or ended up in a snowdrift with the truck wrecked.

His map program told him the nearest gas station was a couple of miles away, on the way to the ferry. He found it easily and pulled in. He rather grimly watched the numbers on the pump roll as he filled the truck's large fuel tank. He'd just finished the hit to his debit card when it struck him that he and Amanda would likely be on the same ferry going back to the other side. And for a moment he seriously pondered either waiting for the next one, some forty-five minutes later, or driving a half hour to the nearest other ferry. But a glance at his watch told him that would dump him in downtown Seattle at a peak traffic hour, and even if he survived to get on the freeway he'd be going through peak traffic there, too. Even though it was less than half as far, it would likely take him four times as long. Not something he wanted to deal with.

At least the blue classic car would be easy to spot. He would just stay several vehicles behind her, and once on board he would stay in the truck, he thought. Then he would never encounter her, because she certainly wouldn't approach him.

He pulled out of the station onto the road and headed for the boat. It was the in-between time on this side, it seemed, too early for the rush of commuters coming back, and too early for those heading over to the city for the evening. And so he had the road pretty much to himself at the moment, only a few cars in sight ahead. His regular glance in the rearview mirror told him it was even sparser behind him, without a vehicle in sight.

Just as he looked back forward, something registered,

like a freeze-frame of an image. His gaze shot back to the mirror. He'd been right. It had been a flash of bright blue that had caught his eye. He waited, realized he was holding his breath and forced himself to suck in some air. The blue got closer, close enough that he knew. Definitely Greg's car; the likelihood of there being two of those classics here, on this road at this moment, was so slim as to be nonexistent. It was still raining fairly hard, so he couldn't see into the vehicle. Not that he needed to, he could imagine Amanda at the wheel easily enough.

He made himself look forward again. Saw that he'd slowed to a creep, only then aware he'd taken his foot off the accelerator.

Good thing there's not much traffic, Kirk. You're driving like an idiot.

He resisted the urge to cut onto a side street and let her go past him, even though it would be easier to stay clear of her if she was ahead of him. But she was close enough to see him now, and if she recognized his truck, which she probably would, she'd know he was dodging. Why that mattered, with everything else she thought of him, he wasn't sure. But it did.

They could still ignore each other, he told himself. Even if she was still right behind him when they boarded. Maybe he'd get lucky and they'd end up getting on at the point where the crew divided the oncoming vehicles, sending them to opposite sides of the vessel. Maybe—

A resounding crash cut off his thoughts. No screech of tires, but the road was probably too wet for that. Nothing in front of him... His heart jammed up in his throat. And even before he looked in the rearview mirror, he somehow knew.

The blue car was not in sight. Another vehicle was

making a wild U-turn, and it sped off in the opposite direction.

He made the same maneuver and sped back the way he'd come. Not after the fleeing vehicle, but with his eyes scanning, searching...

There. A glimpse of blue. The side of a car at an unnatural angle. Greg Bonner's pride and joy, sideways in the roadside drainage ditch. Smoke rising from the engine compartment.

And Amanda, pinned inside.

Chapter 9

There's always a moment of shock. It takes the human brain that moment to process both what has happened, and accept that it's real.

Her father's words echoed in her head, and for the first time she truly understood. Because for a long moment she hadn't moved, in fact had stayed still, waiting to wake up from the crazy dream. Her mind had been in such an uproar since she'd seen Adam at the cemetery she wasn't even surprised it had churned up this nightmare that she had crashed her dad's car. She was, inanely, a little surprised she hadn't dreamed up his truck as the car that had unexpectedly sideswiped her, driving her into the ditch.

It was the pungent smell of gasoline that snapped her out of it. This was real. It was real, she was hanging sideways in the driver's seat, held only by the seat belt. And the smell of gas made her instantly think about fire. She had to get out of here. She'd deal with what she'd done to the car after that. She tried to open the door, but it was jammed, and tight. She needed more leverage, maybe from a different position.

Her first two tries for the seat belt release were futile. The angle she was now at, she simply couldn't reach. She felt the drip of rain on her face, wondered what window had broken. She reached for her keys and pulled them out of the ignition. In an instant she had it, the gift her father had given her when she'd first gotten her driver's license. No useless frippery from Greg Bonner, no, this had been, he'd said, an essential for living here in this land of bridges and water. And so she took the device on her key ring and used it. The slanted blade nestled in the U-bend of the small piece of plastic slashed easily through the seat belt, freeing her.

The other end held a small, spring-loaded bolt that would shatter the window if she held it in the right place.

She didn't want to have to do that, but...

Windows are replaceable, Mandy. You're not.

She maneuvered around to where she could brace against the passenger seat and push at the door with her feet. She still couldn't budge it. At all. Fear started to build in her as the smell of gas grew stronger. One spark, one too hot piece of metal...

Even as she thought it she heard the whoosh as the gasoline caught, flared into fire. Panic spiked through her. She had to get out, and she had to do it now. She chanted what her father had told her, put the bolt against a corner of the window and release it. She would—

Someone was there. Yanking at the door from outside. Fiercely. It didn't budge. It was jammed too tightly. Whoever it was was really trying, but she was going to have to break the window. She scrambled back around in the tilted car, now bracing her feet against the passenger seat. She opened her mouth to call out, tell the person what she was going to do.

"I've got a—"

The door gave. First a couple of inches, but then her rescuer gave a mighty yank and it swung wide, with a metallic scream. *God, he's strong.* For it was a man, she could see that now and—

Adam.

It had only registered when he reached in and grabbed her arm with his left hand. She used it for balance and got her upper body out. Then his right hand came down on her waist, followed by the left on her other side, hauling her out of the car. She was not small at five foot eight, nor was she a lightweight, but he lifted her as if she were a child. Whatever he'd been doing, he hadn't become a weakling, she thought inanely.

"It's okay," she heard him say. "You're out."

"I…"

"Are you all right?"

"I…think so."

"You're bleeding," he said suddenly, sharply.

She realized it hadn't been rainwater she'd felt dripping down her face. And then Adam was touching her cheek. It was so cold out, or she was in shock, because just that touch felt almost unbearably warm. Hot even. And it sent a jolt through her that brought her back to her senses.

"The car," she moaned, hating that she was leaning on him, but unable to quite find her footing. Even as she looked the rain was dousing the flames, but she could see how badly the car was damaged.

Adam was looking at Amanda's head now, gently pushing her hair back to inspect. "Your father would have blown that car up himself rather than see you hurt.

Look at me." She didn't want to look at him, not him. "Amanda, look at me. Forget who I am for a moment, you hit your head and I need to see your eyes."

She looked up then. Odd. She didn't remember his eyes being that dark. They were the same color as the sky, gray, stormy.

And worried.

That was sweet. She almost smiled. Then she remembered who he was.

"I'm fine," she said, trying to pull away. And only then did she realize she was shivering. He moved then, letting go of her. Perversely, she didn't like it. Told herself it was simply because now she was even colder.

And then a swathe of warmth came around her, and she sighed at the wonderful feel of it. She tried to draw it closer, realized it was a jacket.

Adam's jacket.

"Come sit down," he said, tugging her gently toward his truck. She resisted. "Come sit down before you fall down," he amended. "Because if you fall I'll catch you and carry you over there, and you'll be even madder at me."

He had a point. But before they had taken three steps he stopped, lifting his head. She barely had time to wonder before she heard it, too, another vehicle approaching, slowing.

"Foxworth," he muttered.

She looked up, saw Quinn at the wheel of the big SUV. He maneuvered it to the other side of the car—Dad's car, she thought, her eyes stinging with tears—and angled his to guide any oncoming traffic around the scene and flipped on his flashers. Hayley was already out of the vehicle and running toward them, Cutter at her heels.

"Amanda! Are you all right?"

"I'm fine," she said.

"She's bleeding. I think she hit her head," Adam said.

"Paramedics are on the way," Hayley said.

She blinked. "They are?"

Quinn nodded as he came up to them. "We called the minute we saw the car."

"Did you call the sheriff, too?" Adam asked. "It was a hit-and-run."

Amanda blinked. "It was?"

"It was," Adam said flatly.

Amanda heard a whine that sounded as worried as Adam's eyes had looked. She instinctively reached to pet the dog who was nudging her hand. She vaguely heard Quinn saying yes, a deputy was also on the way. Out of the corner of her eye she saw Adam pull out his phone and make a call.

"You all right?" Quinn asked her.

"Fine, I think. Just shaken. You just happened along?" she asked as Adam put his phone away and came back.

"Nope. It was this guy," he said, gesturing with a thumb at the dog.

"What?" She realized both she and Adam had said it simultaneously, but it was the logical question.

"He made us come," Hayley said. "About five minutes after you left he just started barking his head off, headed for the car and wouldn't shut up until we got in."

They both stared at Cutter's people. "He…" She stopped, not at all sure what to ask.

"We've been through it before," Quinn said, rather wryly.

"But how did he get you to come here?" Adam asked, which Amanda had just been wondering.

"Volume," Quinn said, rubbing at his right ear. "Silence, we're okay, barking, we're supposed to make a turn, trumpeting and we missed a turn. I missed one on the way here, and he about took my eardrum out."

They both shifted their gazes to the dog.

"You kind of get used to it after a while," Hayley said cheerfully. "We've learned to just go with it."

The paramedics arrived first, followed quickly by a fire truck. Quinn went to meet them, and directed the medics to Amanda. Then he talked with the fire personnel who were setting up cones to route people around the scene. Adam stayed at her side, a gesture she would probably have found comforting if it had been anyone else. And oddly, when the medics offered her a warmed blanket, she didn't want to give up his jacket. But since he was standing there in the cold rain in shirtsleeves, she let them take it.

"It's his," she said, glancing at him.

And for the first time she realized just how wet he was; the shirt he wore was sopping. And as she looked, she put together the man who'd had the strength to get that jammed door open with the man who stood there now, a wet cotton shirt clinging to every inch of his broad chest and muscled arms. He'd definitely put on some muscle, had Adam Kirk, and he hadn't exactly been a lightweight in that department before.

She finally noticed that she was staring—and worse, liking what she saw—and jerked her head away, making one of the medics drop the pad he'd been cleaning her cut with.

"Sorry," she muttered.

"No problem," the man said. "Do you recall hitting your head?"

"No. Did I?"

"Did you lose consciousness at all?"

Her eyes widened. "No."

"I was here within seconds," Adam said, the first time he'd spoken since the emergency crews had arrived, "and she was conscious and coherent."

"Just covering the bases," the medic assured her. "You've got a bit of a lump there, but not bad. We can take you in if you want, but this looks minor enough you can probably check with your own doctor. I'd guess you'll have some seat belt bruises, but this doesn't look anything worse than a bump. Just don't be alone for the next twelve hours at least, twenty-four would be better, and if you start having headaches, or dizziness, or your vision is affected, then you need to get to the ER."

"I'll be fine. Thank you very much."

"Nothing left but the paperwork, then," the man said cheerfully.

A few minutes later a sheriff's deputy was there, a woman who greeted the Foxworths as if she knew them. But she was all business when she got to Amanda. They already had several reports from witnesses who had called in, she said, but she wanted to hear Amanda's description of what had happened.

"I was heading for the ferry," she said, "and this car came off a side street, the one back by the coffee stand, and went right into the oncoming lanes. I think he was trying to pass me, maybe he thought he was late for the ferry, but he suddenly just veered back into my lane, like he didn't see me at all."

She heard someone suck in an audible breath, thought it was Adam. But the deputy—Lindholm her name tag said—just nodded. "Go on," she said, and her voice was very kind.

"It was weird, because there wasn't a lot of traffic, so they weren't dodging someone else. I didn't see any animals on the road, either."

"What did you do?" Deputy Lindholm asked.

"The only thing I could think of—I cut hard right, to try to avoid him. He still hit me, which sent me into the ditch."

"And he kept going?"

"I…guess so."

"He made a U-turn and left westbound at a high rate of speed," Adam said. "Silver four-door, midsize. I was too far away to get the plate, but they were in state. Had something hanging from the rearview mirror, something rectangular, like a badge or parking permit. White male driver, black shirt, baseball cap, also black I think."

Amanda stared at him. The deputy looked at him as-sessingly. "You our witness call from about ten ago? Kirk?"

He nodded.

"Quinn said you were a cop."

"Once upon a time," he said, his voice flatly unemotional.

"Good," Lindholm said. "We got the suspect vehicle broadcast out right away."

"The crash may have been an accident," Adam said. "No skids, so he could have hydroplaned into her, the road's wet enough. But the running was a definite decision."

Lindholm nodded. "No reports of him being spotted yet, but he may have gone to ground."

"Gone to ground?" Amanda asked.

It was Adam who answered her, although he didn't look at her. "People's first instinct, if they're the sort to hit-and-run in the first place, is to hide the car."

"Maybe he didn't realize," she said.

"Oh, he knew," Adam said, and this time she looked at him, his voice was so cold. "Why do you think he hung that U-turn and got out of here in such a hurry? Didn't even pause to see if you were hurt."

He was, she realized with a little shock, furious. Was there still that much cop in him, that he took such affronts to the law so seriously? It didn't make sense to her, for if that was true, why had he quit? Why had he walked away from what her father had told her was his life's dream?

Of course, not stopping to see if you'd perhaps seriously hurt someone was an affront to common decency, and she supposed she could grant him that much, that he'd be angry at that. She'd never thought of him as a bad person, really, just a guy who'd gotten lazy, careless at the worst possible time, the worst possible moment.

And that moment had gotten her father killed.

Chapter 10

"You'll come to our place," Hayley said as she put an arm around Amanda. "That way you can take your time deciding what to do."

Amanda seemed to hesitate, but then Cutter, who was sitting at her feet, nudged her slightly. She stroked the dog's head, and her expression cleared. Adam didn't know how the animal did it, but right now he was glad of it, for Amanda's sake.

"All right, for a while," she said.

Adam let out a breath of relief. She wouldn't be alone. The Foxworths would look out for her. He hadn't forgotten what the paramedic said. Although the injury looked like little more than a bump on the head, symptoms could show up later to indicate it was something worse.

Quinn came over to stand beside him.

"She's a friend of yours, the deputy?" Adam asked, without looking at him.

"She is now. Foxworth crossed paths with her on a stalking case last month," Quinn said.

"You say that like that's what you do, that kind of case."

"Sometimes. We got into it helping a guy keep a promise." Quinn grinned suddenly. "Well, Cutter got us into it, actually."

Adam blinked. Gave Quinn the quickest of glances, then looked at the dog again. "You guys are making him sound…almost scary."

"Oh, there's no almost about it," Quinn said, still grinning. "And don't ask me for an explanation because I don't have one. He just knows when people need our help."

Adam shook his head slowly, watching the dog lean into Amanda. And finally, looking down at him, she smiled. That alone was worth a lot, he decided.

"He also has another talent, but we'll save that for later," Quinn said, and Adam realized the man was watching him much as he'd been watching Amanda and Cutter. He grimaced inwardly as he once more dodged the man's look. "Right now, he's decided you two need us, so we might as well get started. You can follow us back to the house."

You two? What the…?

"I… I'm fine. Just look after Amanda. The paramedic said— "

"I know the routine. Orientation times five, every hour or so for the next twelve." Adam shot a quick glance at him again. Quinn shrugged. "Been there before."

"The car," he began, looking away.

"We'll take care of it. Obviously, it means a lot to her, so we'll find someone who can put it to rights."

"It was her dad's. It was important to him, so…"

"Of course it's important to her. Very important. So it will get done." Adam still couldn't meet the man's eyes. Not this man, of all men. "You have a problem with me, Adam?"

He made himself meet the man's gaze then. Quinn was looking at him assessingly. "No," he said flatly. "I have a problem with me compared to you. You're the guy who did what I should have done that night. Don't think I've forgotten that." *Or ever will*....

"You're wrong, but that aside, I don't think you'll ever forget that night," Quinn said. "I certainly won't."

"My point," Adam said, barely managing not to sound bitter. At least, he hoped he'd managed.

He realized then that Cutter had moved. The dog had come toward them, and now was sitting at his feet much as he had at Amanda's. And if he'd looked at her the way he was looking at Adam now, it was no wonder she'd surrendered and petted him. He did the same, and again that odd sort of calm spread through him at the first stroke of the dog's fur.

He took a breath, realizing only then how tightly wound he'd been. He'd once been coolheaded all the time, now he lived with such turmoil he didn't even remember what it felt like to be calm. Until now.

Cutter made a low sound and turned his head to stare up at Quinn. Quinn looked back at the dog then, oddly, said, "Okay, buddy. Got it."

Adam barely blinked at the apparent exchange. He supposed any dog that could ease people's inner mayhem like this might just be able to communicate beyond the average dog.

"You can follow Hayley back to the house," Quinn said.

Adam blinked then. "What?"

"It's not far." Quinn gave him a wry smile. "Or Cutter

can ride with you. He'll make sure you get there, but I can't guarantee what shape your ears will be in."

"You don't want me in your house." He said it flatly, with certainty.

Quinn drew back slightly, studying him intently enough that Adam felt the pressure building in him again. And as if he'd sensed it, Cutter leaned into him, making a noise that wasn't quite a whine yet still managed to sound worried.

"Why wouldn't I want the man who likely saved my life in my house?"

"I—"

"We're going to have a little talk about some things," Quinn interrupted, and it sounded like a decidedly ominous promise. Or threat. "But in the meantime, we need to get Amanda off this road, and away from the sight of that car."

"I...yes, but—"

"I'll deal with the car, then have the tow truck drop me off at home."

Adam made a serious effort at thinking clearly. He didn't like the idea of whatever Quinn wanted to talk about, because it had to be that night. But he liked even less walking into the man's home with Amanda there. Quickly he said, "Why don't I stay here until the tow arrives, and then give you a ride?"

He could drop Quinn off and be gone, catch the next boat. It would be too late to start home. He didn't want to tackle a snowy pass at night when it was supposed to drop below freezing, but he could get an early start tomorrow, assuming the storm was done dropping snow on the mountains.

Quinn looked at him consideringly. Seemed to be

weighing the options, although Adam didn't see the problem.

"Or you could leave me your truck and ride home with Hayley," Quinn suggested.

In the same car? With Amanda? No. No way. Even as distracted as she was right now, he didn't think he could stomach being closed up in a vehicle with her.

"No, thanks," he muttered.

"Don't trust me with it?"

Startled, because that hadn't even occurred to him, he shook his head. "Nothing to do with it."

Quinn studied him a moment longer. And oddly, Adam was reminded of the intense gaze of his dog. But finally Quinn nodded.

"All right. But don't be checking that ferry schedule just yet."

Damn. Was the man a mind reader, or just that good at judging people?

If he was that good at judging people, he wouldn't be bringing me to his home.

He watched Amanda and Hayley get in the Foxworth SUV. Cutter looked from it to Quinn. The man only nodded, but the dog trotted off to the back of the vehicle, where the hatch was lifting, obviously opened from the inside by Hayley.

"He understands a nod?" Adam asked.

"And a lot more," Quinn said. "And you'll likely have him to answer to if you try to escape, so I wouldn't recommend it."

Adam stared at him. "You're going to sic your dog on me?"

"He's not an attack dog, although he can do a credible imitation. He'll just herd you where he wants you to go. And I won't have to. He's already decided."

"Decided…?"

"That you need Foxworth help."

Adam wasn't sure what to say to that, because whatever Foxworth did, it wasn't the kind of help that would fix him. So he said nothing.

He walked over to the wrecked car. It was hard to look at because of all the reminders, but it occurred to him that as shaken as she was, Amanda might not have gotten everything out of it. A quick glance inside told him he was right, and he went back to his truck and grabbed one of the bags he kept for trash. He climbed into the awkwardly angled vehicle and began to grab up the scattered items. It looked as if her purse had spilled or split open in the crash, for there were lots of things like makeup and a hairbrush.

He paused for a moment when he saw a long auburn hair caught in the brush. And suddenly a memory shot through his mind, of one of the days she'd come to the station to pick up her father because this very car was in the shop. She'd been fresh out of college, still full of energy and ideals, her green eyes, so like her father's, alight with dreams. But then, so had he been full of dreams. A couple of years ahead of her, but still fairly new to the job he'd wanted since he'd been a kid.

They'd been standing outside the station when Greg had mentioned his daughter was on the way.

I could have given you a ride.

No offense, Kirk, but I'd rather ride with my girl.

He'd said it proudly; Adam had known the man adored his daughter, but he didn't think he'd realized until that moment just how much. And when he'd looked up to see her approaching, looking as good as she had the first time he'd ever seen her, he'd rather inanely agreed.

So would I.

He'd muttered it under his breath, but Greg had given him a sharp look. *Don't even think about it.*

Yes, sir.

He tried to never think about her. Was almost successful, when he focused completely on the job. Greg Bonner was a tough training officer, and he'd washed out more than one cop on probation. But being signed off on by him was nothing less than an honor.

And less than three months later he was dead.

Adam made himself focus. He kept hoping shaking off the memories would get easier with practice, but it didn't seem to be working that way. And he felt another jab of pain as he scooped up a few old audio cassette tapes, remembering how Greg had scoured online auctions for deals on the things, saying the era of the music should suit the era of the car. Adam had understood the idea, but silently thought streaming through his phone was a lot easier.

He heard the approaching tow truck and was backing out of the car when he saw the picture. It was on the floor on the passenger side, nearly up against the door, where it had slid when the car came to rest. Greg and Amanda, taken in front of this very car when he'd first brought it home to restore. Adam wasn't sure how old she was in the photo, maybe twelve. He reached for it, knowing it was probably the most precious thing in the car, for her. And instead of putting it in the bag with the other loose things, he slipped it into his back pocket, where it would stay safer while he worked his way out of the crazily canted car.

Quinn was already talking to the driver of the truck, companionably, as if they knew each other. Maybe he'd towed Quinn's car once or something. Or maybe it was just that everybody knew everybody around here.

Or maybe they'd crossed paths, like Deputy Lindholm, on one of their…cases.

"Friend of yours?" he asked as they got into his truck as the tow truck pulled away.

"We helped him with something a couple of years ago."

"'Something'?"

Quinn gave a half shrug. "His son got caught up in something, a financial deal that went bad. It wasn't his fault, he was set up, but he couldn't prove it." Quinn smiled then. "We did."

"That's…what you do?"

"We help people in the right who have exhausted all options and have no other recourse. Or as my wife puts it, we're all about righteous lost causes."

And what about lost causes in the wrong?

Adam unclenched his jaw as he reached for the ignition.

There was no help for those. And who knew that better than he?

Chapter 11

"I can't believe I crashed his car," Amanda said, feeling cold and shivery inside as she sat down on the couch in the Foxworths' living room. This had been, she knew, Hayley's parents' house, although she and Quinn had made some changes together, fairly major ones, to make it theirs.

"From the looks of things," Hayley said, "you didn't. You were hit. Hardly the same thing."

"If I'd seen that guy sooner—"

"If you figure out how you could have done that, you let me know, because I sure can't."

Cutter came to sit at her feet, resting his chin on her leg, looking up at her with obvious concern. Amanda stroked his fur, feeling a bit calmer as she looked at the woman sitting across the coffee table from her, the wife of the man she admired beyond most in her life now. Quinn hadn't even met Hayley yet when his life had collided so uglily with her father's five years ago. But now Amanda couldn't picture the tough ex-soldier without this woman by his side.

"It's just…it's like the last whole piece of him I had left, and now it's gone, and—"

"It's not gone, and it will be fixed. Quinn'll see to that." She paused and then, her voice low, gentle and commiserating, she said, "I know that's when you felt closest to him, driving that car."

"I had to drive it. Seeing it just sitting, never moving, just pounded home that he's gone." Amanda drew in a deep breath as she stroked Cutter again. Then she slowly shook her head. "Five years. I keep thinking it will get better. That I'll get over it."

Hayley immediately got up and came to sit beside her, putting an arm around her. "Oh, honey, I hate to tell you but you'll never get over it. This kind of grief never goes away, it just changes. It's something you learn to live with, not something that heals up like it never happened."

"But…it's been five years…"

"And in another five years, there will be times it will hit just as hard. It won't happen as often, and you'll recover more quickly, but… I won't lie to you, Amanda. It will never go away. At least, it hasn't for me, for either of my parents. And it's been better than five times as long for Quinn, and there are still times when he just has to go be alone with his memories, even as young as he was when they died."

Amanda cringed inside at the promise of unending pain, remembering that this was a woman who understood, who had lost her own father in much the same way as she had lost hers. And then, more recently, her mother. She'd almost forgotten, in the midst of her self-centered misery, that she was far from alone.

And then, quietly, Hayley added, "And it shouldn't, should it? Isn't it a sign of how great that love was, that you carry a bit of it forever? The pain is just the proof."

She'd never thought of it quite like that. And the ache eased a tiny bit more. Just enough that she thought she could breathe again.

"Thank you," she whispered. "That...hit home."

"Your mother died when you were young, didn't she?"

Amanda nodded. "I was only five. I barely remember her."

"So you and your father were even closer because of that, I'd guess. My mother and I were, after my father was killed."

"Yes. I—"

Cutter's head came up sharply. He let out a low rumble that somehow wasn't threatening but...warm.

"Quinn's here," Hayley said.

"Is that his welcome home sound?" Amanda asked, managing a smile for the first time since they'd arrived.

"It's his Quinn sound," Hayley said. "He's got one for everybody at Foxworth now. I get a happy bark— Quinn and I both get it when we're together—Liam gets this two-note thing, Teague got his own when he and his fiancée got together, and...well, if I told you what Rafe's was you'd think I was crazy."

Amanda stared at her. Hayley laughed, but got up as the front door opened and Quinn came in.

And Adam stepped in after him.

She hadn't expected that. He must have given Quinn a ride home rather than the tow truck. Quinn shed his jacket, then said something to Adam who then, seeming reluctant, did the same. A little awkwardly as he held on to a bag of...something. He switched the bag to his left hand, then used the free fingers to tug at the right cuff and got it off, then hung it up on the rack by the door where Quinn had put his.

He nodded at Hayley, who moved to pour two more cups of the coffee she'd put on when she and Amanda had gotten here. He hesitated, then walked over to Amanda. Cutter jumped to his feet and they got tangled somehow. The dog knocked Adam off balance and he dropped to the couch where Hayley had been sitting. Right beside her.

"Sorry," he muttered, then held out the bag. "Here. From the car."

She gave a little start of surprise, then took the bag and looked inside. Saw several things that must have spilled out of her purse during the crash. "I… Thank you."

He reached into a back pocket. "And this. I didn't think you'd want to leave it in there."

She knew the moment she caught sight of the size and shape what it was. The picture. Taken the day they'd gone to bring the worn, rough-running car home. She'd been as excited as he was, the prospect of long hours spent with him as they worked on it together. Well, he had worked, she had mostly played the oldies on the odd stereo that used the tapes that were also in the bag, as she stood by to hand him tools as he requested them. And so she knew a socket wrench from a torque wrench, but also how to gap a spark plug and change air and oil filters, among other things.

He held it out to her. Gently, handling it so carefully she knew he knew what it meant to her. She kept it in the car because it held everything, the happiness of childhood, the expectations of the future and, above all, the grin of the man who had loved her more than anyone in the world. If it had been anyone else securing this for her, she would have appreciated tremendously the care, but that it was him clashed with her deeply rooted anger, leaving her unsure of how she felt.

She took the photograph as carefully as he held it out to her. Once she had it in her hands, once she had it to look at directly, it suddenly didn't matter who it was who had saved it for her.

"Thank you," she said. She would have thanked anyone short of the man who had actually shot her father for finding this and understanding its importance.

He moved then, and she thought he was trying to get up. But Cutter again got in the way, making it impossible for either of them to move without stepping on him. She glanced at Hayley and Quinn, who were looking at each other, apparently unaware of the problem with their dog. Odd, they didn't seem like—

Her thought was derailed when Quinn turned his head. He looked at her, glanced at Cutter, then back to her, then to Adam, as if he were...assessing somehow. As if he and the dog were—

She broke off her own silly thought; Quinn was an amazing man and Cutter obviously an amazing dog, but to think they were mentally communicating somehow was beyond ridiculous. But then she looked at Hayley and saw not assessment but understanding as her gaze flicked from her to Adam and back.

"I need to figure out how I'm getting home," she said hastily.

"Adam could take you," Hayley suggested blandly, "since he's intent on heading back to the other side."

She nearly jumped. "What? No, I..." Her gaze flicked to the man beside her. He was staring down at the dog now. Avoiding her eyes? Why not, her protest had been a bit sharp.

"Then you'll stay here," Hayley said, as if she'd done

it intentionally. "As you should, so we can make sure you're all right. We'll get you home in the morning." She stood up. "And we're ordering in pizza so you," she said to Adam briskly, "might as well stay for dinner."

"What? No, I—"

He broke off more sharply after saying exactly what she had.

"Cutter, m'boy," Hayley said with a glance at her pet, "you've got your work cut out for you this time."

The dog made a low sound that almost sounded like "Hmpf," as if he were shrugging off her doubts that he could accomplish whatever it was.

Just this morning she would have said she could never sit through an entire meal across the table from Adam Kirk, yet here she was. And she couldn't have sworn to whether it was this or the aftereffects of the crash that was making her feel so stiff. She could have talked easily if it had just been Hayley and Quinn, but with Adam sitting across from her, and studiously avoiding her eyes, she found she had little to say.

Which wasn't missed much, apparently, because Quinn kept the conversation going with questions about Adam's life on the east side of the state.

"I've not been there much," Quinn said. "To Spokane, and the university once."

"Wazoo?" Adam asked, using the nickname for Washington State. "I went there."

Quinn nodded. "So, tell me about life there."

"On the Palouse? It's...very different from here."

"What are your favorite things?" Hayley asked.

Adam looked at the couple, as if gauging if their interest was genuine. She could have told him it was; Quinn had told her once that understanding people was intrinsic to their work.

"Saddling up on a frosty morning, a good horse beneath you as you head out. Just the look of the hills, the way they roll on into eternity. Watching the moon rise over them, where it seems like it's so huge and close you could touch it. The peaceful quiet. And the sounds, like the roar of Palouse Falls."

Amanda stared at him. That had been...almost poetic. And there was no doubting the sincerity, the pure love in his voice.

I'm just a cowboy from the Palouse, nothing special.

His words, spoken to her on that long-ago day when she'd first met him, echoed in her head now.

"I've been to Palouse Falls," Hayley said. "It's so amazing how they just sort of appear, kind of out of nowhere, amid all that flat."

Adam nodded. "Glacial," he said. "Carved out of basalt."

"How far do they drop?"

"Couple hundred feet, give or take."

"Never seen them. Obviously an oversight I need to correct," Quinn said. "I've never—"

He stopped as his cell rang. He excused himself and got up.

"He's always threatening to turn the thing off at dinner," Hayley said, "but Foxworth doing what it does, you just never know when someone might really need us."

"I...never realized exactly what it was you did. It's pretty amazing," Adam said. Since she agreed with him—now there's a shock—Amanda said nothing.

"Quinn, and Charlie, would say it's necessary, as long as there are those who don't play fair," Hayley said. "Or who use their position or manipulate rules to their own ends."

"Charlie?" Adam asked.

"Foxworth's cofounder and the financial genius who keeps it all going," Hayley explained. "And Quinn's sister. The most intimidating human being I've ever met."

Adam blinked, and Amanda saw his gaze flick to where Quinn was standing with his phone.

"Yes, including him," Hayley said with a laugh. "Charlie's intimidating in an entirely different way."

"If I remember right from your wedding, more like a hurricane," Amanda said, earning a grin from Hayley, and a sideways glance and the faintest of smiles from Adam.

But when Quinn came back to the table, his expression was unexpectedly grim. Perhaps someone really had called for help. But he sat back down, and when he did he looked right at Amanda. She drew back slightly, suddenly worried.

"That was Deputy Lindholm," he said, his tone serious. "Apparently, they found the car that hit you."

"Oh!" she exclaimed. "Where?"

"On a rural road off the 101 in the next county. It was abandoned, but the damage matches, paint transfer matches, and it has—" his gaze flicked to Adam "—a parking pass hanging from the mirror."

"Driver?" Adam asked.

"That's the sticky part." Quinn's expression went grim. "It was reported stolen this morning, a couple of hours before it hit you."

Adam went very still. "The owner?" he asked, quietly.

"Older woman who lives at Puget Shores Retirement Village. Hence the parking pass."

"Definitely not," Adam said.

"Agreed," said Quinn. "There's no reason to doubt her story."

"So that's why he ran, then," Amanda said, wondering what the odds were that she'd be hit by a stolen car.

"One reason anyway."

She frowned. "Why else?"

"I'm just looking at all the possibilities," Quinn said.

"But this explains everything," Amanda said, "doesn't it?"

"I just find the timing interesting."

"Timing?"

"What he's saying," Adam cut in, his gaze fixed steadily on Quinn, "is that this might not have been an accident."

Chapter 12

Amanda didn't believe it, Adam could see it in her face, her eyes. He remembered how hard Greg had worked to shelter her from the realities he dealt with every day. Sometimes Adam had thought he worked too hard at it, that if anything ever did rebound on her she would be totally unprepared. But he had never voiced that thought. He wasn't a father, what did he know? And he certainly wasn't Amanda's father.

What he had felt every time he saw her was far from fatherly.

Now that wasn't a problem. Well, not a big one anyway. He might still feel that tug whenever he saw her, but it was hard to feel attracted to someone who hated your guts.

"It's just a possibility," Quinn was saying.

Just a possibility. True, no doubt. But Adam's gut was churning. Greg had always said he had great instincts, but surely after five years they were beyond rusty, if not rusted away completely? Maybe it was just the response of being here, with Quinn and, above all, Amanda.

All he knew for sure was that he was wishing he'd never come. Or at least that his pilgrimage had gone as it usually did—quietly, never running into the daughter of the man he came to honor. And apologize to her yet again for letting him down. He flexed his arm, realized then it was aching in that way that told him the weather was changing. Rain must be on the way out, for a while anyway.

"That's crazy," Amanda said.

"Maybe not," Hayley said gently. "Your father was clearly onto something, something either so big or so sensitive that he kept it completely secret. Except from Adam, whom he obviously trusted."

Amanda glanced at him and he looked away, not wanting to see resentment in her eyes again.

Quinn looked thoughtfully at Amanda. "I'm going to go out on a limb here and guess you haven't personally angered anyone that much."

"I…don't think so."

"Then we're back to it being connected to your father."

"But…why come after me after all this time?" She sounded bewildered.

"You called for help with an encrypted file," Adam said softly.

Her gaze shot back to his face. "But I only called Dad's friends."

He let out an audible breath. He had no answer for that.

Quinn said, "There's always Malachi."

Adam gave him a startled look at the name of the shooter. "That was my first thought," he said. "But why?

He's serving life already, and it's not like he's been coming up for parole and she's stopped it."

"True," Quinn said. "Although that could also mean he's got nothing to lose. But I'd think he'd be much more likely to come after you. For revenge."

"Me?" Adam blinked. "I think you mean you. You're the one who took him out."

"But you're the one whose testimony put him away."

"That was nothing without the dashcam video. We were lucky it got good images of him."

Quinn studied him for a moment. "So you get no credit for anything, is that it?"

Adam went cold. "Ask her," he said, with a nod at Amanda. "She'll tell you what I get credit for. Her father dying."

He shoved back his chair, the pizza he'd eaten now a heavy lump in his stomach. He took three steps toward the door, his gaze already on where his jacket was on the rack. But something bumped him in the shins and he looked down to see Cutter, standing there and looking up at him reprovingly.

"Y'know, dog, I've had enough of that accusing look," he muttered.

"And how often is it aimed at yourself in the mirror?"

It was Amanda's voice, low and quiet, and the shock of that spun him around on his heel. "Not nearly often enough for you, I'm sure."

"Enough," Quinn said, not quite sharply but still with a snap of command. "You two can hash this out later—and if Cutter has anything to say about it you will—but right now we need to focus on who might be trying to send Amanda a message. Or worse."

Worse. Adam's gaze snapped to Quinn, then Amanda. He hadn't thought that far. That perhaps that accident that apparently wasn't an accident might have been more than a warning.

That it might have been intended to be much worse.

That it might have been meant to kill her.

It was odd, Amanda mused. All this time she had despised the very thought of Adam Kirk alive and well, had felt a spark of anger and resentment every time he popped into her mind. Practically had a mantra to chant about how unfair it was that he had walked away, how he was to blame.

So why did she feel so unsettled when she realized he felt the same way about himself?

Perhaps it was because she had always imagined him going blithely on with his life while her father, his life cut short because Adam had been careless, was in his grave. That had been the foundation of that resentment. To realize that he had been tortured by the memory of that night just as she had was…rattling somehow.

Quinn's crazy idea that the guy in that car had been trying to kill her was…well, crazy. If Trevor Malachi wanted her dead why would he wait until now? And as Adam had said, wouldn't he be more likely to come after the man who had actually shot him?

"It doesn't make sense that he'd come after me," she said.

For the first time Adam turned to look straight at her. And again she saw how stormy his gray eyes could look. When he spoke, his voice was full of both confidence and bitterness. "I'd play video of the statement you made about your father in court for anybody with a child and guarantee they'd vote for the worst penalty possible," Adam said. "The evidence made him look like a killer. You made him look like a monster."

She stared at him. The prosecutors had told her she didn't have to make a statement, that it wouldn't be needed since the case was so clear-cut, but that it couldn't hurt. She had spent agonizing hours trying to pour her heartbreak, her grief into those words. And in the end she had veered off what she had written, and instead had simply told the jury who her father had been. Not just the cop willing to lay down his life for them, but the incredible man he'd been, the single father who had adored her, who had sacrificed time after time to see that she had the best he could give her, including himself.

She thought she had reached them, and they had told her later she had brought several of the jury to visible tears. When the killer had been convicted and sentenced to the harshest punishment possible under the present governance, she considered the draining effort worth it.

And in the aftermath, it meant nothing.

The man who had destroyed her life had been taken away, the attorneys went back to their office, the cops back to their work, while she went home to a shattered ruin.

She remembered standing in the living room, feeling numb. And that she simply couldn't go back to the condo she'd been renting any more than she could let go of the place where she had grown up, where she had shared so much with him, where every room was a reminder. Any more than she could pretend everything was normal.

He'd told her once he'd only kept the place for her sake, that as soon as she moved so would he.

Some fancy condo, where somebody else can fix the pipes and the roof and do the gardening.

And where will you work on the car?

Okay, a condo with a garage.

She felt moisture gathering in her eyes at the sweet

memory of that teasing exchange. And the fact that he hadn't actually done it, after she'd told him it would make her sad to let go.

And then she heard Adam swear under his breath. "I can't do anything but hurt you, can I?" he said, his voice quiet.

For once, he hadn't. It had been the poignant memory, not anything he had done. Or not done. "I… It wasn't you."

She didn't say "this time," but he looked as if she had.

And she didn't understand why, but had to admit his expression made her feel guilty somehow. Just as the realization of how he felt—after five years—had surprised her.

She'll tell you what I get credit for. Her father dying.

She'd spent five years blaming him nearly as much as she blamed the actual shooter. And it had never really occurred to her—or if it had she had dismissed it as deserved—that he might blame himself just as much.

Not so long ago, maybe even this morning, she would have said as well he should.

Now she wasn't quite so sure.

Chapter 13

Heedless of the light rain still falling, Adam stood out on the Foxworths' back deck, staring out through the trees toward the Sound visible between the evergreens. Toward the Cascades.

Toward home.

Quinn came up beside him. "Still in a hurry to get back?"

"I was," he said, looking at the sky and trying to gauge by the ache in his arm how much longer it would last.

"But?"

He looked Quinn then. "Do you really believe she's in danger?"

"I think it is a possibility," Quinn said.

"You think whoever it is will try again?"

"Depends on if this crash was a success or a failure."

"At warning her."

Or killing her.

He couldn't even say it out loud—it made it too real. A shiver went through him. He suppressed it, tried to think. "How would...anybody even know she was here? She's a ferry ride away from home."

"Wouldn't take much imagination to find her at the cemetery on yesterday's date, if they know anything at all about her. Maybe they would have tried there, if Hayley and I—and you—hadn't shown up. And then we went back to her place with her."

"You think she was followed from her place over here?"

"Could be. I didn't notice a tail on us, but Amanda left a couple of minutes after we did, so they could have hung back and waited for her."

"So...follow her over here, steal a car, come after her, then abandon the car a county away and leave in the original car?"

"Thought out a bit, if so. Not using their own car because it could be caught on the ferry cams coming or going, then abandoning the stolen car a county away, although that might have backfired on them."

"Because it was discovered fairly soon?"

Quinn nodded. "Same day. They may have been hoping for a week or so."

"City thinking," Adam said. "Figured dumping it in a rural area would buy them time, without realizing that things like that stand out like crazy to locals."

"Exactly. The person who called it in said it didn't belong to anyone in the area because he knew all their cars."

"They," he said slowly, realizing Quinn had been saying that all along. "It would have to be at least two. One to drive their vehicle and one to pick up the other, who did the hit-and-run and then abandoned the car."

"Yes."

The rain was getting lighter, and the weather ache in his arm lessening. He flexed it again to be sure.

"They haven't talked you into a joint replacement yet?" Adam drew back sharply. Quinn shrugged. "Seems logical at this point." Then, with an upward quirk of his mouth, added, "And, Foxworth has friends everywhere."

He blinked. "You've been…what, checking up on me?"

"You've been on our radar since that night. Lot of people worried about you."

"Lot more probably glad to see me gone."

"They weren't there that night. I was. It wasn't your fault."

"But—"

"All you had to go on was what you'd been told."

"Right." He'd been through this so many times it barely registered anymore. He looked up. The rain had stopped, his arm an accurate gauge once again.

"You know, one of Foxworth's best has that same over-size sense of guilt you've got. When he was in the military he saved thousands of lives, but all he could think about were the ones who'd died before he'd been able to hunt down and take out the threat."

"Sniper?" Adam guessed, not arguing with Quinn's assessment of the size of his guilt, although he didn't think it oversize at all.

Quinn nodded. "He ended up with a knee in about the same shape as your elbow."

"Let me guess, though, he's tougher than me so he had the replacement done."

"Actually, no, he hasn't. I think he wants the reminder."

The words were was so close to his own frequent thoughts Adam was a bit taken aback.

"That's what I thought," Quinn said quietly. "Guilt,

especially survivor's guilt, is a hellish thing. What you do to yourself is far worse than anything anyone else would. For a while there I was afraid he was going to be one of the twenty-two."

"Twenty-two?"

"The twenty-two veterans who commit suicide every damned day."

Quinn's voice had gone suddenly cold, harsh and distant, and Adam realized it was anger. And if that statistic was right—and he had no doubt it was—then it was a righteous anger. Which Foxworth seemed to specialize in.

"And what's Foxworth doing about that?" he asked.

Quinn seemed to snap back instantly. "What makes you think we're doing something?"

"What you told me about what Foxworth does. And you don't seem the type to let something that means that much to you slide."

Quinn's gaze narrowed. And then, slowly, he smiled. "No. We're not. You've got potential, Kirk. Don't let that slide."

Adam couldn't think of a thing to say to that except that he was wrong about the potential. He tried to come up with something, anything to say, to divert the way Quinn was looking at him. He didn't know much about Quinn Foxworth's personal background, only what he'd guessed from the man's bearing and demeanor, but he knew enough of the man himself to know he didn't want to cross him.

"I get the feeling you could have walked that path yourself," Quinn said quietly, gently.

The easy lie leaped to his lips, but again something about this man made it impossible to say it. So again, he gave him the truth. "I thought about it," he admitted. "Maybe riding out onto the Palouse and never coming back. Middle of winter, maybe. But that'd endanger a good horse."

Quinn just looked at him, waiting. He let out a breath and went on.

"My grandmother committed suicide, when I was a kid. It nearly killed my mom, and tore up my dad because he couldn't help her. I…couldn't make them go through that again."

"And that," Quinn said, very quietly, "is why you have potential, Adam. A weaker man might have taken that out."

"Weaker?" He gave a wry laugh. "I always thought I just wasn't strong enough to do it."

"And that's the deadly trap, the mind game that lures some people into doing it, heedless of the devastation left behind. If you're at a natural, unavoidable end anyway, that's one thing, but to throw away so many years with potential…that's the biggest waste I can think of."

Adam stared at this man who had taken a childhood tragedy and turned it into a calling. And couldn't think of any words at the moment that were enough to express his admiration.

"Now," Quinn said briskly, "about you heading home."

Adam shook his head. "I don't think so."

"Why?"

He met Quinn's gaze then. "She could be in real danger. I'm staying."

"Why?" Quinn repeated.

"I know I'm not much use, but—"

"That's not what I meant. And I think you know it."

He drew in a deep breath. This was a man who required the truth. And so he gave it to him. "I may have failed her father, but I'm not going to add not protecting her when I could have to my list of sins."

"I'd argue that first part with you, but now's not the time. We've got plans to make."

"I don't think she believes it."

"Agreed. It's only natural. Anybody not used to threats hangs on to their normalcy bias as long as they can."

He heard a faint sound and turned to see Cutter coming out through his own door. The dog crossed over to them, paused to nuzzle Quinn's hand, then went to Adam and sat at his feet. He looked down into amber-flecked dark eyes that were fixed on him intently.

"Got an answer for me, dog?" he asked softly, not even certain what the question was.

"He's got more than you might think," Quinn said. "And interesting ways to get you to see them."

"We've got ranch dogs, always have," Adam said. "Smart ones, too, who can read a herd like a book, and stand watch over them like the Praetorian Guard. But I've never seen anything like him."

"I'm halfway to being convinced he's an alien in a dog suit, like Liam says," Quinn said, sounding only half joking. "And…he agrees with you. Staying, I mean."

Adam blinked. "How do you know that?" He looked at the dog again. "How does *he* know that I even am?"

Quinn smiled wryly. "If you weren't doing what he wanted, he'd be herding you."

"And just what is it he expects me to do?"

"What we're all going to do. Keep Amanda safe."

Chapter 14

It had to be Malachi.

Amanda was lying awake, so far from sleep she knew it was useless to even try. She'd been lying in the Foxworths' guest room for a couple of hours, wrestling with her thoughts. She couldn't quite believe someone wanted her dead, but if she had to accept that possibility, her first thought was him.

The evidence made him look like a killer. You made him look like a monster.

She hadn't even noticed Adam had been in the courtroom that day. She had been so focused on what she had to do that for all she knew there could have been only two people in that room, herself and the cold-blooded killer who had shot her father.

She felt a flicker of…something, that Adam had thought she'd done so well. Which made no sense, because the last person whose opinion mattered to her was Adam Kirk.

A light tap came on the door and she sat upright. Apparently, the Foxworths had meant what they'd said, that they'd be checking on her regularly. "I'm fine," she called out.

The door swung open, enough for her to see who it was.

Adam.

She felt a flush of heat that had her suddenly checking to make sure she wasn't revealing too much in the T-shirt Hayley had loaned her to sleep in. Instinctively, she pulled the covers up around her, then regretted the move. She didn't want him thinking…whatever a guy might think at that reaction.

"What do you want?" It came out sharper than she'd intended. Only then, when he slipped past Adam, did she notice Cutter was with him. The dog came into the room and walked over to the bed.

"I'm just doing the first check," Adam said, his voice inflectionless. "Don't worry, you'll get Hayley next. Then Quinn. That way nobody has to get up every two hours."

She stared at him. "Except me, apparently," she snapped.

He looked the tiniest bit sheepish. "Well, you are the one we're worried about."

Cutter whined softly, and she automatically reached out to pet the dog's head. And immediately felt calmer. Amazing. Weird, but amazing.

"I'm fine. You can go back to—" She stopped suddenly, her brow furrowing. "Why are you even still here? I thought you were leaving, going back to the other side so you could get an early start in the morning?"

"Cutter thought otherwise."

She blinked. "Excuse me?"

"Long story, which would require you listening to me far more than you want to."

"That boat's already sailed," she pointed out.

His expression didn't change. "I know." Then, more briskly, "Have you slept at all?"

"A little," she fibbed.

"You know where you are?"

"Of course I do. And if I didn't you would have given it away mentioning Hayley and Quinn."

He sighed. "Yeah. Well, not my forte."

"What is, these days?" She stroked Cutter's head again. "Talking to dogs, apparently?"

"I could do worse," he said, and she thought the tiniest edge had crept into his voice. Then, even more briskly, "You remember why we're doing this?"

"Of course."

"Tell me."

"I hit my head."

"Remember what day it is? No checking your phone."

"Tuesday by now, no doubt."

"All right." He started to back away.

"Aren't you supposed to ask if I remember who I am?" It just figured he'd do a half-assed job at this.

"I don't have to. It's obvious you know."

Her brow furrowed. "Why?"

"Because you remember how much you hate me."

And then he was gone, closing the door quietly behind him. She stared after him, feeling oddly chilled by his words. She wondered why. It wasn't like it wasn't the truth.

He'd left Cutter with her. She could see the dog looking at her by the faint reflection of what light there was in his dark eyes. He put one paw up on the bed, politely.

"Are you allowed?" she asked.

He gave an almost indignant sound that nearly made her laugh. "All right, then."

And the moment the animal jumped up and plopped beside her, she was able to think more clearly. Even if she still didn't understand why Adam's words, the look in his eyes, had made her so unsettled. Over the last five years she'd never questioned her feelings about this man. She'd always solidly placed the biggest chunk of blame after the shooter himself squarely on Adam Kirk's shoulders. So why on earth would the knowledge that so did he change anything? Shouldn't she be pleased, or at the least satisfied that he knew his own culpability?

She vaguely remembered when, in the depth of her grief, a few of her father's colleagues had tried to defend him, saying any one of them might have done the same in that situation. She hadn't wanted to hear it.

She still didn't. Did she?

She gave herself an inward shake. Cutter nudged her slightly, and she began to pet him again. If she was going to be lying sleepless thinking about anything, it should be what had happened today—yesterday—not Adam Kirk.

But he was the one who pulled me out of the car. The burning car, at the time.

She pushed away the reminder, focused on the puzzle. Although she supposed it was possible Trevor Malachi had orchestrated this from the state prison—she'd heard of such things—she couldn't see what it would gain him. Adam had been right about that, at least. He wasn't eligible for parole, so it wasn't like there were parole hearings that she attended to stop them from releasing him. She'd been spared that, at least.

But she hadn't encountered anyone else in these five years, or in her entire life for that matter, that seemed capable of this kind of thinking and plotting. And maybe

Malachi simply wanted revenge, maybe locked away as he was, that was all he could do.

It almost had to be. Because the other theory made no sense. It couldn't be a result of her contacting anyone about her father's secret file; she'd called only friends of her father's, people who would never, ever hurt her.

She didn't even realize she'd fallen asleep until Hayley gently woke her, and she managed to get through the litany of questions to prove she was aware. Asked if Cutter was bothering her, she immediately said no, half joking that he was probably the only reason she'd slept. So Hayley left him with her.

Since there was none of the high emotion there had been with Adam, she was able to go back to sleep until Quinn arrived for the next check at 6:00 a.m. She sleepily sat up, but he told her to go back to sleep until she woke up hungry, but this time he collected the dog.

That wake-up turned out to be a couple of hours later, right on time to show she was fine yet again. And not only was she hungry, the smell of fresh coffee was a lure she couldn't resist. She got up and took a quick shower, glad the Foxworth amenities ran to an en suite bathroom in the guest room. She looked in the mirror and grimaced, but did what she could with what she had on hand, most of which had been rescued by Adam.

She found the clothes she'd been wearing yesterday folded neatly on the foot of the bed when she came out, and realized Hayley must have taken them last night and washed them. Or maybe Quinn; the man certainly didn't seem to think he was above such tasks. She dressed quickly, then stepped out of the room. The first thing she noticed as she went into the living room was the neatly folded blanket on the end of the couch, topped by a pillow. Adam had slept on the couch?

She glanced toward the kitchen, where she could hear lowered voices. She walked that way. Adam and Quinn were there, talking quietly. She got close enough to hear just as Quinn said something about sugar. Adam quickly switched his coffee mug to his right hand and reached for the small bowl with his left, handed it to Quinn, then switched the mug back to his left hand and took a sip of coffee. It seemed odd to her, but he'd done it with the ease of long practice.

"How much bend do you have?" Quinn asked.

Bend? What did that mean?

Adam shrugged. "About a hundred degrees."

"Must make things interesting, back home."

"Driving a tractor is an adventure," Adam said with a wry expression.

"But you do it," Quinn said quietly.

"Have to," Adam answered. "But I went to an automatic in the truck. Save the energy for work."

"Come on in, Amanda," Quinn said. "Coffee's still hot."

He had never even looked her way, yet he had known she was there. Adam glanced at her now, turned and left the kitchen without a word.

Quinn got two more mugs out of a cupboard, and handed one to her. "Hayley'll be in for hers any moment now," he said with a smile and a nod at the second mug.

"Thanks," she said as he filled her mug, then the other. She waited as he put two spoons of sugar in Hayley's, then reached for the bowl herself. Which reminded her.

"What did you mean by bend?" she asked.

Quinn put the spoon in the dishwasher before he looked at her and said, "Just wondering how much function he has." He held up his own arm and bent it a bit past a right angle. "A stop at a hundred degrees is pretty limiting."

A stop? Was he saying Adam couldn't bend his arm? She stared at him. "A… I don't…"

Quinn gave her a puzzled look. "Pretty hard joint to put back together, the elbow. I'd go for the replacement myself, but after all those surgeries I don't blame him for wanting to avoid the knife for a while."

"Elbow?" she said, rather faintly. "Surgeries?"

Quinn drew back slightly. Understanding was dawning in his eyes. "Amanda, that bullet shattered his elbow. He's lucky he can move it at all."

"I…didn't know." Suddenly, the memory of that half salute he'd given at her father's graveside shot through her mind. Along with what she'd thought at the time. It had never occurred to her that his hand had only gone halfway because that's all he could do.

"What, exactly, did you think?" Quinn asked.

"I thought… I only heard he was shot in the arm."

Quinn drew in an audible breath. "And so would have been physically able to shoot back."

She nodded, starting to feel faintly nauseous.

"You never watched the store video, did you?" he asked softly.

"I tried, once. But I knew what was coming, and I couldn't."

"If you had, you'd have seen Adam go crashing back right through the store window. Cut him up pretty good, too. But he still got up, and fought to get to his weapon with his left hand."

"I…didn't know."

"Who do you think held Malachi for the backup units after I passed out? And probably saved my life, slowing down the bleeding?"

She drew in a deep breath of her own. "I'm beginning to realize I wasn't thinking much at all."

"And my pain was nothing compared to having a major joint shattered. He held on until he passed out standing up. One of the medics had to catch him. It's amazing he was on his feet at all." He took a sip of coffee before going on. "Too bad he couldn't come back. They lost two good cops that night."

"You must be talking about Adam." Hayley's voice came from behind her. She patted Amanda on the arm as she passed, Cutter at her heels. The dog nudged Amanda's hand as if reassuring himself she was all right. Then, oddly, he sat at her feet, as if he'd sensed her inner turmoil.

Hayley reached for the coffee Quinn had prepared, giving him a loving look as she did so. "It's still sad, him having his lifelong dream taken away."

Amanda knew she was still staring, but that nausea was expanding. "Taken away?"

Hayley gave her the same sort of puzzled look Quinn had. It was Quinn who answered her. "I'm sure they didn't want to retire him, but not much choice with his arm in that condition."

Amanda set down her mug rather sharply. She opened her mouth to speak, but no words would come. She felt as if the ground under her feet had shifted, or worse, turned to slipping, sliding sand. Cutter whined, and the worried sound was the impetus for her to move.

She whirled and ran back to the guest room, where she sank down on the edge of the bed, shaking. The dog had followed her and leaned against her. She felt the warm comfort, but this time it wasn't quite enough.

For five years she had hated Adam Kirk. For not doing what he should have when her father had been shot. And for quitting.

He hadn't just been shot in the arm, some flesh wound as she'd always thought. The very thing the function of that arm hinged—literally—on was destroyed.

He hadn't been physically able to do what she thought he should have.

And he hadn't quit, he'd been forced out, medically retired. Unable to come back even if he had wanted to.

Everything she had thought about him for the last five years was wrong.

He's a good man. I trust him completely.

Amanda lowered her face into her hands, right now hating herself more than she had ever hated Adam Kirk.

Chapter 15

"We're a little shorthanded right now," Quinn said. "Liam's the only one here. Teague won't be back until nearly Christmas."

"And who knows when Rafe will be back, now that he's got another line on that mole." Hayley tapped her finger on the big table. They'd come back to the Foxworth building as soon as everyone was ready. Adam found he couldn't settle, even after the little sleep he'd gotten. He stared out the big window looking out over the meadow, wondering how things were going at home. He'd called this morning, and Nat had assured him things were fine.

"You're useful, but not indispensable," his sister had teased. "Do what you have to."

He turned back now. "Mole?" he asked.

"Long story," Quinn said, rather grimly. "We've been after someone who betrayed us for over two years now. Got Cutter shot."

"And you," Hayley said rather pointedly, as Cutter woofed softly as if to say it was nothing.

"That, too," Quinn allowed in about the same tone as the dog. "Thought we had him a couple of times, but it was never the top guy behind it."

"Took out a few slimy folks in the process, though," Hayley said, in a much lighter tone. "And we'll get him, or her, eventually."

"You're awfully cheerful about it," Amanda said. It was the first time she'd spoken since they'd gotten here.

"Because if that mission had gone any differently, Quinn and I might not be together."

"There is that," Quinn said, looking at her, and Adam thought he'd never heard quite that note in a man's voice before.

He sat down rather heavily, but safely across the table from Amanda. He'd never thought much—or at least tried not to—about whether his future, such as it was, would ever include a woman, marriage, kids maybe. He couldn't quite make the jump to imagining a woman who would want him, want his life. Not in the way Hayley wanted Quinn and his.

And it was all he could do, when that old familiar thought came into his mind once more, not to look up at Amanda.

She'd been acting rather odd since this morning. Quiet. Almost withdrawn. And more than once he'd caught her watching him. With those green eyes that were so familiar, but this morning reddened, as if she'd had a sleepless night just as he had.

Or as if she'd been crying. And why not? If there was ever a time when she had the right, this was it.

But most disconcerting of all, when he did catch her watching him, that barely banked anger seemed…missing. Which made no sense. Unless maybe she'd just decided all hands on deck was the wisest thing until this was resolved. He got the feeling she still didn't believe someone was after her, but when they'd arrived here and Quinn had asked her for a list of everyone she'd called, she'd written it out without question or comment. Then he'd asked Adam for a list of Greg's friends on the force, and anyone he had regular contact with.

"Back to our manpower situation," Hayley said with a beatific smile. "It's a good thing we have Adam here. Between him, Quinn and me, Liam and Cutter, we should be able to cover things."

"Liam can do any immediate online digging we need, the rest we'll give to Ty," Quinn said. "We need to know if ol' Trevor has had any interesting visitors lately. And I think I'd better handle poking at the people you called for help, Amanda. You or Adam would likely get more of an assist, but either of you would obviously tip anybody worried about what your father was investigating."

Adam doubted Quinn was right about he himself getting more help from that quarter, but Amanda surely would. But there was another aspect he hadn't thought of until now.

"Think out loud," Quinn said, and it took Adam a moment to realize that was aimed at him.

"I... Just thinking it wouldn't have to be someone she called." He gestured at the list Amanda had made, lying on the table. "I know—knew—most of these people, and she's right, I can't imagine any of them ever wanting to hurt her. Her, of all people."

"Why so sure?" Quinn asked.

Adam studied him for a moment. "It's not just that they're cops," he said. "They all were friends of Greg's. And..." He hesitated, glancing at Amanda, who seemed to be studying her list as if it might have changed since she wrote it. When he went on, his voice was very quiet. "They all know she's living their worst nightmare. That any day, their own family could be where she is."

Amanda's head came up then. She looked at him, straight on, and his breath stopped in his chest. Not at something that was there in her eyes, her expression, but what was not.

The hatred was definitely gone.

Was she really capable of setting that near-fury aside so completely?

"But?" Quinn prodded.

"They could have said something to somebody else. In fact, it would be only natural to say to anybody who'd known Greg that they talked to his daughter, wouldn't it?"

Quinn nodded, a slight smile on his face, as if of approval. "Excellent point."

"I still can't believe it was someone there, if this is really happening at all," Amanda said. "But if so...there are a whole lot of people still there who knew my dad. How in the world could you narrow it down?"

"Good question," Hayley said.

"I'll just have to be very clever about getting people to talk to me, I guess," Quinn said.

"I think you'll just have to show up and you're in," Adam said, meaning it sincerely. "You're golden around there."

Quinn only shrugged.

"That leaves me, Adam, and Cutter to keep Amanda safe," Hayley said briskly then. "I think we can manage that, thanks to the Cutter early warning system."

Adam smiled; he imagined the dog was rather efficient at that.

"I don't need bodyguards," Amanda protested. At her sharp tone, Cutter got up and walked over to her. Adam couldn't see the dog, but he guessed by the way she looked down and slowly smiled, he'd rested his chin on her leg in that way he had, that uncannily comforting way.

"Perhaps not," Quinn said. "But as long as there's a possibility…"

"But—" Amanda began again.

"We're not taking that chance," Adam said, rather sharply.

He waited for her to light into him, to tell him it was none of his business, that he'd surrendered any responsibility to her the night he'd let her father be murdered. She didn't say it. In fact, she didn't say anything.

"Agreed," Hayley said. She picked up the two odd-looking cell phones that he'd noticed sitting on the table. She slid one across to him, and the other over to Amanda. "These are Foxworth phones. They function like any smartphone, but with a couple of extras. Like that red button there. You tap that and you've got us directly, on an encrypted connection."

Adam picked up the phone and looked at it with interest.

"Now," Hayley went on, "we just need to work out coverage."

"I have work to do," Amanda said. "Consultations."

"Give us your schedule—we'll work with it," Quinn said.

"My clients are already victims," she pointed out, "and some of them are very uncomfortable having strangers see them grieving."

"Cutter can help with that, I think," Quinn said. "And

Hayley can cover those times. She's very good at putting people at ease."

Amanda studied Quinn's wife for a moment. Adam knew that she knew her, but didn't know how well. Then Amanda smiled.

"Yes. Yes, she is." She skated a sideways glance at Adam. "And she's less intimidating than Adam would be."

He nearly gaped at her. Intimidating? Him? He was so stunned at that assessment it took him a moment to realize that this was the first time she'd called him by name to his face. He'd assumed she had a few choice, less socially acceptable terms for him that she politely didn't use in front of Quinn and Hayley, and so didn't refer to him specifically at all.

"Adam, you said you'd worked with Greg on the car before?" Quinn asked.

Adam's throat was suddenly too tight to speak. Those were some of his best memories of Greg. So he only nodded. He heard Amanda make a small sound, and yet another memory flooded his weary brain, the day Amanda had come home for something she'd forgotten in her move to her new place, a condo about fifteen miles north of Seattle, on the other end of the ferry ride from the more rural side where Foxworth was situated. She'd been loath to leave her father living alone, but Greg had convinced her on her twenty-third birthday it was time for her to stretch her wings.

He'd been there working with Greg on putting a new set of spark plugs and wires in the car. It had been a hot summer day, and he'd pulled his shirt off after about an hour. And when she'd pulled up in the little SUV her father had picked out for her for its safety record, he'd considered finding wherever he'd tossed it and putting it back on, except that it seemed a little obvious. And in the next moment he didn't know whether to be glad or regret that he hadn't, because the appreciative look she gave him had brought on a tangle of reactions in him that he never had been able to properly sort out.

If I'd known you were here, I would have stopped by sooner.

If I knew you stopped by, I'd come more often.

The unexpected, flirtatious exchange had made him feel impossibly awkward, with her father standing right there. He'd been wishing he hadn't teased her back when he caught Greg's assessing look at him. But then his partner had grinned at them both, made a comment about suddenly feeling like a third wheel, and the tension had vanished.

"When we get it home to her, that can be your cover, then," Quinn said, snapping him out of the reverie. And slamming home to him that he would be back at that house. Greg's house. His gut tightened.

"I really don't think all this is necessary," Amanda protested again.

"We'll stay out of your way," Hayley promised. "We'll just be around, just in case."

"'Precaution is better than cure,'" Adam said without thinking. But Amanda's expression made him wish he had thought. Because the old quote was something Greg had often said, when teaching Adam to cover all the bases. She simply stared at him, and he felt that familiar ache inside.

"All right," she said, but sounding wary.

Hayley laughed. "We aren't moving in on you permanently. We'll just be at hand. Until we sort all this out and find out for sure what's going on."

Adam wished he was as confident as Hayley sounded.

And he couldn't deny that Quinn had been right when he said as a private entity they could sometimes do more because they weren't hamstrung by regulations or political interference that sometimes kept police from doing their job. Or at least what cops like Greg thought was their job, which was protecting innocent people.

He made a silent vow then and there that this time, unlike last time, he would do that job.

Chapter 16

This was ridiculous.

Amanda pronounced it silently as she turned on the water in the kitchen to rinse out her coffee mug. It was ridiculous, annoying, disconcerting and a few other things she could mention. Not solely because she still couldn't seriously believe she was in any danger, but because it had upended her entire life.

Not Hayley, she didn't mind having her around at all. She was sweet, charming and smart. Quinn had been right; her clients hadn't been the least concerned about her. In fact, more than once in the three days since this farce had begun, she'd been quite helpful. Once she'd even offered Foxworth help to a victim's widower who wanted to set up an ongoing scholarship in his murdered wife's name but didn't know how to go about it.

And she didn't mind Cutter, either; the clever, kind

animal had her thinking she should get a dog of her own. And Hayley was all for that.

"A therapy dog might be very helpful in your work. And it never hurts to have a protective watchdog around," she had said about day two, when Amanda had commented yet again on Cutter's nearly miraculous ability to both guard and to calm and comfort. But then Hayley had ruined it all by adding rather archly, "Unless, of course, you prefer the watchdog out in the garage."

Adam.

There was the true discomfort about this whole thing. And not for any of the reasons she would have given just days ago.

She was still so angry with herself she could barely think about it sanely. All the assumptions she had made, all the anger and loathing she'd carried for five years was scoured out, and she only now realized how much she had let it consume her. She thought she had relegated it all to some back corner of her mind, only escaping at the occasional sharp, jabbing reminders, but apparently while it had been hiding there it had been gnawing out a bigger and bigger space for itself. And only now that it had been blasted out of existence by the truth she had never known—had never bothered to find out, she corrected herself harshly—did she understand how large it had become.

Now she was looking at a weekend, without much work to distract her. Not that she worked a weekday job— tragedy struck at any time and she was always on call for clients. She worked mostly by referral, from both prior clients and friends of her father who had learned of someone who could use her help. Sadly, it happened often enough to keep her busy; there weren't many with her primary motivator and specialty, a police officer killed in the line. Mostly she stayed on the West Coast, but for the grieving loved ones of a cop, she would go anywhere she was asked.

She should be thankful not to be needed for that just now, she told herself. Because someone needing her meant they'd suffered the ugly kind of loss that had nearly crippled her. And she usually was glad when things were slow, for just that reason, but now she was perversely feeling anxious, wondering what she was going to do this weekend with…all this going on.

Be honest. You mean Adam. To whom you owe a huge apology you haven't made yet.

It was true. But she'd been left so reeling about how wrong she had been she hadn't quite been able to put the words together yet. "I'm sorry I thought you were a coward and a quitter," didn't seem nearly enough.

But she had to say something, and soon. And thought if anyone was a coward it was her, not wanting to admit in front of the Foxworths how awful she'd been. No wonder Quinn had been so surprised that she still blamed Adam.

Adam, who had been quietly here, as Hayley had said, in the garage. But what stuck in her mind, so horribly, was the look of pale, grim determination that had been on his face when he'd seen her father's portrait on the wall. Tension had radiated from him as he stared at it, and his expression had made her stomach knot up.

She remembered the moment when Quinn had asked if she still had her father's weapons. She'd nodded and gone to the safe where he'd kept them, and brought back the two handguns.

"His department-issued weapon went back, but the Colt .45 and this—" she pointed at the small, five-shot .38 "—were his."

Quinn had hefted the 1911 model Colt, and looked at Adam. "Ever shot one of these?"

"I've shot that one," he'd answered.

"Can you still?" Quinn asked, neutrally.

Adam had answered just as neutrally. "I'm better with a rifle, but still decent with my left, adequate with the right."

"Good." Quinn had reversed the weapon and handed it to him. Adam had taken it with only a nod. And she supposed he'd had it with him or on him ever since.

She didn't even know where he'd been spending his nights, while Hayley and Cutter stayed here. But he must have slept, because he spent the days working on the car that Foxworth magic had already brought home. What couldn't be repaired or replaced here at home had been done or farmed out, and now Adam was working on the rest. If it had been anyone else she would have been out there with him, because that car connected her to her father in a way nothing else did. And she knew enough to at least know what tools he might need—

It hit her suddenly. How was he doing this, with his arm not working properly? It was a sign, she supposed, of how thoroughly she'd been discombobulated that she hadn't even thought of that until now. She should go and see. Perhaps this wasn't just a case of her being able to help, perhaps he genuinely needed that help.

She dried her hands and braced herself. After the way she'd treated him, he was bound to be wary of her, anyone would be. She—

"Amanda?" Hayley's voice came from the other room. "Quinn's here to update us."

Diverted, and embarrassedly relieved, she called back, "I'll put on fresh coffee."

She had had no idea how Quinn would go about getting information from people at the department without saying why he wanted it, but she knew Foxworth often worked, in a way, undercover. And Quinn was one of the most competent men she had ever met, so she decided she wouldn't worry about how he did it and simply be glad that he could. And wondered what he'd found out in two days of playing casual visitor to the department that held him in high regard for what he'd done that night.

She noticed the bowl of water she'd put down for Cutter was low and refilled it as she waited for the coffee. Once it was done she poured four cups and set them and sugar and milk out on her small dining table. Quinn and Hayley thanked her—as did Cutter for the water with a wag of his tail—but Adam just glanced at her warily. As if he thought she might have poisoned the coffee in his particular mug.

That apology is going to have to be extraordinary.

"First," Quinn said, with a smile at Amanda, "if you didn't already know, your father's friends are immensely proud of you."

She blinked. "Proud?"

"Of what you've done, how you've taken what you went through and turned it into something good."

She felt her cheeks heat, but she couldn't deny the pleasure those words gave her. "I... Thank you for telling me that."

"And I think there are several who would jump in in a hurry, if we need official help."

She drew back slightly then. "Official?"

"If this turns out to be related to what your father was working on, we may need to turn it over to them."

"Oh."

"That said, none of them seemed to have any idea that he was working on anything special or big at the time. But they also agreed he was very careful, a step-by-step sort of guy who wanted all his ducks in a row before he took any action." Quinn shifted his gaze to Adam. "Agree?"

"Absolutely. He was meticulous," Adam said.

"'Make sure of your landing before you jump,'" Amanda quoted.

Adam gave her a startled glance, and a split-second smile curved his mouth as she quoted her father's oft-spoken words. And in that split second it hit her again, how attracted she'd been to the new partner her father had brought home. He'd smiled at her almost hesitantly then, and she'd found the nervousness over meeting his partner's daughter charming. Not to mention those lovely gray eyes, with thick, dark lashes she couldn't help but notice when he looked down rather shyly.

But then he looked down again now, staring into his coffee, as if he regretted his own reaction. And she was right back to staring at the dark semicircles of his eye-lashes as she had that long-ago day.

"By the way, they all mentioned you, too, Adam. Wondered how you were doing."

Adam made a sound that, if it was even a word, she didn't understand.

"They were all sorry you couldn't come back. And they knew how hard you tried to, even after the doctors said it could never happen."

Amanda shot a glance at Quinn, wondering if that was for her benefit. But her gaze was drawn back to Adam as if by a magnet, and she thought that if Quinn and Hayley weren't here she would apologize right now, just because she couldn't bear the guilty feeling any longer.

"I…had a hard time believing it was really perma-nent," Adam said lowly, still staring at his coffee.

"That why you turned down the desk job?"

Adam's head came up, and Amanda looked at Quinn, startled yet again. One more thing she hadn't known.

"I didn't want to spend my life being that cop who got shot and couldn't do the job anymore," he said, still not looking up. "And being tied to a desk would have been..." He waved a hand as he shook his head, apparently at a loss for words bad enough to describe how that prospect felt to him.

Amanda was still trying to process, her disgust at herself building at every moment, when Quinn briskly went on.

"Liam's been running all sorts of checks, trying to find any correlation between the dates in Greg's file and anything else, but it's a pretty broad search so it hasn't turned up much so far. He's already sent what we have to Ty Hewitt—" he glanced at Adam again as he spoke "—our tech guy at our headquarters in St. Louis, to see if he can come up with anything."

"I've been thinking about those dates," Adam said. "Or more accurately, that time period. In between radio calls he would stop a lot to talk to people. Most of the time it was following up on something we'd handled, and I remember thinking I liked the way he did it, that he was working the community to build trust."

He glanced at Amanda then, as if he wasn't certain he should say what he'd been going to in front of her. "Go ahead," she said quietly.

He looked back at Quinn, who was waiting silently; obviously he felt this was worthwhile. "But about six months or so...before, he started talking to people about things I knew we hadn't handled. At the time I assumed it was something from before we rode together. But now..."

"You're thinking it was this," Quinn said. "What was on that flash drive."

"More wondering if it could be," Adam said. "If that's why I didn't recognize a lot of the cases in that file as ones we handled. Because we didn't handle them, but Greg was linking them as he went, because of…whatever it was he was onto."

"Liam ran that, too, trying to match the dates and names to reported cases or crimes." At Adam's look he added rather blandly, "It's good to have friends. And computer proficient help."

"Did he find anything?"

"No trail that went beyond the same officers handling two or three cases because they were in their beat."

Adam nodded. "Didn't figure it could be that easy."

"Do you think you could remember those instances when Greg talked to someone about things you didn't know about?"

"Been a while, but I can try."

"All we ever ask," Hayley said.

Chapter 17

Adam looked at the list he'd made. At the top there were maybe a half dozen items, times he remembered Greg talking to people about situations or people he himself had never heard of. He had at least a reasonable guess on the time periods on these, and had included that with each. Below that were another half dozen encounters that he couldn't put even an approximate date to, although he generally recalled who the people were.

"Best I can do for now," he said when he'd gone to find Quinn, who was taking advantage of the rain clearing out and was outside throwing a rather grubby ball for the apparently indefatigable Cutter.

"That's great," Quinn said as he scanned the list. "Enough for us to get started checking into these people. And I'll bet more will come to you, now that you've started thinking about it after all this time."

"I hope so. But I've spent five years avoiding even thinking about it."

"Can't blame you for that." Quinn studied Adam for a long moment, enough to make Adam a bit edgy. "Speaking of blame," he said after a moment, with a glance back at the building where Amanda was.

Adam knew instantly where he was going. He opened his mouth to try to stop whatever was coming, but couldn't think of anything to say. Finally, he just muttered, "She's got every right."

"No, she doesn't," Quinn said. "But she didn't know that until now."

Adam blinked. "What?"

"You're not the only one who's been avoiding thinking about that night."

"Of course she doesn't want to think about it. Her father died, because I—"

Quinn held up a hand and he stopped. "We're going to have that discussion, but first you need to know that until I told her the other day, she had no idea how badly you'd been hurt. Or that you'd been medically retired."

Adam stared at him. "What, did she think I just quit? That I could have come back but chose not to?"

"Exactly that." Quinn looked at him steadily. "She only heard you'd been shot in the arm. She had no idea how badly."

"Oh."

He didn't know what to think about that. Not that he expected her to know, or even care. Why would she? He wasn't sure what to think. It felt…significant somehow. And it clearly was to Quinn, who didn't miss much.

"But right now we need to plan our next steps," Quinn said, "so if you plan on heading home—"

"Not until we're sure she's safe."

Quinn nodded as if he'd expected no other answer. "All right. Come on in, then. Cutter!"

The dog had been investigating something at the edge of the backyard. Adam smiled when he saw a small black cat shoot out of the bushes and leap to the top of the fence between them and the house next door. Cutter looked torn for a moment but answered the call.

"Somehow it's reassuring to see him doing something so normal," Adam said wryly.

Quinn grinned. "It is, isn't it? Makes it easier to believe he's just a dog."

When they went back inside Hayley and Amanda were already back sitting at the table. Adam took the chance to study her for a moment, as if some unruly part of his mind wanted to know if this was the explanation for the sudden vanishing of that hatred he'd always sensed from her, that she hadn't known before how badly his arm had been hurt, but knew now. Knew that he hadn't quit, he'd been forced out by the injury. It seemed…too much to hope. He told himself sternly it didn't matter, but he couldn't seem to look away.

He could see the man he'd admired so much in the tilt of her nose and the dark auburn of her hair. And he knew if she looked up, it would be like seeing Greg's eyes again, those vivid green eyes that saw so much. And yet they were different, because of the person behind them.

Her head moved and Adam quickly looked away, although she looked up at Quinn, not him.

"I've been telling Hayley I really don't think this is necessary," she said. "Nothing more has happened, and maybe it really was just an accident. Maybe he was just driving recklessly, trying to get away with that stolen car."

"That's possible," Quinn said mildly as he sat down.

"Then you can all go back to doing your good work," she said, sounding relieved.

"This is our good work," Hayley said quietly.

"But—"

"She's right, Amanda," Quinn said. "Why take the chance when you don't have to?"

To Adam's surprise, Amanda looked at him then. As if she were waiting for him to say something. For his input. Now, after all the years of hating him, his opinion mattered?

"Adam?" she said, clearly wanting exactly that. When he didn't answer right away, because he couldn't think of what to say, she prompted, "Don't you need to get home?"

An hour ago, before Quinn had told him what he had just now, his answer would have been a resounding "Yes," and he would have gone for his keys right then. At least, that's what he told himself. But now, looking at her, remembering the girl he'd first met, the woman who had hurled angry words at him in a hospital room, the woman who had wept so brokenly over her father's casket, he thought of the man he'd so admired, the man who had died when he should have stopped it. And he knew if he didn't stay to make sure she was safe, he might as well slide back into that dark pit he'd escaped and end himself as he'd once thought about.

"Quinn's right," he said. "We stay as long as there's even a slim chance."

"But...you don't have to."

It was clear to him she didn't want him to, didn't want him here. He couldn't blame her. What Quinn had told him had dug its way a little deeper into his mind now, and the word *pity* was beginning to surface. And he'd had enough of that in his life. He would have preferred her anger to...that.

"I'll stay out of your way," he said, his voice tight.

"Adam—"

"I think we need to expand our parameters a bit," Quinn said, cutting off the growing tension. "Amanda, we'll need a list of people in your life that aren't connected to your father."

She blinked. "You think one of my friends could be behind this?" Her tone was even more disbelieving than before.

"No. But they still might know or have seen or remember something you haven't."

"Oh."

"We'll also need to know about any ex-friends. Especially ex-boyfriends."

"But…there aren't any. Not since Dad was killed."

Adam couldn't help it, he stared at her. No one? In five years? How the hell had that happened?

"What about the professor?" he asked.

Greg had told him about the man that very evening, that it had been going on for several months now. He'd sounded none too happy about the relationship. And Adam remembered wondering, after she'd blown up at him in the hospital and they were wheeling him into surgery, why the guy wasn't with her.

Her head came up. "He was…less than supportive when it happened. In fact, he dumped me the day after. Said he couldn't take it, and he'd never liked dating a cop's daughter anyway."

Adam stared at her for a moment. No wonder she'd been so broken, to have that dropped on her at the very moment where any decent human being would have stood by her at least until she was through the worst, even if they knew they'd be leaving after.

Then he looked at Quinn. "If that guy ever turns up dead, you'll be looking for me."

"If that ever happens, we'll be looking to help you," Quinn said mildly. "Unless, of course, I run into him first."

Adam blinked, then nodded.

"If you two men are finished with your chest-beating, can we get to something mundane like scheduling coverage?" Hayley suggested. Her tone was teasing, but there was nothing but love and pure female appreciation in her eyes and face as she looked at her husband. It was so apparent even a slow-witted guy like himself couldn't miss it. He'd never in his life had a woman look at him that way. Without thought, and for reasons his mind refused to acknowledge, he glanced at Amanda. Who was looking at him.

He had to quickly look away. Reminded himself to stop looking at her altogether. Not because it kept making him think about how lovely she was, or how vivid those green eyes were, or how alive with that crackling intelligence. He had to stop looking at her because his imagination went crazy every time he did. Crazy enough to imagine he'd seen a bit of that kind of look in her eyes when she was looking at him.

And if there was anything he could do that was crazier than that, he couldn't think of it.

Chapter 18

This was so pointless, Amanda thought on Monday morning after a very quiet weekend. She stared around at the bedroom her father had converted into an office, not really seeing it.

With each hour that passed, she was finding it harder and harder to take seriously the idea that there was any true threat to her. The more distant that day became in her memory the more convinced she became that it had simply been an accident, caused only by the reckless driving of someone trying to escape with the car he'd just stolen. She was using up the Foxworths' time needlessly, when they could be helping someone who needed it. Not to mention she felt guilty because they were apart because of her.

Besides, she had other things occupying the forefront of her mind now. She couldn't remember a time when she'd been so unhappy with herself. And it was rubbed home to her every day that Adam was around. Not that she had seen him all weekend. She knew he'd been here because Hayley and Quinn said so, but where she didn't know.

He'd finished with the car, at least all that could be done here. It now needed paintwork done, and that was going to take a pro, and she'd decided that could wait until this was resolved. But this also meant he was no longer in the garage every day, and she no longer had the option of finding him there now that she'd worked herself up to what she knew she had to do and was only waiting for a moment alone with him to do it.

If that guy ever turns up dead, you'll be looking for me.

Adam's words echoed in her head. As did the tone of his voice when he'd said them. He'd been angry. That had been more than obvious. What she wasn't sure of was exactly why. Because of Geoffrey's awful timing, choosing the moment when she most needed support to walk away? Or because he didn't like anyone who would feel that way about a cop's daughter?

Or because it was her specifically?

That last thought made her even more restless. Her mind was careening around rather wildly. She no longer felt anger when she thought of Geoffrey, which wasn't often. She only thought she should have taken her father's advice when he'd told her he didn't think he was trustworthy. Because he'd clearly been right.

He's a good man. I trust him completely.

Her throat tightened as the words came back to her again. He'd been right about Adam, too.

And suddenly she couldn't put it off a minute longer. She shut down her computer, where she'd been pretending to revamp her scheduling program. She spent a grim amount of time checking her news alerts, set to notify her of any police officers down in accidents or shootings. Ironic, she supposed, since she used to avoid such reports scrupulously, as if not admitting it happened could somehow keep it from happening to her. And now that it had, she hunted them down, to see if she could help.

And it was a process that was taking hideously longer than it used to. She wondered if things would ever get back to normal. If vicious people would ever let it get back to normal. That was a bigger question than she alone could possibly answer.

"It's two weeks to Christmas and you want normal?" she chided herself. Not that she had any idea what normal was anymore.

She got up from her desk, only then realizing Cutter was there. The dog was curled up beside the desk, as if he'd been waiting there for some time. He lifted his head when she stood, watching her with what she'd have sworn was concern in those intense, amber-flecked eyes.

She bent to pet him, and as she stroked the soft fur her inner turmoil eased, just as it had before. It was truly amazing, the effect he had.

"Thank you, my furry therapist," she said softly.

He made a tiny little sound that still seemed worried, as if he wished he could do more. Deciding she was carrying the anthropomorphizing a bit too far, she headed for the door. Her inner turmoil had indeed eased, but it didn't change the decision she'd made. She couldn't move on until she at least tried to make this right.

But she couldn't do it if she couldn't find Adam.

Hayley was on her laptop at the kitchen counter.

"Do you know where Adam is?" she asked without preamble.

Hayley met her gaze, not looking in the least surprised at either her abrupt words or her rather fierce tone.

"Hopefully asleep."

Amanda blinked; she hadn't expected that. "Asleep?"

"He's been taking the night shift outside."

She truly hadn't expected that. "Outside? At night? It's December."

"He pretty much insisted. And Quinn let him, because he got the feeling Adam has something to prove."

"He doesn't need to prove anything to me," Amanda said. "Not anymore. I know the truth now."

"So Quinn said. That you didn't, I mean." Hayley studied her for a moment. And then, softly, she said, "I don't think it's you Adam needs to prove it to."

"Then who does—" She broke off her own words as Hayley's meaning got through. "Himself."

"Exactly."

This further proof that Adam blamed himself as much as she ever had jabbed at her like a serrated blade. She wondered if he ever would have felt that way if she hadn't lost it and screamed at him that night in the hospital. Oh, she was sure he would have felt a certain amount of responsibility—any cop who lost a partner did—but to blame himself entirely? Had that been her brutal gift to him as he'd already been facing so much?

"I need to talk to him," she said. "I owe him a...very large apology."

Again Hayley showed no surprise. Had she expected this, or was she just that unflappable? She was married to Quinn after all, so the latter seemed entirely possible.

"Do you want to wake him up?"

She thought of the last two nights, when it had been down into the midthirties. He'd really been outside in that, watching over her?

"Not if he's someplace warm," she said, with a hint of the self-disgust she was feeling.

She would have to wait until tonight, she thought. But she couldn't let it go any longer. It was eating at her in a much different, harsher way than her anger ever had, for this was her failing and she needed to make it right.

And if what he'd felt had been like this, she felt even guiltier for so misjudging him.

By the time night fell, even as early as that happened this time of year, Amanda thought she was going stir-crazy. She normally thought nothing about spending a day at home, and often did, but somehow feeling it was being enforced by circumstances beyond her control changed everything. There was a world of difference between staying home because you wanted to and staying home because you had to.

Especially when she wasn't at all convinced she had to.

Hayley was in the bathroom when Cutter suddenly trotted to the door and whined. He looked back over his shoulder at her in a very clear signal that he wanted out. Hayley had assured her that he knew he was working and thus wouldn't stray, and while this sounded a bit much to her, it had proved true ever since they'd been here.

Still, she would step outside and keep an eye on him at least.

Oddly, the dog trotted with purpose, not toward the yard where he usually went, but down the sidewalk toward the three cars parked at that end of the street. When he reached the vehicles, Cutter paused at one, then put his head down, nose nearly to the ground. His head came back up and he spun and headed for the small grove of alder trees that began behind the house next door and wrapped around behind hers. Again with obvious purpose.

He was nearly getting out of sight, so she went down

the porch steps and headed out toward the sidewalk. Belatedly, she realized the vehicle the dog had paused at was a pickup. A familiar one.

Adam's.

And it wasn't covered with frost as the other two cars were, the windows were clear, and she could hear the pop of cooling metal. Had he just arrived? Was that why Cutter had wanted out?

She headed that way, smiling at the idea that the obviously clever dog could lead her to the man she needed to see more than anyone right now, to at least get her piece said. Her father had always told her apologies were one thing that didn't keep. And right now she felt as if her entire life was dammed up behind this intense need to apologize to Adam, and nothing could move on until she did.

Three things happened in rapid succession. She heard a sudden cacophony of ferocious barking from the trees. Cutter, sounding fierce even at this distance.

She stopped in her tracks.

And then the third thing happened.

A rush of footsteps behind her and an arm coming around her neck.

Chapter 19

Adam had heard the faint rustle in the underbrush. He'd frozen in place, only turning his head to make sure the sound was coming from as low as he'd thought. After a couple of seconds he was sure, and so wasn't surprised when Cutter appeared out of the darkness, his plumed, lighter-colored tail more visible than his dark head and shoulders. What faint light there was on this overcast night was caught by the dog's eyes, a dark sort of gleam, as if nothing could completely mask the glow of intelligence there.

He'd greeted the dog with a scratch behind his right ear as he'd seen Quinn do. He'd been wondering how to tell the dog to go back to his watchdog duties, remembering about something he'd read once about how to puncture your ego by trying to give orders to someone else's dog, when it happened.

In an instant Cutter went from amiable pet to ferocious guardian. The dog let out a spine-tingling growl as he whirled around. He was gone so fast, back the way he'd come, that it took Adam a split second to react and follow. But he figured there had to be a reason Quinn trusted the dog's instincts so much, and given he was headed back toward Amanda, he wasn't about to ignore the obvious signals.

As they burst out of the trees Cutter's vocalizing changed to a half bark, half snarl that would send anyone with an ounce of self-preservation running. Or if they were smart, climbing, because it was doubtful anybody would be able to outrun the dog who was running full tilt, head down, teeth bared.

The instant he saw where the dog was headed Adam's heart jammed up in his throat. There were two figures on the sidewalk in front of Amanda's house, one larger, hulking, the other smaller, slender, and struggling, kicking. Amanda. He didn't think he'd ever run so fast in his life, even when he'd had to qualify at the academy.

He could tell the moment when the man heard them coming—Cutter, no doubt, that vicious-sounding, snarling growl seemed to echo in the night air—because suddenly there was space between him and Amanda. Time slowed down in that crazy way it did when things were happening fast. She kicked at the man, threw an elbow toward his head, which Adam could now see was swathed in a kind of covering that reminded him of some of the violent street protesters he'd encountered while in uniform.

He also saw something in his hand, the barest glint on metal. A knife.

He saw the man's head turn toward him and Cutter. He was still a good hundred feet away, although Cutter was gaining ground fast. Lights had come on in the house. As if he only now realized he was in trouble, the man finally shoved her away and ran. Amanda stumbled, went down, just as the front door of the house burst open. Hayley.

"Take care of her!" he yelled and kept running.

Cutter was closing on the man, but Adam knew it was pointless when he saw the man yanking open the door of a car that had been parked in the deep shadows of a row of cedars just north of the house. The passenger door, and he could hear that the car was already running.

"Cutter!" He yelled it, afraid the dog would get hurt. He hadn't really expected the animal to listen to him, but as the man he was pursuing got into the car, he slowed. The car's tires squealed as they made a wild U-turn and sped off. Apparently, the dog was clever enough not to waste energy on a moving vehicle and stopped.

Adam immediately turned and ran back, the image of Amanda falling to the ground when the guy let her go seared into his mind. He was terrified she'd been hurt. Or worse.

Hayley glanced at him as he knelt beside them. Breathed again when he realized Amanda was alive. Hayley was helping her sit up, but she looked at Adam and nodded toward Amanda's left side. He looked down, saw a long, thin line of blood across her ribs.

"Anywhere else besides your side?" Adam asked urgently.

"I… What?" Amanda sounded so shaken he wanted nothing more than to sweep her up in his arms and hold her until she felt safe again.

"You're bleeding a little," Hayley said then; she'd pulled out her phone and turned the flashlight on, scanning Amanda from head to toe.

"I am?" It was the shock, the aftermath of fear for her

life that put that quaver in her voice, Adam knew. He put a hand over the spot on her ribs. She winced slightly. "Oh. He…had a knife."

Adam's jaw tightened as he probed, found the long but thankfully not deep slice across her ribs, which had done what they were designed to do and protected her. "I saw. Anywhere else?"

"I don't think so…but I didn't even feel that."

"Adrenaline is an amazing thing," he muttered.

"Let's get you inside," Hayley suggested, "where we can see how bad that is, if we need to call paramedics or get you to the ER."

"Oh! No, no, it's not bad, really. I—" Adam gave in to the urge he'd felt before and picked her up. She stiffened and let out a gasp, but he thought it sounded more like surprise than pain. "What are you—"

"Just getting you inside, like Hayley said," he said gruffly, not giving her a chance to argue. He carried her easily even with his arm; he'd had to learn how to manage bales of hay that weighed more than she did. He heard Hayley speaking behind them as they walked toward the house, realized she had called Quinn. But he focused on getting Amanda inside.

A little to his surprise she had relaxed, in fact was resting her head on his chest. She was still shivering slightly, whether from the aftermath or actual cold he didn't know. Nor did he allow himself to savor the feeling of holding her, although he wanted to. He focused on the porch steps, and then on turning sideways to get through the door Hayley held open for them.

Hayley, who was now on the phone again, and this time it was obviously to the sheriff's office. And Adam knew they were likely to have a long night in front of them.

* * *

Amanda still felt the sting and slight pull when she moved a certain way, but other than that the slice along her ribs wasn't bothering her all that much. Or maybe it was just the distraction of everything that was keeping her from thinking about it.

The distraction that Adam and the Foxworths had been right all along. Someone was trying to kill her.

She shivered anew at the thought. She could feel the exhaustion hovering, the post adrenaline crash Quinn called it, but her racing, swirling thoughts wouldn't let go.

It had been a very long night. It felt strange being on this side of things when the police arrived, even though it wasn't her father's department. She'd told them what she could, although she'd barely gotten a glimpse of the man as he'd shoved her away. She hadn't even been able to give them an idea of his size, other than bigger than her. And stronger. And what she had smelled.

She grimaced inwardly. That he smelled of beer wasn't going to get them very far.

But she noticed that Adam told them much more; he'd given them a clothing description, when she remembered only the head wrap, and height and build. Also something she'd completely missed, that he'd been holding that knife in his left hand. He also gave them a vehicle description—no front plate, he'd said, and the rear had been covered with what had looked to him like duct tape.

Right now Adam and Quinn were in a deep discussion with the tall, lean man in a black coat over slacks and a white dress shirt that they'd introduced as Detective Dunbar, from the sheriff's office. He was clearly well-known to them, and Hayley had pronounced him as one of the good guys, the best in fact. Amanda believed it. He'd been amazingly kind as he gently led her through it again, so he could hear firsthand. And hadn't made her feel at all guilty for going outside, which was good because she was doing a fine job of that herself.

"I just couldn't believe someone was really after me," she had admitted.

"That's a normal reaction," the detective had assured her. "But now you know."

She barely managed to suppress a shudder. "Lucky me."

He'd said then, with quiet confidence, "You've got the best on your side, Amanda. Let them do what they do and it will all work out."

It was much later—or at least it seemed so to her—that things finally calmed down. Hayley and Quinn had their heads together over near the kitchen, and Adam stood beside the couch she was lying on, staring out her front window. It played through her mind again, the way he'd never hesitated to chase that man. And nearly caught him, probably would have if that car hadn't been there waiting.

"What were you doing out there?" she asked, almost without thinking, because her brain felt so scrambled.

Adam turned to look at her, his brow furrowed. "What?"

"You were out there in the trees."

"Yeah. There's a good spot there, up the hill a little, where I can see the house, front and back." He frowned. "Obviously it's too far away, though. Although I didn't expect you to come outside."

It was her turn to frown. "I took Cutter out. I saw him stop at your truck and then track you."

"He's usually on his own when he comes to visit up there."

It finally registered on her weary brain. "You mean you have been up there...what, every night?"

"Like I said, it's a good spot."

"But it's nearly freezing out at night."

He merely shrugged.

"Adam—"

"You should try to rest. The crash is going to be ugly enough without you pushing so hard."

"I will—when you tell me why you've been up there, out in the cold."

He looked genuinely puzzled now. "I told you, to watch the house. But I need a new spot. It's close enough to the back, but not the front." Cutter had padded over to them, and nudged Adam's hand. He stroked the dog gently. "You still almost had him, didn't you, boy?" he said approvingly.

Amanda took a deep breath and tried again. "You're watching the house because of me, right?"

"Of course." His brow was furrowed again.

"Then why," she asked, scraping up what little patience she had left, "aren't you doing it inside, where it's warm?"

Adam blinked. "Because…you don't want me in your house. Your father's house."

He said it as if he were saying the sky was blue. A given. Accepted. It flooded back to her now, that thing that had been all-important to her until the moment when that man had grabbed her.

And Adam came racing to your rescue. Even after you treated him so unfairly.

Now. She had to say her piece now. She shouldn't have taken this long, nearly a week, but it had been so hard to process, to change the mind-set of the last five years. It was the last thing she felt like doing right now, but she couldn't let this go on another moment, no matter how tired she was.

She gestured at the space beside her on the couch. "Will you sit down?"

He looked beyond startled. Then wary.

And Amanda hated that she had caused those feelings in him. It was past time to fix that.

Chapter 20

Adam had no idea what was going on, but sitting next to Amanda on the couch where she'd been lying, no doubt still warm from her body, was the last thing he wanted to do just now.

"Please?" she said, and it was so clearly heartfelt he couldn't say no. But that didn't mean he had to sit next to her. He didn't think he could take that. So he went to the chair that sat at right angles to the end of the couch and slowly, reluctantly sat.

"What?" he said, without looking at her.

"I'm so sorry."

The moment she spoke he wanted to get up again. Wanted to leave, get out of here before she said what he now knew was coming.

"I've been so angry at you for so long, and it was all wrong. I was wrong. I made a horrible mistake, and I truly am sorry. I—"

"Amanda—"

She kept going. "But I must say this. Even though I don't have words for how awful I feel for misjudging you so." She grimaced. "As if I had any right to judge you at all."

"If anyone does, it's you," he muttered.

"All I can say in my defense is I didn't know. When they said you were shot in the arm, my brain—no, my emotions—put an 'only' in front of it. You would think I'd know better, but... I wasn't thinking straight at the time."

The memories of that night rose up with fierce suddenness and clarity, nearly swamping him. He fought the shudder that began down so deep he wasn't even sure where it originated, only that if he let it start he'd be on his knees. And while he'd often thought he should do just that in front of her, it was for him to apologize, not her.

"Are you done?" he asked, his voice so tight it sounded even to him as if it would shatter.

"Adam, please. I've treated you so horribly—"

"You've treated me exactly as I deserved."

"No!" She reached out then, and before he could pull away she'd grabbed his hand. Her touch sent a lick of fire through him, which was the only thing that immobilized him long enough for her to go on. "No, you don't deserve the awful things I thought, not at all. All these years I blamed you for something you couldn't help. All this time—"

He jerked away then, and stood up in a rush. "I don't want your pity."

"Pity? Is that what you think this is?"

"Isn't it?"

"More like admiration, Adam Kirk. You've come back from that night, adapted where you had to, built a life—"

"Come back? Is that what you call it? I ran home and hid out like a scared kid. And I've stayed there."

He turned away, back toward the front window. The sky was lighter, and he realized it was nearly dawn. Tried to calm down, picturing the sun rising over the rolling hills of home. Might even be able to actually see it there, for it appeared the storm had passed.

The physical one anyway.

"You went home to your family," she said softly. "Just what I would have done."

Except she didn't have any family now. Thanks to him.

Silence stretched out between them. His mother, he realized, would say he was being rude not to accept what was clearly a genuine apology. The problem was, he didn't deserve it. She was only doing it because she felt sorry for him now. Amanda Bonner would never kick someone when they were down, and obviously that's the category she had put him in now.

He was thankful when Hayley and Quinn walked into the room.

"Ah, good," Quinn said when he saw them. "I need to talk to both of you."

Adam turned sharply at that, but he didn't sound as if they had discovered something momentous.

Quinn got to the point quickly. "I'm going to make a quick flight to Walla Walla."

Adam blinked. "To the prison?"

Quinn nodded.

"Then...you think he had something to do with it?" Amanda asked, her voice a little shaky again now.

"I tend to agree with you that none of the people you talked to about that file would ever want to hurt you. So I think Malachi is a possibility we need to either eliminate or prove, if we can."

"All right," she said, although she still sounded a bit uncertain.

"So the question is, do either of you want to go with me?" Amanda drew back slightly, staring. Quinn shrugged. "I didn't really think so, but thought I'd ask in case either of you wanted to confront him at this point."

And give him the pleasure of seeing the lives he's ruined?

Adam's thought sent a new sort of shiver through him. "No, thanks."

"Ditto," Amanda said, rather fervently.

"I'd rather focus on messing up his plans, if it is him," Adam added.

"Good choice," Quinn said. "Just wanted to be sure. We need to continue the coverage now that we're certain it's necessary. Liam will cover our shifts this weekend, because we have a trip of our own to take, one we can't really change."

"The wedding?" Amanda asked, clearly knowing about it.

Hayley noticed Adam's look and explained. "My brother's wedding. He's marrying my best friend."

Adam managed a smile. "I'll bet there's a story there. Congratulations to them both."

"There is quite a story," Hayley said, "and one I should tell you, now that I think about it. But right now I think Quinn needs to get going if he's going to get back this afternoon."

"This afternoon?" Adam asked. "I think there are only a couple of flights a day, and the return is later."

"He'll be flying Air Foxworth," Hayley said with a grin. "He hasn't had a chance to break out the toy in a while."

They had their own plane. Adam stared at Quinn for

a moment. He had obviously built the Foxworth Foundation into something bigger than Adam had ever realized.

"You're not going alone, are you?" Amanda asked, sounding a bit anxious. "I mean…you're the guy who shot him."

"And vice versa," Quinn said. "Evens that ground a bit. But I'll take Liam with me. He's working on finding out if the guy could have arranged this from his cell."

Adam nodded slowly. "You mean who his visitors have been, cell mates who may have been released, or had visitors with potential, that kind of thing?"

"Exactly. So far nothing. He hasn't had many visitors, but Liam's just getting started on the connections once removed."

"I just don't see what he'd hope to gain out of it," Amanda said.

"Maybe," Adam said, "we need to think more about whether he's got anything to lose."

"Exactly," Quinn agreed. "And these days the answer is, not much. So we'll dig."

It was after Quinn had gone that Amanda approached him. "You can leave, after Quinn gets back. I'm sorry this has kept you away so long, I know you hadn't planned—"

"I'm not going anywhere."

"But—"

"I'm staying, Amanda." He turned away then, but she came after him. Tenacious, Greg had always said. Obviously, he'd known his daughter well.

"Look, if you're staying because you feel guilty or responsible or something, don't. You shouldn't and you're not. So you can just go home."

He turned back then. "I'm staying so I can live with myself," he said flatly. "Which is hard enough already without adding abandoning you when you're in trouble to the list."

For a long moment Amanda just looked at him. There was something different about her gaze, something beyond just the absence of the anger. Something…warmer? That the idea even occurred to him rattled him, and he was about to be rude and turn his back on her when she spoke so softly he felt the urge to lean in to be sure he heard her.

"For all the horrible things I said and thought, it's still nothing to what you've said to yourself, is it? You blame yourself more than I ever could."

"Then you're not blaming me enough," he said, his voice harsh.

He did turn his back then, and headed for the kitchen, where Hayley was preparing more coffee. He took the cup she silently poured for him, cooled it a bit so he could gulp it down, needing the caffeine hit more than anything.

"I'm going to make a circuit outside," he said.

Hayley nodded. "Take Cutter."

"I will. He's…a good partner." He'd hesitated on the words, remembering yet again what had happened to his last partner.

"He is," Hayley said. "And unlike humans, he doesn't feel guilty when he does all he can do and it doesn't work out right." Startled, he met her gaze. She took a sip of coffee before adding, "You know, some of the standards we hold ourselves to are more than anyone else would ever require."

You blame yourself more than I ever could.

He needed to get out of here. Before he started believing what two kind, generous women were saying.

Chapter 21

Amanda felt oddly disoriented. She had taken a shower
in an effort to wash away the feel of the attacker's hands
on her, and even the familiar process seemed strange.
When she'd finished she'd stood there dripping for a minute before she remembered the next step was to get out
and grab a towel.

She knew she was tired. She had been up all night
after all, but just the idea of lying down and trying to
sleep made her recoil. She didn't want to relive this night
in dreams. She had some vague idea of staying up until
she fell asleep involuntarily, thus saving herself from
lying awake trying to keep from thinking about what
had happened tonight.

The incontestable proof that someone was after her
was part of it of course, but it wasn't all of it. She was
only now realizing how much time and energy her con-

demnation of Adam had taken up. She felt like a compass needle that had lost North, spinning a bit.

And now that she knew it was both unfair and unfounded, she also understood that it had done damage to her as well as to him. Holding on to anger always did, the counselor she'd seen right after her father's death, the one who had inspired her to her current work, had said.

And you quit seeing her because she told you it wasn't healthy to hate so much, and you didn't want to hear it.

She didn't like admitting that, even to herself, but there it was and it was true. It had given her purpose, and sometimes it had been the only thing that had gotten her through the next day, the next hour, the next minute.

The horrible things she'd screamed at him in the hospital, when he'd been lying there helpless, awaiting the surgery that apparently had only put him partly back together, played back in her mind. Would he still be blaming himself if she hadn't poured her anger and fear and grief onto him that day?

In the space of a week her entire perception of the most momentous event of her life had been turned upside down. And this new view—the truth—made her feel like sitting in her room and calling herself every vile name she knew. But it still wouldn't be enough.

She had never bothered to find out the truth. Because she assumed she knew the truth. She'd heard the phrase "blinded by grief" before, but she hadn't applied it to herself. Because she'd thought her vision was crystal clear and she'd laid responsibility right where it belonged.

Except she'd been completely wrong.

And Adam Kirk was everything her father had thought he was.

The real problem now was that he didn't believe it. And a big part of that could be laid at her door.

Quickly, she put her wet hair in a single braid, fastened the end and let it hang down her back. A glance in the mirror told her her eyes were reflecting the lack of sleep, but the last thing she felt like doing was trying to hide the ravages of what had happened. She felt better, if not good, and figured that was the best she could do for now.

She found Hayley with her phone in hand, sitting at the kitchen counter. "Quinn's getting ready to take off," Hayley said. "Good thing he at least got a little sleep yesterday."

Amanda blinked. "Already?"

"Airport's only about a half hour away, and he called ahead to have them ready the plane."

Amanda smiled. "He looked like a kid at Christmas."

"That's how he feels, I think. It's a great little plane. Prop, not a jet, but one of the few with a pressurized cabin, so it's more versatile." She grinned then. "And it's pretty. Even he admits it."

Amanda's own smile widened. Hayley had such a way of making her feel better. Just like her dog. Speaking of which… "Where's Cutter?"

"Out with Adam."

"Still?" She'd heard him say he was going to make a circuit, but that was over an hour ago.

"He texted an all clear, and said he'd be looking for a better lookout spot." Hayley grimaced. "He was really stressed about not being able to get to you in time."

"But he—they—did," Amanda said. "If that guy hadn't seen him and Cutter charging them, I… I…" Hayley reached out and laid a warm hand over hers. "Sorry," Amanda muttered.

"Don't worry about it. When Quinn first kidnapped me, before I knew who and what he was, I was a wreck. My brain wouldn't shut off."

"Exactly." She grimaced. "But Adam should get some sleep. He was up all night."

Hayley gave her a considering look. "He's been up all night every night."

Remorse flooded Amanda again. "He's really been standing guard."

"Yes. And sleeping in his truck, so he could still be close."

In his truck. In this cold.

Because you don't want me in your house.

The sudden knot in her stomach seemed to suck all the strength from the rest of her, and she swayed on her feet. Hayley quickly urged her to sit on the stool next to her.

"Quinn told me, before he left, that you hadn't known how badly Adam was hurt. I was glad to hear that."

Amanda stared at her. "Glad?"

"Because I didn't understand why you blamed him so…fiercely. You didn't seem to me the type to blame someone unfairly. Now I get it."

"I feel so awful," she admitted. "He didn't deserve any of the things I thought. Or worse, said."

"You've told him that?"

"Yes, today, when I finally was able to talk to him alone. I should have done it sooner but I couldn't think straight, and it took me a while to work up to it."

Hayley nodded in gentle understanding. "It's not easy to change your entire way of thinking. And it would be especially tough for you right now, when you have your own situation to deal with at the same time. But I'm glad you told him."

"I'm not sure it did much good," Amanda said rather glumly. "Now he thinks I just feel sorry for him."

"Do you?"

"In a way, because of the permanent damage. But I admire him more, for how he's adapted."

"He's done well. Although it is curious that he's refused the joint replacement surgery."

Amanda frowned. "Joint replacement? I didn't realize they did that for elbows. But I guess if they can do knees, an elbow isn't all that different."

"I'd think it would be even more durable, without the putting weight on it issue."

Amanda nodded. "But…you said he's refused it?"

"That's what Quinn told me."

"But why, if it could help?"

"Quinn said he said he was tired of surgery. But he suspects there's more to it than just that."

"Like…what?"

Hayley shook her head at the question. "Quinn's a guy, he doesn't speculate on stuff like that, or dig at somebody to talk about something they don't want to talk about. Well, except me," she added with a grin.

Amanda sighed. "If I didn't like you both so much I'd envy you. You're amazing together."

"We are," Hayley agreed simply. Then, with a speculative look at Amanda, she said, "That story I promised… I know a little bit about…misjudging people."

"You? I can't imagine that."

"Then you should talk to my brother. I thought the absolute worst of him for a very long time. Because I didn't know the truth."

Amanda listened with increasing amazement at the story Hayley told her then, of terrorism and courage and a man who kept his word even when it hurt. "So…heroics run in the family?" she said rather faintly at the end.

Hayley grinned. "On all sides, now. Amy's no slouch

in the nerve department, either. And Walker's running the Southwest office of Foxworth now."

"Wow."

Hayley became serious then. "I told you that to show you that damaged bridges can be repaired. And sometimes they're even stronger, after."

"I…but how do you make up for that damage, when they believe the horrible things you thought are true? And when it may well be your fault that they believe it?"

"That one I don't have an answer for, except keep trying."

"Maybe if I grovel for five years," Amanda said glumly.

Hayley seemed to be looking at her rather intently. "Or maybe when this is over he just goes home and you go on with your lives."

"No!" It broke from her harshly. "I can't let him go on feeling that way when it's not true. And I just know what I yelled at him in the hospital that day was the start of him feeling that way, because nobody else believed it except stupid me."

"Grieving you," Hayley corrected softly, "which makes it much more understandable."

"But not acceptable," Amanda said with renewed determination.

"Luckily, he's here now, and you have time to fix it." She gave Amanda a wry smile. "At least now we know why Cutter acted the way he did at the cemetery."

"What?"

"That look he gave Quinn? That's his 'fix it' look. He knew something was very wrong between you and Adam, and that was his signal that we, Foxworth, needed to help."

You and Adam.

Even being coupled together in a sentence like that sent an odd sort of sensation through her. And the thought she'd had a moment ago, about Hayley's brother, echoed in her mind.

A man who kept his word even when it hurt.

Adam had done that. He'd stayed here, to protect her, even when she'd made it clear what she thought of him. Even as she'd proved her own ignorance and judgmentalism time and again. That it had been born out of her own unbearable agony wasn't an excuse, not after all this time.

She wasn't sure if this bridge could be repaired.

She might just have to build a new one.

Chapter 22

"I don't think it was him," Quinn said as he sat at Amanda's table, Cutter at his feet and clearly delighted he was back. "Nothing fit, no strange visitors. He's had the same cell mate all along. And he seemed genuinely surprised by my showing up and asking questions."

Adam imagined Quinn Foxworth didn't get fooled often, so he accepted his determination without much doubt. But he did voice the little he had. "You don't think he might just be out for revenge, for her putting him in there?"

"I didn't get the vibe, but I could be wrong." Quinn looked thoughtful for a moment. "In fact, I didn't get the angry lifer vibe, either. He seemed...strangely content."

"Some cons are like that," Adam said. "We arrested a guy once who admitted he'd let himself get caught because he wanted to go back inside. The outside world was too chaotic for him, he liked the regimented life and not having to worry about anything more than ticking off one of the gang leaders."

Quinn nodded. "There's a mentality that fits that existence. Don't get it myself, but that's just me."

"And me," Amanda put in rather fervently.

"Still, I do think he's hiding something. I'm just not sure it's related to this. Anyway, Liam did a little digging into his family on the way back."

"I remember his mother and grandmother at the trial," Amanda said.

Quinn nodded. "The grandmother passed a couple of years ago. As far as we could find, his mother and a younger brother are the only ones left. He wouldn't talk about her, but Liam found out she's living there in Walla Walla now."

"What an awful reason to move," Adam said. "Kind of…sad, I guess. For her, I mean."

Amanda gave him a surprised look that turned thoughtful as Quinn said, "We'll keep digging on that front, but I don't think he's the answer to our immediate situation." He looked at Adam. "I've hit everyone on the lists you gave me, and a few more, and nothing. I think we're at a standstill on that front for the moment. So I'll take the night shift the next couple of nights, and you can catch up on sleep."

"Good," Amanda said. "He needs to."

Adam gave her a sideways look before he said to Quinn, "Don't you have to pack?"

"Fifteen minutes. Much to my wife's dismay, since that's what she's doing already."

Adam smiled at that, but Amanda sniffed and muttered, "Men. Dark suit and you're done."

"Gives me more time to appreciate how great Hayley's

going to look in that dress she'll be wearing," Quinn said, turning Amanda's teasing complaint into a wide smile.

Adam wondered what it would be like to be at such ease with her. Quinn was just as connected to the tragedy of her past as he himself was, but with none of the guilt and remorse attached. No, Quinn Foxworth was the hero of the piece, and nothing could change that.

Except... Amanda had apologized. And he didn't know how to feel about that. He'd never expected it. The only thing that he could see that had changed was that she hadn't known the details of his injury, and now she did. Which in his mind added up to only one thing. She felt sorry for him. A little to his surprise, he found he preferred her anger to her pity.

"So," Quinn said to Adam, "you can crash here tonight, while I stand watch."

Adam's gaze flicked to Amanda, wondering how she felt about Quinn giving away her guest room to him, of all people.

"Of course," she said quickly. So quickly he wondered if they had already discussed it.

"I'll leave Cutter with you in the house, just in case somebody gets past me. He'll let you know."

"Can't see that happening," Adam said. After that fateful night he'd learned a bit about the man who'd done what he couldn't. And he doubted the former Army Ranger had forgotten much.

"Always a chance," Quinn said. "And you," he said to Amanda, "don't go out alone."

She flushed. "You don't need to remind me, believe me. It was stupid to do it the first time, but..."

"You didn't really believe any of it, did you?" Adam asked gently.

"No," she admitted. "No, I didn't. I know better now."

"I'm sorry," he said, meaning it completely differently this time. He was sorry that she was having to deal with this, face the fact that someone was trying to hurt her. Or worse. He couldn't even form the word for that "worse" in his mind, let alone say it. The injustice of that, if they succeeded, first her father and now her…it made him want to go blow something up. A feeling he'd had only once before in his life, that moment he'd known Greg was truly dead.

She was looking at him as if she somehow knew exactly how he'd meant it this time. And then, quietly, she said, "If it wasn't for you I might not even be here to dwell on it." He started to shake his head, but she spoke again, quickly. "You pulled me out of the car, you chased that guy off last night. That's twice you've saved me from serious injury, or last night likely worse."

He hadn't really thought about it like that. But even if she was right, it still didn't make up for that night.

When he finally lay in darkness that night, he was aware of being more comfortable and, thankfully, much warmer than he had been for days now, but he was much more aware of being in Amanda's house. The house that she'd once shared with her father.

In the end, renewing his vow to Greg that he would not let her be hurt was the only thing that let him slip into much-needed sleep.

Amanda pondered the food in the fridge as the coffee brewed the next morning. Hayley had seen to it that they had all the basics. Foxworth handled that sort of thing when they moved in on somebody, she'd said.

She could tell by how she caught herself staring at the shelves that she was still a little fuzzy after a restless night. She'd expected to have nightmares about the attack, and so her mind had been reluctant to let her slip into deep sleep. But when she did, it wasn't her attacker she dreamed about. It was her rescuer.

How many times had she awakened from one of those dreams to the startling realization that the man himself was right down the hall? Was that what had brought them on?

She closed the refrigerator door rather more firmly than was necessary, and the bottles in the door racks rattled. The movement, and muscle aches it caused, jarred the fuzziness—and the thoughts—out of her head. She'd thought she was in decent shape, but every time she moved a certain way she was rather fiercely reminded of how hard she'd fought.

Which brought her right back to the attack, and seeing Cutter and Adam charging out of the darkness, heedless of any danger, as they came after the brute who had her so helpless.

On the thought Cutter appeared at her side, plumed tail wagging slightly. She'd already let him out first thing this morning when she'd given up on sleeping any longer, and he wasn't looking as if he wanted out again. Especially not when he sat at her feet and stared at the fridge intently.

"Hi, furry one. Can I get you something?"

Even as she said it she remembered something Hayley had told her and opened the fridge again. She reached into the produce drawer and pulled out the small bag of baby carrots. Cutter sat politely, but his eyes were glued to her movements. And when she tossed him one of the little carrots he caught it and crunched with gusto. It made her smile, and she thought once more that she might just have to get a dog. She supposed dogs like Cutter were few and far between, but just the companionship made it worth thinking about. She reached out and stroked the dark head.

And then the dog's head came up, his ears alert, as he looked toward the back door. He listened for a moment, then trotted over to the door and looked back at her. Quinn had said if he scented or heard danger she'd have no doubt, so she assumed the wagging tail and no barking or growling meant there wasn't any, and he just wanted outside. She opened the door for him, and he went out eagerly. Maybe he'd heard Quinn, she thought. She should try again to think about some breakfast for her guardians. It seemed the least she could do.

She had a mug of coffee at her fingertips and was starting eggs and bacon when she heard a sound from the hallway. And she caught herself holding her breath as she listened, wondering if Adam would appear. Oddly, it felt a little like when she had met him for the first time, when she'd been so startled that her father hadn't mentioned, amid all his approval of his new partner, that he was also drop-dead gorgeous. How could you describe him and not mention those stormy gray eyes and thick dark lashes, or that he was built like some walking, breathing example of her ideal male.

Not that she had ever told her father what her ideal male was. She'd been a little embarrassed to admit that he was the one all males in her life would be measured against, and that most of them came up far short.

I wish I'd told you that, Dad.

That, and so much else that she'd never gotten to say, because in her youthful ignorance she had thought they had all the time in the world.

She heard the bathroom door close, and breathed normally again. She'd told him there were clean towels in the bathroom, and he'd brought in a small duffel bag last night, politely thanking her for the chance at a real bed.

The rest of the brief conversation played back in her head.

If I'd known you were sleeping in your truck I would have offered sooner. The couch at least.

You wouldn't have before Quinn told you about my arm.

Was he right? She hadn't wanted him around, true, but would she really have been that ill-mannered when he was here to help?

Of course, she now knew he was likely only still here because he felt guilty. Which was at least partly her fault, so now she felt guilty.

Guilt's a useless emotion, Mandy, unless it drives you to do something about it, to fix what you feel guilty about. And if there's nothing to be done, resolve to do better and cut it loose before it drags you down.

God, she missed her dad so much. Unlike many of her peers, who had dismissed parental advice in the youthful certainty they knew better, she considered her father the wisest person she knew, and when he shared that wisdom she took it seriously.

She heard Adam in the doorway just as she was putting the bacon on a paper towel to drain. "Good timing, breakfast is—" she looked around, and her tongue stumbled. "Ready," she finished with an effort.

She'd looked a hair too soon. He'd been pulling on a long-sleeved knit shirt, and she'd gotten a blast of his bare chest and abs. If that was what ranch work did to a man, they should tear down most of the gyms in the world and replace them with memberships at a working ranch.

The only thing that saved her from complete humiliation was that he hadn't yet pulled the shirt down over his head when she'd gotten that eyeful. So he didn't know she'd quite literally gaped at him.

Kind of like I did the first time I met him.

She'd never denied that she'd been fiercely attracted back then. That had made what happened even harder to take. In a strange way it was another layer of grief, that he hadn't been what she'd thought he was, what her father had thought he was.

But now she knew he had been exactly that, all along. It was she who had been wrong. Completely wrong.

And she didn't know how you made up for a mistake that big.

Chapter 23

"You don't have to cook for me," Adam said, his voice still a bit husky with sleep.

It had taken him a while to get there, mentally working his way past being in this house, and then past her bedroom being just down the hall. But he'd been beyond weary after days of little sleep, with what he did get restless while trying to jam his too-tall frame into the small crew seat of his truck, so the lure of an actual bed with warm blankets had finally won.

Amanda was staring at him rather oddly. Then she looked quickly back at the skillet she was standing over.

"I… I'm fixing them for Quinn and myself, too," she said.

"Oh." He glanced around, looking downward, looking for Cutter before he asked, "Where is the Foxworth contingent?"

"Outside. At least I assume that's why Cutter wanted back out when he'd just been."

He nodded, hesitated as he studied her for a moment, then asked, "How are you feeling this morning?"

"I... All right."

Why did she sound so tentative this morning? "I'll bet you've got some sore spots. You fought hard."

She glanced at him then, and gave him a little smile he found oddly warming. "I tried to remember what Dad taught me. About elbows and feet and knees, fighting someone bigger."

"He was that," Adam said sourly.

"If you hadn't come running when you did, and scared him off—"

"That was Cutter. He looked and sounded like he wanted to rip the guy's throat out. No man in his right mind would stand his ground with a dog intent on mayhem, and big enough to inflict it, coming at him full tilt."

She studied him for a moment before she said, "Not to mention a big, strong guy who was heading for him, not running away like most would once they saw that knife. But you never hesitated."

He stared at her. What was he supposed to have done, hidden somewhere, maybe called 911? A lot of good that would have done. He knew too well the truth of the old saying, when you need help in seconds, the police are only minutes away. They would have gotten here, but long after she'd been dragged into that car. And she'd likely have been dead before they found her.

A shiver went through him at the thought. Amanda, who had gone back to stirring the scrambled eggs, spoke as if she'd read his last thought.

"I wonder why he didn't kill me right there? He had that knife, he could have easily cut my throat."

Adam stared at her anew, she said it so calmly. Matter-of-factly. He himself had to fight for calm to answer her the same way.

"Probably had a plan, of where to do it, how to hide the evidence, how to deal with…the aftermath."

"You mean dispose of the body? I suppose that would be the most problematical."

He couldn't stop himself then. "This is *you* we're talking about. Not some random stranger you'd hear about in the news the next day. How can you sound so…unruffled?"

She looked up from the eggs. "Oh, I'm ruffled. Matter-of-fact, now that I've had time to think, and when I woke up feeling those aches you mentioned, I'm pretty hacked off."

"You're…mad?"

"Furious. Taking my father from me wasn't enough?"

"So you're convinced now, it's connected to him?"

She went back to stirring the eggs, and turning over the pieces of bacon she had cut into thin slices. "It's the only thing that makes sense. And if Quinn's right, and Trevor Malachi isn't behind it, then it has to be that file, doesn't it?"

"Pix," Adam muttered. "Whoever or whatever the hell that is."

"Yes."

"I'll go through it all again," he said wearily. "If I read it a few more times, maybe something will pop."

Amanda's head came up sharply. He realized belatedly that was a phrase he'd picked up from Greg. He had his mouth open to apologize when she spoke.

"His old whiteboard," she said. "We could set it up, like he used to."

I like having it all there in front of me, because sometimes seeing it all at once makes something pop.

The explanation was given shortly after they'd first been partnered and they'd taken a string of burglary reports in a neighborhood. The detectives had been working it, but it was Greg who, after setting up his board and marking locations and patterns, had broken the case. It had turned out to be what they called "buddy burgs," burglaries committed by a supposed friend of the teenager living in each house. The kid had cultivated the fake friendships for exactly that reason, to get into the house for a look at the layout and for anything worth stealing.

Before he could answer her Quinn and Cutter arrived at the back door. And he supposed he should be grateful for that, but he wasn't sure he was.

"It can't hurt," Quinn said later, as they sat over the breakfast Amanda had prepared and she told him about the whiteboard idea.

She smiled, and sipped her coffee. Then she set down the mug rather purposefully.

"I've been thinking," she began. And stopped abruptly when Adam choked on a swallow of coffee and coughed. He gave her a darting look that made her ask, a bit miffed, "Something funny about that?"

"No, I—" he coughed again "—it's just that…" He hesitated, then looked away as he said softly, "Your dad always used to say some of the most challenging moments of his life started with that phrase from you."

I've been thinking, Dad.

Uh-oh.

How many times had it happened, that loving teasing? Countless. And she couldn't stop the sudden welling of moisture in her eyes.

Adam swore under his breath. "I'm sorry, I didn't mean to—"

He stopped when she held up a hand. "Please. Don't apologize. Too many people are afraid to even mention him, like they want to forget he ever existed, and it just pounds home even harder that he's gone."

"I will never forget him," Adam said quietly, meeting her gaze then and holding it. "After my own dad, he's the best man I've ever known."

"Thank you," she said, meaning it with her whole heart.

Quinn had tactfully let the exchange play out, but now he asked, "What, dare I ask, were you thinking?"

She shifted her gaze back to him, this man who had taken the last bullet meant for her father, and then taken down the man who had fired it. "That maybe you should leave."

Quinn blinked. Glanced at Adam, who looked as shocked as he did. She realized suddenly that Quinn was wondering if she and Adam were on the outs again, and went on quickly.

"I just meant pull back, let them think I'm alone, maybe draw them out."

"You want to be bait?" Adam asked, sounding incredulous.

"Aren't I already?" Amanda countered. "They're coming after me anyway."

"So you want to give them a better shot at you? And maybe that'll be what it is next time, a shot. I'm surprised they haven't tried already, if this is big enough to set them on you five years later, just because you asked for help with an old file."

"Excellent point," Quinn said.

"So what am I supposed to do?" she asked. "Just hide

in the house until…what, we figure out what that file's about?"

"Excellent idea," Adam said, echoing Quinn's word.

"I won't live like a prisoner," she said, realizing she sounded almost sulky and a little foolish even as she said it. When she saw Adam's mouth twitch slightly, she knew he was thinking exactly that. "Something you want to say?" she said with an edge in her voice.

"Just that your dad also said you could be a bit… obstinate when your mind was set on something."

"Calling me stubborn?"

"That's not always a bad thing. Sometimes it's the only thing that gets you through."

At those words her irritation vanished. Because the truth of it rang in her mind, all the long, awful days when sheer determination had been the only thing that had allowed her to put one foot in front of the other. And what she hadn't known until now, the kind of determination, and yes, stubbornness, that it must have taken for him to recover and adapt as well as he had, sparked that newly born admiration she'd found for him again.

And she smiled at him.

He looked surprised. No, more than that, he looked startled, and quickly shifted his gaze back to his now empty plate.

"I don't think we need to resort to that yet," Quinn said. "We'll consider it when Hayley and I get back. In the meantime, Liam will be around—he'll take the night watch, Adam, so you can stay here and focus on that file. And he's got a Foxworth phone, so the red button will reach him live."

Adam nodded, but he didn't look up. Quinn went on.

"You're probably going to have at least one deputy at least in the neighborhood on a regular basis, if I know

Brett Dunbar. So more help won't be quite so far away. Although Adam and Cutter are clearly capable of handling the likes of those two who showed up Monday night."

Yes, they were. Amanda knew she'd never forget the feeling of relief that had flooded her when she'd realized they were coming, when she'd heard Cutter's frightening snarl and seen Adam running straight for them.

"If this trip was anything else," Quinn began.

"I understand. You absolutely have to be there for this wedding. And I'll be fine," Amanda assured him. She looked at Adam. *He's a good man. I trust him completely.* "I have complete faith in that."

Adam glanced up then. He looked surprised all over again. And right then Amanda set herself a task she'd never expected to undertake; apologizing wasn't enough, she wanted to convince Adam Kirk not to believe what she had believed for years.

Chapter 24

Why was she being so nice?

Adam watched her pour another mug of morning coffee and wondered it for the… He'd lost track of how many times in the two days he'd been under her roof. And it didn't really matter, because the only answer that made sense to him was the same one it had been since he'd learned she hadn't known how badly he was hurt. She felt sorry for him. And that grated more than he would ever have thought possible.

It wasn't that he hadn't encountered the feeling before. Often, even back home, he had caught that look in more than one person's eyes. Thankfully, most of them seemed to have forgotten about it as he doggedly kept doing everything that needed doing. Even if he did have to change his approach as he tried to rebuild a life in the home he'd never stopped loving but had thought he'd left behind.

It was one of the reasons he loved his little sister more

now than ever. She'd never gotten that look in her eyes, that pitying expression that his brain insisted on narrating with the words *poor guy*. No, Nat had refused to cut him any slack at all, in fact had pushed and prodded and poked at him from the moment he got out of the hospital, saying his job now wasn't to figure out what he could still do, it was to figure out how to do everything he used to.

"That's a nice smile."

Amanda's soft voice jolted him out of his thoughts as if she'd shouted. He was feeling better after two nights of decent sleep—thankfully uninterrupted by a return of Amanda's attackers—but he hadn't quite realized how unnerving staying here in her house would be. He thought again that it would be easier to deal with her anger. That at least, he understood. Now, he had no idea what she was thinking, only that he was sure it arose out of an emotion he had never, ever wanted from anyone, but most especially her.

"Just…thinking. About my sister."

She smiled at him. "Natalie? How is she?"

"All grown up," he said, rather wistfully.

"You don't sound…entirely happy about that."

He wasn't sure he sounded entirely happy about anything anymore. But he said only, "I miss the little girl. But I wouldn't trade the amazing woman she is now for anything."

She walked around the kitchen island and put her hand over his on the counter. He nearly jumped out of his skin, and told himself it was just because the move had been unexpected. Not because it sent an electric jolt through him, like touching a live wire.

"That's wonderful. I'm glad."

He risked a glance at her then. For some reason, perhaps the absence of the sun on these December days, the vision that flashed through his head was the very first time he'd seen her. As had happened a few more times after that, he'd been keeping Greg company as he waited for a ride after a shift. But that time it had been a brilliantly clear, what they called a severe clear, summer day, when she'd gotten out of Greg's prized Camaro and stepped into the sunlight, and the hair that had looked merely brown inside the car was suddenly a glorious blend of brown, red and gold.

And then she had started toward where they were standing outside the station. Moving with that easy, supple, and ultra-feminine grace, dressed in snug jeans, a simple white sleeveless blouse, her slender, small feet in strappy white sandals that had him wondering why he'd never noticed how pretty feet could be before. And whatever Adam had been saying died in his throat.

"You're allowed to notice how beautiful she is," Greg had said. And Adam hadn't been sure that time if that sudden glint in his partner's eyes had been amusement or warning.

"I… She is.".

"Yes."

"She is what?" Amanda had asked cheerfully as she reached them. After, Adam had noticed, a glance around to make sure she was the only she in sight.

"You," Greg said teasingly as he hugged her.

"The youest you?" she asked with a loving note in her voice that warmed Adam. He knew they were close, since her mother had died when she was so young, but it was something to see it up close.

"That ever was or ever will be," Greg had answered, finishing what was obviously a familiar exchange to the both of them. And then Greg had introduced them, and Adam had stumbled through some awkward greeting and—

Amanda again snapped him out of a reverie. "Where did you just go?"

"I…was just remembering. The first time I met you."

She smiled, and there was a touch of sadness in it. Of course. "I remember that, too. I was upset with my father for telling me all about how smart and quick you were, what a good cop you were going to be, but failing to mention how good-looking you were."

He blinked. Opened his mouth, then shut it again, figuring saying nothing was better than saying something stupid, which was all that came to mind. He was glad—at first—when she kept going.

"I'm afraid I was a bit snobbish about it. City girl bias, I guess. I knew you grew up on a ranch, and I guess I had some preconceived notions about country boys. Then I saw you standing there and they all blew up." She laughed, clearly at herself, which he found…he wasn't sure what. "I should have known cowboys have been a thing with women for so long for a reason."

He stood up suddenly. The last of his coffee sloshed in the cup. "Why are you doing this?"

"What? Remembering? You started it, if you recall."

"Talking to me. Talking to me like…a friend."

"We're not friends," she said, in what he could have sworn was a sad tone. "I know that it will take a lot more than an apology to make up for a mistake five years long."

"You have nothing to make up for."

"Oh, but I do. I misjudged and blamed and— "

"Amanda—"

"I had someone within reach who knew, admired and respected my father, and whom he felt the same way about, and I turned my back on him because I was too wrapped up in my own pain to see the truth." She gave a quiet little sigh. "And if you hate me for that, it's only what I deserve."

Adam gaped at her. He felt disoriented, as if the entire world had flipped on him. She thought *he* hated *her*?

"And," she went on when he kept staring at her, speechless, "I can see I have my work cut out for me." Then, with the flashing smile he remembered from that day, she added, "But my father was right when he told you how stubborn I can be."

He still didn't believe her.

Amanda kept her gaze fixed on the whiteboard they'd set up in the office, the large rectangle her father had used so often in this very room. It had taken her a while to find the pens for it, and only two of them still wrote after all this time. But by limiting things to the two basic categories— what they knew and what they were guessing at—it was enough. They were looking for connections. And right now she couldn't see any new ones, most especially anything that would connect Malachi to the mysterious Pix.

"You don't need to worry at the moment about whether we can prove it," Quinn had said before he'd gone to catch a few hours of sleep. Leaving the ever-watchful Cutter with them again.

But out of the corner of her eye she saw Adam, also staring at the board, reach down to scratch behind Cutter's right ear. "So when do you get a solid night's sleep, dog?"

She gave up pretending she wasn't watching them and turned her head in time to see the animal lean his head against Adam's arm. His right arm, she realized. And after a moment the movement stopped, and Adam looked from the dog to…his elbow. The injured elbow. Then he flexed it, as far as it would apparently go. And he had an oddly puzzled expression on his face.

"What's wrong?" she asked.

She supposed it was a measure of how unsettled he was that he answered her in a tone that matched his expression. "Nothing. I mean…it was aching a bit but…it stopped. When he did that."

She crossed the two steps between them and stroked Cutter's dark head. "Well, aren't you the wonder worker?"

The dog looked up at her rather intently, then shifted his gaze to Adam. And then looked back at her. She wasn't sure what he was trying to communicate, but she looked at Adam, as well.

"Does it always ache?" she asked.

That quickly he shut down, his expression going stiff, his eyes chilly and his voice just as cool. "Not your problem."

"I know. I just…hate to think of you dealing with constant pain."

Something flashed in his eyes, like lightning behind gray clouds. "Shall I tell you exactly what you can do with your pity?"

"It's not pity," she said with exquisite politeness. "But why don't you take it and stuff it wherever you keep your usually good manners at times like this?"

For an instant he looked taken aback. It took her a moment to figure out that if she really had been feeling pity for him, it probably would have made her just ignore his rather rude question as only to be expected if he was hurting. But would he see that? Was that too fine a point to expect him to pick up, under the circumstances?

"I'm not sure I brought them with me," he muttered finally.

She smiled. "Oh, you did, I've seen them," she said.

"The best kind, the quiet kind, that opens doors, cleans up after himself and never complains. And I'll bet when you're wearing that cowboy hat, you probably tip it to the ladies."

He let out a snorting burst of laughter. She grinned at him, happy she'd gotten at least that much out of him.

"You do, don't you?"

"It's part of cowboy hat etiquette," he said. "Rule number two, I think."

Was he actually joking with her? Delighted, she took the obvious bait. "And rule number one?"

"Never touch another man's hat."

She laughed then. "Are there more?"

"Of course. And superstitions."

"Hat superstitions?"

"Like never set your hat down on the brim, because all your luck will pour out."

"What else?" she asked, enjoying the silliness more than she ever would have imagined. This was the Adam she remembered, the Adam she'd first met and been so attracted to.

"It's bad luck to wear a hat backward."

She raised her eyebrows. "Lot of boys missed that one."

"I don't think it applies to baseball caps."

"Lucky for them," she said. "Are there more? Do they all apply to luck?"

"Most," he said. He seemed about to say something more, then caught himself. "We should get back to this," he said, and his voice was once more the flat, lifeless thing it had been until now.

And all trace of the younger, happier Adam Kirk had vanished.

Chapter 25

Adam stared at the whiteboard, not quite able to believe how close he'd come to quoting that other superstition, that it was also thought to be bad luck to put your hat on the bed.

Talking about beds in any way to Amanda Bonner was near the top of his list of things never to do. But damn the way she'd smiled at him, even grinned at him…how was he supposed to take that?

I should have known cowboys have been a thing with women for so long for a reason.

He hadn't really thought of himself as a cowboy lately, although he rode, herded cows when necessary and wore the hat. His father called himself a rancher, but he owned the place. So what was he?

A failed cop. That's what you are.

He stared at the whiteboard. He wasn't really focused on the two columns, one in blue, one in a noxious shade of yellow brown, the blue one topped with what they knew—Pix—the other with what they didn't, who or what Pix was. He didn't have to focus; he thought he had it all memorized by now. But it kept his gaze off Amanda, which was his wisest course just now. Because the memory of the way she'd looked at him that very first time kept haunting him.

And it was not, he told himself firmly, because the way she looked at him now reminded him.

Back then, the immense impediment of her being his partner's daughter had kept him sternly in line. That was a complication his fledgling career as a cop hadn't needed.

And now you've got a complication your entire life didn't need, and it's here for good.

He clenched his right hand into a fist, as tightly as he could. Tried to be grateful he could do that at all; they'd done an exquisite job of keeping those nerves intact. Except for his little finger, the hand worked fine, it just didn't go where he needed it to half the time.

He shook off the thought with the ease of long practice. As much as he couldn't stand pity from others, he hated self-pity more, and had fought it down more times than he could count. The only thing stronger was the guilt he felt, for which there was no way out. There was no adapting to it, no altering it. It was simply a fact of his life now.

"You know what I've never understood?"

Amanda's voice snapped him out of it again. For an instant he thought she was going to come at him again with this newfound gentleness, which he knew was born of that hated pity. He didn't think he could take much more of that. But then he saw that she was studying the map they'd pinned up next to the whiteboard, and on which he'd marked the locations of every one of the contacts he knew about that were mentioned in Greg's secret, encoded file.

"What?" he asked cautiously.

She pointed at the map. "Why was he where he was?"

Adam's stomach knotted up when he realized what she was talking about, that she had been pointing at the spot on the map he hadn't bothered to mark because it was etched into his mind more permanently than if it had been done with acid.

The spot where Greg Bonner had died.

And it was a question he had asked himself more than once.

"I mean, why on the side of the building?" she said with remarkable calm, as if it were just another part of a puzzle. "I get that it was dark and he wouldn't be seen, but…"

"You can't see all of the front of the store from there."

"Exactly," she said, and he wondered if she, like him, had gone back there and stood in that spot, trying to understand. He'd done it more times than he could count.

"They're probably right," he said cautiously.

"You mean that he was checking the back of the building?"

For us. "We did park there sometimes, for the view down the street and that stop sign everybody blows."

"I guess that makes sense, but wouldn't they have done that first? By the time you got there the clerk thought they were gone, so wouldn't he have already checked?"

Yes. "Maybe it was an afterthought, like they said."

This was old ground to him, and probably her, too, but he'd never been quite able to let it go. Not that he didn't believe the reasonable conclusion the exhaustive investigation had come to, but it just nagged at him a tiny bit.

Not that it made a damned bit of difference to anything. It had still happened, and Greg was still dead, and nothing ever changed about that.

He heard her let out an audible breath. "I'm sorry. I didn't mean to bring it up again. I know it's old, tired ground, but—"

"Don't apologize. I understand."

She turned to face him then. "You can't let go either, can you?"

It was more of an assessment than a question, but he answered anyway. "Never."

Then, quietly, she said, "The difference is I can't because he was my father. You can't because you feel responsible, no matter who tells you or how many times you're told it wasn't your fault."

"The people saying it weren't there."

"Quinn was there. And he's about the most level-headed guy I know."

"He is. But he's not a cop."

She continued to look at him in that assessing way. "If it had been my father who had gone inside, believing what the clerk said, that they were gone, and you had been the one Malachi shot...would you blame him?"

He nearly groaned aloud as she asked the question he'd asked himself so many times, although not in quite that way. He'd only asked it of himself because he'd been certain Greg would have reacted differently, would have somehow known the robber's accomplice was there in the shadows, even if Adam couldn't explain how he could have. Greg had had those instincts he himself hadn't had time to hone, the instincts of a man who'd spent a career learning how the bad guys thought so he could protect the good guys.

"He wouldn't blame you," Amanda said, with quiet certainty. "I know he wouldn't."

"You did," he pointed out.

"I know. Unjustly. I told you, I was in so much pain I...had to strike out. And you were the likeliest target, no matter how undeserved. And that is something I will be sorry for until you can forgive me. And if that's never, then I'll just have to live with the guilt."

He was torn between saying she had nothing to feel guilty about and telling her good luck with living with it, since he'd learned firsthand what a useless effort that was; you learned to live in spite of it, not with it, which implied some kind of accord reached.

And then it hit him, what she'd actually said. *Until you can forgive me.*

She wanted him to forgive her?

What she'd said before... *If you hate me for that, it's only what I deserve.*

The world really had turned upside down.

Liam Burnett was a very different presence, Amanda quickly realized when he took over the night watch. While Quinn was imposing, even intimidating, the man with the hint of Texas in his voice, who looked younger than she guessed he was, was quick, lively and had a ready grin.

And, after observing Cutter with her and Adam, and the way his herding instincts seemed to kick in at the oddest—and frequently most inconvenient—moments, that grin had appeared often.

"At it again, hey, dawg?" he'd said, clearly purposefully drawling out the last word.

"At what?" she'd asked.

"His other talent. Of which I am an eternally grateful recipient, along with almost everybody else at Foxworth Northwest."

He wouldn't explain beyond that, simply gave her another of those grins and said she'd find out.

But other than that, they saw little of him. He was in the area from dark to dawn, which this time of year was a long stretch. He borrowed Cutter for a security round at night, but sent him back to them afterward. He asked the last one of them to go to bed to let him know, and the first up ditto, and he always answered immediately when they hit that red button on the Foxworth phone. She didn't know where he went to sleep, if anywhere. It bothered her, but she couldn't deny having him around made her feel safer.

Having Adam in the house with her made her feel anything but, in an entirely different way.

She had, in the end, agreed to not take on any new work and indeed stay home for a while, although she justified it with her intention to spend every bit of that time going over what information they had as many times as necessary to come up with the solution.

That she was having more than a little trouble focusing on that was also the fault of having Adam in her house.

Her father used to tell her that if you had two different problems to deal with, that sometimes focusing on one freed up part of your subconscious mind to deal with the other, and when you went back to it sometimes you'd have the answer you couldn't come up with when it was all you were thinking about. She'd found that to be true a great deal of the time, but right now the one problem—who was after her—and the other—Adam—were so intricately entwined it was hard to separate them.

She hadn't meant to, had in fact specifically intended not to, but by the time she remembered that she was already at the kitchen window that looked out into the backyard. Where Adam was throwing a tennis ball for the apparently tireless Cutter. For the first few moments she just admired, loving the way his long, leanly muscled body moved, trying not to dwell on what his backside did to a pair of jeans. Trying not to picture him astride a horse, like some Western hero, maybe tipping that cowboy hat to her as he passed.

Then she threw caution to the wind and decided to enjoy the view instead, at least while he didn't know she was staring at him.

Hungrily.

She realized it with a little jolt that took her back again to that first day she'd laid eyes on him, when she'd nearly glared at her father for his stunning omission of his new partner's looks. Hardly important to him in a partner, but she would have appreciated a little warning. Then again, her father had set so little store by looks he probably hadn't even noticed.

But she had. Instantly. And Adam Kirk hadn't gotten any less attractive since that day.

It was in that moment that she belatedly realized he'd been throwing the ball with his left hand. Well enough, she thought, and wondered if maybe that was something he practiced. They had dogs on the ranch, he'd mentioned.

Even as she thought it, he switched the ball to his right hand. For a moment he just looked at it, while Cutter sat at his feet, politely waiting, with his lolling tongue the only sign he'd been running full tilt for a good quarter of an hour. Adam tightened his fingers around the ball, flexed his arm slightly as his face took on a very tight expression.

Then, with a motion that was as much push as it was

throw, he tossed the ball again. It didn't go as far, and went somewhat sideways, steered awry by the elbow that wouldn't allow a natural motion. She thought about what Hayley had said, that Quinn thought there was something more than just being tired of surgery behind his decision not to go for the joint replacement.

And suddenly, as she watched Cutter—who hadn't cared a whit that the throw had gone sideways—bring the ball back and Adam reach out to take it with his left hand again, as she thought about what it must be like to live with that constant, physical reminder of that grim day, it struck her what that something more was.

He was punishing himself.

Chapter 26

"I'm glad you're here."

Adam's head came up from the file he'd been pretending to read yet again. Amanda had said it softly, gently, and he expected to see Cutter leaning against her as he often did to both of them. The effect the dog had was uncanny, and—

She was looking at him. Cutter was five feet away, curled up on the rug in front of the fireplace where Adam had earlier built a fire to ward off the damp as much as the chill, since the rain had returned. The dog had his chin resting on his paws, his amber-flecked eyes watching them alertly, his gaze flicking from where she sat on the couch to the chair he was ensconced in.

As words he'd never thought he'd hear died away he didn't know what to say. Decided the safest course was to assume she simply meant it was better than the alternative.

"Nobody would want to be alone with this going on."

"Then let me rephrase. I'm glad it's you here."

He went very still. "You'll be better off when Quinn gets back."

"Why?"

He blinked. "Because…this is his thing. He looks out for people."

"It used to be your thing, too."

"And you of all people know how that turned out."

"Stop it." She said it sharply enough that he drew back a little. "Don't you ever get tired of blaming yourself?"

"Yes," he said, and it was heartfelt.

"Then stop."

It should be so easy. "Being tired of it doesn't change the facts."

"Yes, facts are facts, but your interpretation of them sucks." She said it so bluntly he was at a loss for words. "And I know, I was the one who accused you of the same thing you're blaming yourself for. That's why I can see so clearly how wrong you are, because now I know how wrong I was."

He opened his mouth, shut it again and only shook his head wearily.

Amanda stood up suddenly, putting down the pad she'd been writing on. She'd told him she'd begun making notes on her phone, as she usually did when dealing with something complex, but had decided she didn't want any of this on a hackable device. Quinn had agreed. He'd also suggested the hard copy of the file Adam had just been reading—he'd lost track of how many times—just in case, as long as it never left the house.

"Look," she said as she came over to stand in front of him, "I understand a lot of this is my fault, for making you feel this way, yelling at you in the hospital when you were down and in pain. I'll never forgive myself for that, so I understand about that, too."

"You only said what I was already thinking."

"But I cemented it good and solid in your head, didn't I."

It wasn't a question, and so Adam didn't answer.

"I can't go back and undo what I said, although if I could, I'd do it in a minute. So tell me, Adam, what can I do? How can I make it up to you?"

A dozen answers to that, mostly involving things he'd never dared think of in conjunction with her before, raced through his mind. He cut off the string of thoughts. Just because she apparently no longer hated him didn't mean she was ready to stroll down the path he was suddenly imagining.

"Amanda," he began and then stopped abruptly, because to his ears his voice sounded as if he'd said everything he'd just been thinking. Rough. Tight. Aching.

And then, suddenly, Amanda let out a sharp sound of surprise. Before Adam could even react she was falling forward. Onto him. He knew it wasn't intentional by the way she grabbed for something, anything, to stop the fall. What she got was his arm, as he tried to turn her so she wouldn't hit the arm of the chair he was in, or worse, crash to the floor.

She ended up on his lap. And the first thing he saw when he caught his breath was Cutter, standing right there, and looking immensely pleased with himself.

"He bumped me," Amanda said, a little breathlessly. "I didn't mean to…fall on you, but he came up right behind me and—"

"Pushed?" Adam suggested.

She looked at him quizzically. "Yes. How—"

"I've been told he…herds people where he wants them to go."

She laughed. He was afraid to say any more, to explain any further, because he thought she would get up. And he didn't want her to. Holding her like this, on his lap, felt better than anything had in…at least five years.

"I'd buy that," she said, as if she didn't even realize where she was sitting. Or on what, he added silently as he finally had to admit to his body's fierce and instant response to her position. "I've seen him do it. But why…"

Her voice died away, and he had the feeling that only when she had wondered why Cutter would want her on his lap did she realize that's where she was.

"I…" she began, but it trailed off as she stared down at him.

He could feel himself breathing hard, felt his lips dry as his breath rushed over them. But he couldn't stop staring back at her. And because of that he saw the moment when something changed, shifted, when her eyes widened as if in surprise, then, impossibly warmed.

She kissed him.

In all his imaginings, and he couldn't deny he'd had them, he'd never imagined this. Oh, not her kissing him, because sometimes on a sleepless night long ago he'd imagined exactly that. He'd just never known how it would feel.

Because he'd never in his life felt anything like it.

Heat blasted through him as if he'd stepped into the path of a flamethrower. Her lips on his, the taste of her, even the tentativeness with which she did it seared him. Maybe that most of all, that she was shy about this, held him motionless for an instant. But the heat was too much to be denied and then he was kissing her back, even as he was aware he was throwing gasoline onto a flame that should never have been kindled.

But I didn't. She did.

And he wasn't sure what to think about that. But then he felt the featherlight touch of her tongue over his lips and stopped thinking at all.

Amanda felt as if every muscle she had was quivering. She hadn't really realized how much she'd wanted this until the split second when she knew she was going to do it. But then it flooded her, the awareness of how long she'd waited for this moment. Some small part of her mind wondered again if this was part of the reason for the fierceness of her anger at him, if she'd only been so angry because she'd known somehow that this was there, between them, just waiting to be awakened. But she spared it only a fleeting thought, to be filed away for future scrutiny, because right now all she wanted was more. More of this, more of this amazing heat, more of the feel of him, the taste of him.

He'd obviously been startled at first, and she couldn't blame him for that. But when he'd begun to kiss her back, fiercely, hotly, something surged along every nerve in her body, something new, electric and impossibly exciting. It was the sensation she'd had the first time she'd ever seen him, multiplied a hundredfold.

His hands came up and cupped her face as he deepened the kiss she'd begun. She felt his fingers threading through her hair, then one hand slipped to the back of her head and held her as he tasted her deeply. She stroked his tongue with her own and heard him make a low, rough sound that sent a renewed burst of heat and sensation through her.

She shifted, wanting to be closer. Instead he broke the kiss and pulled away with a sharp gasp. In the same moment she realized the relative intimacy of their positions, realized exactly what it was that her thigh was pressed against. This proof she was not in this alone buoyed her, and when she pulled back far enough to look into his eyes…he was staring at her, his brow furrowed in obvious puzzlement.

"Adam?" She hadn't meant it to sound so breathless, but she seemed to have forgotten how to breathe.

"Sorry I'm a little confused," he said, and there was an edge in his voice she couldn't put a name to. "A week ago you wanted to shoot me on sight."

She felt her cheeks flush, although she was so warm all over she wasn't sure how she could tell. "A week ago I was holding on to a lie."

He let out a long, weary-sounding breath. "It wasn't a lie. It's still not. I should have—"

She lifted a finger to his lips—God, those lips—and silenced him. She felt a sadness rising in her, chasing the heat with its chill. "No. I'm sorry for what I said that day, and for what I believed. So consider this another in the long line of apologies I owe you."

"You don't—" he began the moment she moved her hand.

"I do." She gave him a smile that let some of that sadness show. "And someday I hope you'll accept."

She couldn't help herself, she touched his lips again. Then she drew back, aware she was expecting too much too fast, from a man who knew she had hated him for five years. That it was all a mistake didn't matter, not yet. She could only hope that one day it would.

"If you ever get there, let me know," she said softly.

"You want a registered letter?"

She didn't blame him for the sarcasm. Anybody would feel that way, she supposed, after what had to seem like an abrupt about-face. Going from a fierce hate to…whatever this was.

"No," she said softly. "Just you kissing me would do it."

She got up then, reluctantly, but determinedly. And the ache that was growing inside her told her just how much pain she'd just set herself up for. Because he was looking at her not like a woman he'd just enjoyed kissing, but a woman he wasn't sure he even wanted to be around.

Chapter 27

Adam sat out on the deck, savoring the chill in the air as his overheated blood gradually cooled. There were certain things he had always acknowledged in his life. That the wide-open spaces of home would always call to him. That his family was his rock, his foundation, the source of his gravity. That a good dog and a good horse were among the most important things a man could have.

And when he'd started the next phase of his life, he'd known from the day Greg Bonner had sat down and talked to him about what his chosen career meant that this man was as solid as they came. He'd quickly come to both admire and respect the man. And in a way, he'd come to know the daughter his partner talked about so much before he'd ever met her. The love and protectiveness in Greg's voice had warmed him, because it reminded him of his own parents. But Greg had done it alone, and being a single dad was hard enough, but a single dad and a cop?

Which was why, on the day he'd first set eyes on his daughter, Adam had quashed the instant response of both his mind and body to Amanda Bonner.

You're allowed to notice how beautiful she is.

Notice, but no more. And even spoken teasingly it had been a warning, and Adam had taken it as such. Greg had even joked about it. "Don't take it personally, I warn every cop off her. Not a life I want for her."

He'd understood immediately what he'd meant. Amanda had lost her mother so young, the last thing her father wanted was for her to invite more tragedy into her life by living with the knowledge that yet another person she loved worked at a job where not coming home was a distinct possibility. And so Adam had ruthlessly crushed the surge of attraction, both physical and otherwise, he'd felt every time he'd encountered her. After that horrible, bloody night, of course, it had all become a moot point, because Amanda would never look at him with anything other than loathing. And rightfully so.

But she kissed me.

She feels sorry for me.

The internal argument hammered at him as he sat trying to read through the file yet again. He doubted he would find anything they'd missed, but he did it anyway, because it was something to do while he was here in her home. Which was the only place he could be. Quinn had been adamant— —thankfully, since he felt the same way and would have hated to try to go against the guy—that keeping Amanda safe was the first priority.

"If it takes twice as long to pin this down because they know you're under watch, so be it," he'd said bluntly when Amanda had again suggested luring them out by appearing to be alone. "We're taking no chances with your life."

Quinn had looked a bit concerned when she'd wiped at her eyes and turned away, but when she'd gone Adam said quickly, "You sounded just like Greg used to, when he was in protective mode. Which was all the time."

"Ah," Quinn had said in understanding.

And now Quinn, the one most likely to be able to do just that, protect her, was gone, leaving her to the man least likely.

Then again, maybe not, he thought grimly. Because he knew deep down that if it came to it, he wouldn't hesitate for a moment to lay down his life to keep her safe. In fact, it was the only thing he could think of that might make up for failing to save her father.

But she had Liam looking out for her as well, and Adam had a suspicion it would not be wise to underestimate the smiling, easygoing Texan. And then there was the dog, who was quite unlike any dog he'd ever encountered, even among the dozens of ranch dogs he'd lived with over the years. The smartest of those had been Joker, half German shepherd, half who knows what, and the memory of the animal still made him smile.

"That was a…wistful smile."

He managed not to jump, or snap his head up and betray how she'd sneaked up on him.

"Just…remembering." And before things could veer into the dangerous territory still smoldering between them, he clarified, "Joker. A ranch dog we had when I was a kid."

She sat down on the deck chair next to him, glanced over to where Cutter was lying on the deck, his ears twitching occasionally as he heard something. Nothing that apparently was of interest, since his chin stayed on his paws.

"Was he like Cutter?" she asked.

"Not as people smart," he said, then regretted it as he remembered just who had facilitated that action that had ended in the most amazing kiss of his life. He went on hastily. "He had a personal vendetta going on with the local coyotes. If he spotted or even sniffed one, the chase was on, and from the way he snarled you'd swear he'd rip their throat out if he ever caught one."

He noted belatedly the imagery was a bit grim, considering, but she only smiled. "And?"

"One day when I was working out in the barn he came in, carrying something. He brought it over to me, set it down in the straw and whined. That dog never, ever whined."

Her brow furrowed. "He caught one?"

"No. He found one. A pup, hurt, looked like it had tangled with a hawk or something. And Joker looked at me like… Cutter looks at the Foxworths. The look Quinn calls his 'fix it' look."

She was smiling then. "So this dog with a coyote vendetta brings you an injured baby coyote to fix?"

"Exactly."

Her smile widened, and it was a warm, wonderful thing. "What did you do?"

He grimaced slightly. "Well, I knew what my dad would do—coyotes were a pest to him, like most ranchers— but I couldn't do it. So I cleaned him up as best I could, bandaged him and hid him out in back of the well house, in a little lean-to I built. Joker guarded that thing like it was his own kid."

"And you?"

"I checked on him. Stole a bit of food to give him,

enough to keep him going. He could have used a vet, but I knew there was no way my dad would go for that. In fact, he started talking about going on a hunt, because there were a couple of coyotes hanging around too close. Started nagging at Joker, because he wasn't doing his job."

"The parents?" she guessed.

"Yeah. At least, that's what I figured. It was the only reason I could think of why Joker didn't run them off."

She looked utterly entranced, leaning forward with her elbows on her knees, as if he were reading some fascinating story to her.

"What happened?"

"When he was strong enough and healed enough, I carried him out close to where the pair of adults had been hanging out. Put him down and Joker and I walked back to the well house and waited. After a few minutes, they came and got him."

"Do you suppose he made it?"

"I know he did." At her look, he explained. "Couple of years later, when I was out riding the fence line, I saw him. I could tell by the scar on his shoulder. And the way he and Joker stopped dead and stared at each other."

"That's amazing, Adam. What a great story. Did your father ever find out?"

He gave her a wry smile. "He knew. All along."

She blinked. "What?"

"He saw the lean-to and went to look. He never said a word, then."

"Then how do you know he knew?"

"We were talking about something else, a few months after. About exceptions to the rule. And he told me the young of any species, except maybe rattlesnakes—he'd been bitten by a baby one once—should be off-limits.

Then he gave me this look he had, we call it the Dad look, and added, 'Even coyotes.'"

She stared at him, a half smile on her lips, belied by the sudden sheen of moisture in her eyes. The slight husky note in her voice was like a feather down his spine when she said, "I think I would like your dad."

"And he you. He's a good man." He tried not to think of how much he would like for them to be in a place where her meeting his father would happen.

She settled back in the deck chair, as if planning to stay despite the cold. She had on a heavy sweater and a pair of sheepskin boots, but he wasn't sure even that was enough. He was feeling it, but then he'd come out here without his jacket precisely for that reason, to cool down after...

He caught himself sneaking a look at her, wondering if she regretted kissing him. She didn't seem to, but he didn't know what that meant. If it meant anything.

"Tell me about your sister."

That startled him. "Nat? What about her?"

"Does she look like you?"

His mouth quirked. "Nah, she's pretty."

Amanda gave him a grin then that nearly stopped his heart. "So are you." She didn't give him a chance to react—a good thing since he was speechless at the moment—but went on. "Who does she resemble?"

"More Mom," he managed to get out. "Lighter hair and blue eyes."

"What's she like?"

"Smart. Kind." He hesitated, then added, "Content."

The smile she gave him then held a touch of the wistfulness she'd mentioned before. "That's something to aspire to."

"Yes," he agreed, meaning it wholeheartedly. "She's been really happy since she finished school."

"Did she go to WSU also?" she asked, referring to Washington State, the college he'd graduated from.

He nodded. "Another Wazoo-ite, just like Mom and Dad. She graduated with honors."

"You sound proud."

"I am. She's a great kid." He grimaced. "Well, she's twenty-four now, so not a kid, but she'll always be my kid sister."

"I'm glad she's got a big brother looking out for her."

"It's been more the other way around lately." He regretted the words the moment they were out, but he'd been lulled by the surprisingly normal conversation.

"I'm glad she's been there for you."

"Nat's…special."

"Dad talked about you a lot," she said in a seeming non sequitur he didn't know how to answer and so said nothing. "He said it was rare to meet a kid—he called you that, too—with such a solid foundation. He said he'd like to meet your parents someday, because it had to be from them."

"If I did, it was them," he agreed, his throat tight.

"But not solid enough?"

He blinked, drew back a little. "What?"

"If it had been, it wouldn't have been eaten away by guilt. You'd know there was nothing you could have done, no matter what an emotional wreck of a woman screamed at you."

"But—"

"I know, I know, you shouldn't have taken the clerk's word as anyone would have, you should have stayed outside even though your partner and superior told you to go in, should have been somehow magically sensed that

the already escaped robber's partner had for some inex-
plicable reason lingered until it was too late to escape.
Don't ask much, do you?"

Adam was stunned into silence as she presented what
had happened that night in an entirely different light.
She'd not only made what he'd done—and not done—
seem reasonable, she'd made what he kept telling himself he should have done sound unreasonable. Impossible,
even.

She tugged on her sweater to wrap it more tightly
around her. He seized at the chance to end the uncomfortable discussion. "You should go inside. It's cold out here."

"Which perfectly explains why you're out here," she
retorted. Then, more softly, she asked, "Missing home?
Open spaces?"

He glanced around then. "This isn't bad."

"It was a lot better when we first moved here. Now
the city's kind of spread until we're in it."

"You sound like you don't care for it."

"I don't. I've been thinking of moving."

"Leaving this house?" He was startled at the thought.
"Your dad's house?"

"It's not like he won't come with me, if I do," she said,
in the tone of someone who'd had this discussion with
herself many times. "But sometimes I want…to not have
it so close around me. Does that make sense?"

It did, to him. Perfectly. Going home, to those open
spaces, was the only thing next to his family that had
kept him from eating a bullet in those horrible early days.

I never wanted you to be a cop.

His father's words, spoken the day he'd come home,
weak, wobbly, his shattered arm still held together by
bolts that looked like something out of a horror movie.

It was the only thing his father had ever said about

it, and from that day on he'd treated Adam as if he was there because he wanted to be. It had made it easier and more difficult at once.

I warn every cop off her. Not a life I want for her.

Greg's words followed his father's through his mind. The memory was sharp, jagged. But what could slice him to bits if he lingered on it for an instant was the thought that followed, which was his own.

He wasn't a cop now.

Chapter 28

Except for the kiss, this was the closest they'd come yet to having a normal conversation. Yes, there were undercurrents, but then there always had been between Adam Kirk and her.

Amanda leaned back in the deck chair, not looking at him but at the line of evergreens along the edge of her backyard. She had often wondered, back in those days, if what she had felt had been one-sided. If only she felt that sort of electric crackle when she was around her father's partner.

Now she knew better. Because a kiss like that didn't happen unless it was on both sides. She knew that down deep, in some instinctive place that had never been awakened before that moment when their lips had met.

She wondered now if he'd truly been as shocked as he'd seemed. And if so, why? Because of that instant, almost jolting electricity?

Or because she'd done it at all?

She supposed her change of heart had to be as hard for him to accept as this whole situation was for her. Had he been surprised that it was still there, that attraction, that connection that had been there—at least on her side— since that first day she'd walked up to the back of the station to pick up her dad, and seen him standing there?

You don't want this, Amanda. It's just a reaction. Too much adrenaline.

As he left her to come out here and sit in the cold, his words echoed in her mind. She hadn't immediately denied or discarded his words but had considered them, carefully. Because he was right about one thing, this situation, and what had happened in the last couple of weeks, had been extraordinary, and indeed adrenaline filled in a variety of ways.

But that was not the basis of her reaction to him for the simple reason that she'd felt this from the first moment she'd laid eyes on him. The current situation might have amplified it, but it didn't cause it. So she was certain of her own feelings in the matter. It was his she didn't know. Had she destroyed any feelings or attraction he might have felt back then? She could hardly blame him if it was true, but...

That kiss certainly hadn't felt that way, but maybe he'd just been startled, shocked. Or maybe it was just a thing with guys; why turn away from a good, hot kiss? Adam didn't seem the type, but it wasn't like she had that much experience to compare it to. Dating hadn't been high on her priority list for the last five years.

In the end she decided she couldn't be sure. It had been so long, and the circumstances now were so unusual and unexpected, she couldn't be sure of anything.

Well, maybe one thing. Because underneath it all was

the unwavering thought that you didn't go seeking out cold unless you were…hot.

Oh, he's hot all right.

She nearly laughed aloud at the emphatic declaration that popped fully formed into her head. But it was so true. She thought she found him even more appealing now, with that slight stubble and in the charcoal sweater that made his eyes look even darker gray. And jeans worn by work, not paid extra for as some designer feature.

Oddly, she found herself focusing on his feet, and the gray shoes he wore. The heavy-duty moc-style slip-ons that were so popular in the city, for him a piece of style that somehow surprised her. She was wondering if he normally wore cowboy boots at home when it hit her. Of course he wore slip-ons instead of lace-ups, because how would he tie them? She tried to imagine how she would do it, how she would get her dominant hand in any position that would work if her elbow wouldn't straighten completely and would only bend halfway. She couldn't come up with a single scenario that didn't involve positions worthy of a yoga master.

"Something wrong with my feet?"

Her gaze shot to his face. His voice had been edgy again, as it had been inside. "No," she said. "I was just thinking."

"Again?" he said, and what he'd said earlier, about her father's joke about her thinking made her smile. But it didn't last. It couldn't, not in the face of the idea she was formulating in her mind.

"You lost a lot, too, that night. Not just…physically, but the life, the career you'd planned and worked so hard for."

He stared at her, his eyes going from merely bothered to icy. "How can you even say that? I've got no room to complain. You, you lost your father. And Greg lost… everything."

She watched him, saw the pain in those gray eyes, before she said softly, "When is it enough, Adam? When will you have paid enough?"

He looked away then, stared out toward the trees. "About as soon as Greg walks back in that door."

She heard Cutter make a sound, a quiet cross between a growl and a whine, as if he didn't like either the words or the tone. But she kept her gaze on Adam, his profile now; he looked just as good from this angle.

"Is that really why you're here?" she finally asked, even though she wasn't sure she wanted the answer. "You're trying to make up for what happened to my father by taking care of me? Because if the only reason you're staying is because you feel you owe it, I'd just as soon you go."

He didn't look at her. Didn't react. She would have thought he hadn't heard her if she wasn't sitting within three feet of him.

"So here we are," she said wearily after a moment. "You think I pity you, and I think you're only helping because you feel guilty."

Cutter barked sharply. She hadn't realized the dog had gotten up, he'd done it so quietly. But he was standing in front of them, looking from her to Adam and back. And that bark had sounded suspiciously like "Stop it!"

And now the animal was practically glaring at them.

"I feel suddenly like I did in fourth grade when Mrs. Gage snapped at me for whispering in the middle of geography," she said ruefully.

She heard Adam make a sound, and from the corner of her eye saw him fighting a smile.

"Hayley told me he practically runs things at Foxworth, but lets them think they're in charge," she said.

"Quinn said he's very patient with them, even when it takes them some time to catch on."

They both said it very seriously, but then they were smiling and the tension had eased. Amanda only wished she could figure out how to keep it that way.

But right now the cold was starting to get to her, and she stood up. "You should come back inside. It's too cold to be sitting out here when you don't have to." He gave her a sideways look. She felt herself flush. "I promise not to…jump you again."

"Then I might as well stay here."

The instant he said it he looked as if he regretted it. But Amanda barely noticed that, she was too busy trying to quash the leap of excitement that had jammed through her at his words. It truly had been as amazing for him as it had been for her. Which changed everything.

And Amanda suddenly wasn't sure she wanted the tension to ease at all. At least, not this kind of tension.

"I'm sorry," he said tightly. "I shouldn't have said that."

"I'm sorry you're sorry," Amanda said, letting her voice echo what she was feeling inside.

His gaze shot to her face. "Amanda—"

"But I'm sorriest about the fact that you'll turn your back on the good that's between us because my grief overwhelmed my judgment."

"He deserves that huge grief." Adam's voice was almost hoarse, and he looked away, as if he could not bear to look at her as he said it. "He was the kind of man who holds the world together, one of those pillars they talk about. The kind who leaves a hole behind that can never be filled."

"And you know if—"

She broke off suddenly. She had thought before, in the midst of that nightmare time, about what it would be like if it had gone down the other way. If it had been Adam who had stayed outside while her father had gone into the store. In fact, in her darkest moments she had wished it, that it would be that other family ripped apart. After all, hadn't she paid enough, losing her mother and now her father? And only the certain knowledge that her father would look at her as if she were the child she'd once been, and say in that way he had that wishing her ill fortune onto someone else was only human, but also useless.

Adam looked at her again. "If what?"

"If it had been the other way around, if you had died that night, he would feel exactly like you do. That it was his fault. That he should have, by some unknown power, have known that the second robber had lingered after the first had gone. That he'd left you to face it alone."

"But—"

"So do us both a favor, and cut yourself as much slack as you would him." She gave him the best smile she could manage. "And come inside and get warm."

She turned and walked back into the house.

Chapter 29

Come inside and get warm.

After five years of long, hard practice, he usually managed to keep his imagination mostly under control. The therapist the department had assigned to him before they'd officially retired him had warned him that would be one of his biggest jobs, reining in his mind when it wanted to race down all the fruitless paths of all the myriad what-ifs.

But somehow that simple phrase careened around in his mind now, with what she'd clearly meant, the literal sense of the words, crashing into all the other ways it could be meant. Because she could warm him, in a way no one ever had. One kiss had proved that.

But she deserved better.

And he shouldn't even be thinking about it like that, weighing as a possibility something that should—and would—remain impossible. Even if he were looking for someone, she shouldn't even be on the list. He had no right. Not with her. He should—

A sharp nudge jolted him out of his thoughts. Cutter, bumping him rather fiercely, his nose feeling cold even to Adam's chilled hand.

"Go ahead, go in where it's warm," he told the dog.

But the animal just stood there, staring at him. His fixed gaze was almost unnerving. He wondered, rather inanely, if there was a difference in the instincts of dogs who excelled at herding sheep versus those who excelled with cattle. He'd always heard sheep were dumber, but he'd seen some pretty stupid cows in his day. Either way, it would take a very strong-willed creature to ignore that stare.

He wasn't sure he was one of them.

"Go on, dog."

Cutter never moved. Adam tried to look away. He found the top of a dead tree in the distance that was rather sculptural to stare at. And after a moment of that he knew he was losing it, because he would have sworn the dog's stare was burning a hole in his skin.

Again Cutter nudged him, and almost against his will he looked back at the dog. Back at that compelling, staring gaze. He resisted, fighting the urge to do what the dog clearly wanted him to do, which was follow Amanda's… order? Request? Invitation?

"Damn," he muttered, shaking his head sharply.

And then Cutter came forward, sat in front of him and rested his head on Adam's right knee. It was, in its way, a gesture as compelling as the stare. Maybe more, because it warmed him in an odd sort of wave, reminding him of just how cold he was after sitting out here for a couple of hours.

Slowly, unable somehow to resist, he laid a hand on

the dog's head. His right hand, since the dog was almost exactly within reach of his damaged arm. As if he knew just how close he had to be for Adam to be able to reach him. Which was as insane a thought as the rest he was having.

Cutter gave a low, worried whine. Adam sucked in a long, deep breath. And gave in. "All right, dog. You win."

He stood up, and the animal backed up slightly. And stood between him and the steps down from the deck to the yard, as if blocking that path, leaving him only one way to go. Inside.

"I already said you win," Adam said to the dog wryly.

Cutter woofed quietly, as if saying "Just making sure."

This, Adam thought as he headed for the door, was one determined—and different—dog. He thought of Joker again, which made him think of his dad. Who might be worried about him by now, although he hadn't been very specific when he'd called to say he'd be staying here on the rainy side awhile. He'd said only that Greg's daughter needed some help, but that was all Dad had needed to hear. He understood about responsibilities. Hadn't he been the one to teach Adam, growing up?

Still, he should call. Even if Dad wasn't worried, Mom would be. Because that's what she did, worry about her kids. She'd probably still be worrying about him when he was fifty. So when he got inside—where it was indeed blessedly warm—and after pausing for a moment to determine that Amanda was in the office, he walked over to the kitchen counter where he'd plugged his phone in to charge. It was at 100 percent now, so he unplugged it and made the call.

Nat answered. "Are you all right? I've been worried."

"I'm fine, sis. It's just…more complicated than I expected."

"Amanda's all right, though?"

"So far."

"Does she still blame you?"

Adam almost smiled at the indignation in his little sister's voice. Nat had been his fiercest supporter, telling him repeatedly it hadn't been his fault. His mother had been too glad he was alive to talk about it much, and his father had only said blaming himself accomplished nothing.

"I think she mostly feels sorry for me now," he said, barely managing to keep from sounding bitter.

"You think everybody does, when in fact most admire you for how well you've done," his sister said.

"Funny, she said pretty much the same thing."

"Smart, huh?" Nat said in an arch tone. He grinned.

"Yes," he agreed. "She's very smart. Maybe even smarter than you."

"Ha. As if."

The grin broke into a laugh. Nat could always do that for him, even when he was down so deep he wasn't sure he'd ever surface again.

"You will be back for Christmas, right?"

"I…hope so."

He waited for her to protest even the slight doubt, but instead, quietly, his sister said, "I love you, brother mine."

"And I love you, sis. More than you know."

For a short moment after he ended the call he just looked at the phone, blinking a bit rapidly as his eyes stung. He sucked in a breath, shoved the phone into his pocket and turned.

Amanda was there. Watching him. Automatically, he raced through his side of the conversation in his mind as he wondered how much of it she'd heard.

"You think I'm smart?"

He shook his head, saw the flicker in her gaze before he said, "I know you are."

That made her smile. "Your sister?" she asked.

He was sure she'd heard that much, since it was the last thing he'd said. So he only nodded.

"It's nice. That you're so close."

"Sometimes she was the only thing that kept me from going under for good," he said, feeling he owed it to Nat to be honest about what she'd done for him.

"She made you laugh."

"She's usually the only one who can," he said, that honesty still prodding him, that need to acknowledge.

"I wish I could," Amanda said quietly. "I wish I could do for you what your sister does."

Adam's breath jammed up in his throat. He stared at her. And before he could stop himself the words were out, low, harsh and apparently unstoppable. "Believe me, Amanda, I don't feel anything like brotherly toward you."

The smile that lit her face then took what little breath he had away. "Thank goodness," she said.

She crossed the short distance between them in two quick steps. He felt frozen, unable to move, to dodge. On some buried level he knew he didn't want to dodge, he wanted to stay right there and just luxuriate in that smile. He wanted to carry that smile in his mind forever, until he took his last breath.

She reached up and brushed her fingers over his jaw-line, making him wish he'd shaved. But she didn't seem to mind.

"Mandy." It was all he could get out, then regretted it because that was her father's nickname for her, and only her father.

Even as he thought it she said slowly, "I think I'll allow you that name."

He stared at her, tried to swallow, couldn't, which told him just how tight his throat was. In his mind he swore harshly, but he couldn't think of a damned thing to say out loud.

"It's not adrenaline, Adam," she whispered. "This never has been. Not from the first time I saw you."

And then she leaned up and into him. And kissed him. Again. And it was even more than the first time, because his blood, his body and every nerve in it was prepped and waiting. He still stifled a gasp at the hot shock of it, but didn't manage to stifle a groan as she deepened it, tasted him, probed, until he could no more resist than he could fly.

He not only couldn't resist, he couldn't stop himself from kissing her back, with all the hunger he'd buried since the first time. Her lips were hot beneath his, soft and tempting and he was helpless to resist. And when she nipped very lightly at his lower lip he thought he would lose it completely. He pushed deeper, tasting, his tongue sliding along the even curve of her teeth. And he groaned again as her tongue teased his, danced over it, and sent a renewed burst of fire through his veins.

He wanted to taste more, not just her mouth, he wanted to trace every inch of her skin with his tongue. And when he realized his hand had slid up and was cupping the soft curve of her breast, he wanted nothing more than to taste her there, wanted to tease that nipple into a tightness that would make her gasp, make her feel at least something of what he was feeling right now.

He wanted her pressed against him head to toe, naked skin to naked skin more, much more than he wanted his next breath. He wanted her mouth on him as much as he wanted his on her. He wanted—

She was gone.

She had broken the kiss, that sweet, sweet kiss, and pulled away. He felt himself sway a little, like a building that had suddenly lost a crucial support.

For a moment she just looked at him, and he would have sworn he saw in her eyes, in her flushed face, the same fierce heat that had nearly swamped him. But she had still pulled away. He tried to say her name, but only an odd little gulp came up.

She drew in a very deep breath. He tried to keep his gaze on her face and not stare—okay, gape—at the full curves of her breasts as they rose with her breath.

"That's twice," she said, her voice so husky it nearly put him on his knees.

"I...what?" He wasn't sure exactly what she meant. That she'd kissed him twice? She was counting?

"I've never done that before, Adam. Made the first move. And I won't do it again." Kiss him? Was that what she meant? The heated fog in his brain was taking its time to dissipate and let him think. And that low, rough note in her voice wasn't helping any. But then she added, more steadily, "The rest is up to you."

And she walked away.

Chapter 30

Up to you.

She didn't mean that. Because if it was up to him they'd be naked on the nearest flat surface as soon as he could get her there.

If it was up to him, this whole nightmare that had brought them together would be over, leaving only the together part.

If it was up to him…

Greg's daughter. She's Greg's daughter.

Up to you.

He thought he knew all there was to know about a body at war with his mind. All the long days of trying to force a body part to do what it was supposed to do but no longer could had taught him the hard way. But now a body part that was clearly still very functional was applying a force he'd never felt before. It made all the sexual urges of his life pale by comparison. Because he knew, deep in his gut, that strings came with this one. Amanda—Mandy? She'd give him back that precious nickname, after she'd coldly told him never to speak it again?—might have made the first move, but that didn't mean she didn't expect…everything.

And he had nothing to offer her. Even if she could set aside that horrible night, he wasn't sure he could. Whatever her reason, pity or not, she apparently didn't blame him any longer, but that didn't mean he didn't still blame himself.

Which made him realize he'd been wrong. She might be the kind of woman who would expect—and who deserved—everything, but there was no way she'd want that from him. Of all people.

So what was this about? Sympathy sex? No way she could feel that badly, to offer that. Not the daughter Greg had raised. She would never hold herself so cheaply.

And he wished he could say he wouldn't take it if she did. But as the ache in him at the very thought grew, he wasn't at all sure.

He turned to look in the direction she'd gone. Belatedly realized it was toward her bedroom. He was moving before he consciously decided to. Following. Unable to stop himself. So when he reached the doorway he grabbed the doorjamb on each side of him and held on so tight his knuckles whitened.

She was there. Sitting on the edge of the bed. Just sitting. Waiting?

"What did you mean…the rest?"

It came out hoarsely, but he was surprised it came out at all past the tightness of his throat.

She rose, slowly, and he was struck anew by the lithe grace of the way she moved. "You know what I meant."

"Amanda…"

She shook her head, but smiled. "I definitely think it's Mandy, for you."

He nearly doubled over, feeling like every muscle in his body had cramped. He felt like only his fierce grip on the doorway kept him off his knees. "You can't…you don't want this."

"This may surprise you, but sometime ago I stopped letting other people tell me what I want or don't want."

"I mean…with me."

"And I repeat," she said. "But I meant what I said. It's now up to you. I've made myself as clear as I can."

"We… I'm…not prepared for this," he said, sounding desperate even to himself. And he suddenly remembered the day when, in one of his blackest moods, he'd thrown out the condom he'd once always carried in his wallet.

Gesturing toward the nightstand she said, "I am. In the drawer." She gave him a faint smile. "I have ever hopeful friends."

He couldn't speak. And for a long, silent moment something taut and tempting spun out between them. And then she made a small, sad sound. And she looked away, as if her courage had suddenly failed her. He saw a faint tinge of color rise in her cheeks, and then she spoke in a tone that matched that tiny sound of regret.

"And apparently I was wrong. Again." Her head came up then. "I guess my judgment is really off when it comes to you, in more ways than one. I thought you…wanted this."

He groaned aloud. "If I wanted it any more I'd tear this doorjamb apart."

The blush faded, but her eyes went hot and wide. And when she bit her lower lip before speaking, he felt as if a firebomb had gone off in his gut.

"Then why are you still over there?" she whispered.

Because I can't believe you want this. Want me.

And then, as if she'd read him again, she slowly began to unbutton the silky blouse that was the exact green of her eyes. By the time she reached the second button that bared the upper curve of her breasts, he was lost. He had a better chance of doing that flying he'd thought of when she'd kissed him than to stop himself now.

He was barely aware of crossing the room, so focused was he on her. He pulled her upright, into his arms.

Just you kissing me would do it.

Her words echoed in his head, in the fraction of a second before he was doing just that. His mouth came down on hers hungrily. Still he held back, just a little, giving her a last chance to change her mind. Instead she met him eagerly, welcoming him, giving a tiny moan that fired every nerve in his body to wire-strung readiness. She tugged at his shirt, pulling it free of his jeans.

At the feel of her fingers sliding over his skin he went crazy in a way he'd never known before. He wanted more, he had to have more, and he broke the kiss just long enough to yank the shirt off. Then he took her mouth again, and when she slid her hands over him as if she liked the feel of him he nearly lost himself completely. He wanted to taste every inch of her, wanted to bury himself in her until there were no longer any boundaries between them. He wanted her free of that lacy bra, those lovely breasts rounding into his hands—

It hit him like a dash of ice water. There was no way in hell he'd be able to get her out of that bra. His left hand wasn't coordinated enough, and he couldn't reach the clasp with the right.

"Adam?"

"I…can't…"

She took a half step back. And that quickly it was over,

now that she'd realized how limited he was. For a very brief moment she just looked at him. He saw her take in the multitude of scars on his right arm, and the chill spread. But then she reached out to the thin scar that ran across his ribs, around from the back, where a shard of the plate glass window had caught him.

"Pretty, aren't they?" An edge he couldn't seem to stop crept into his voice.

"I was thinking admirable," she said softly. "Badges of honor, all of them."

Her words seemed to suck the breath out of him. And then she leaned forward and pressed her lips to the puckered end of the scar, just above his navel. A shudder he couldn't suppress went through him, and his abdominal muscles contracted fiercely.

She straightened, then reached back and did what had stopped him, unfastened the bra. She slipped the straps off her shoulders and let it fall to the floor. The sight of her brought back every bit of the heat he'd lost, multiplied. He reached out, without much thought, and cupped the soft curves as he'd imagined. She made a small sound and arched toward him, pressing against his palms. He saw with a jolt of even fiercer heat that his right hand, in the only position he could manage at this angle, was in the perfect place for his thumb to slide over a nipple that had already drawn taut in anticipation.

When he did it, and she gave a little cry of pleasure, it was like the fire racing along his nerves had suddenly reached an explosive core deep inside him. He wasn't sure who undressed who and it didn't matter, not when moments later they were skin to skin on her bed, and she was urging him on. He handled the condom she got for him, then kissed every bit of her he could reach, stroked what he could not. And then she shifted on the bed, parting her legs so he slipped between them. His rigid flesh slid over her, and he felt the slick heat of her.

"Mandy," he breathed.

"Hurry. Please."

Something in the way she moaned it out snapped the last bit of his control. He surged into her, sliding deep in one stroke. She gasped as he groaned aloud at the encompassing heat and tight grasp of her body. And then he was moving, because he couldn't not, and nothing else in the world now or past or future mattered more than this. He reached between them, stroked her, found that swollen knot of nerves and circled it. She cried out and clenched around him.

His last thought before the incredible sensations blasted him to pieces was that hell, maybe he could fly.

Mandy didn't think she'd slept this deeply or peacefully since her father had been killed. That it was here, with the man who'd been there that night and who she'd been so mistaken about, made it unexpected, but no less wonderful. For the first time in so very long her heart was at peace. And these past two nights had been…she had no words for what they meant to her. She wondered sleepily if the Foxworths would be surprised at the change in the relationship between her and Adam, in merely two weeks. In fact, over the course of a single weekend.

She had the feeling if he was, Quinn wouldn't show it. And she doubted Hayley would be surprised at all.

She didn't open her eyes but just lay there in the darkness, savoring the heat of him as he slept beside her. Their coming together had been nothing less than explosive, and the touch of desperate need she'd sensed in him, the need that echoed her own, had been the match to the fuel that had sent them both flying.

She pondered waking him, wanting to feel it yet again, that glorious heat, the building pressure, the luscious feel of him sliding into her, and most of all the way he groaned her name as her body clenched in delight around him. Then she smiled into the darkness, wondering where this hungry, eager woman—who was now Mandy in her own mind, because it was who she was to him—had come from. This woman for whom three times in a night wasn't enough. She—

The sharp, loud cacophony of barking slammed against her ears. She'd barely gotten her eyes open before Cutter raced into the room. Adam was already sitting up, and he took one look at the dog, who was dancing on his front paws as if barely keeping himself in place, and was on his feet.

Mandy blinked, then focused with no small bit of pleasure on Adam, on his lean, strong body as he picked his jeans up from the floor and pulled them on. She noticed but didn't care a whit about how he had to shift his right arm to do it. She was so admiring that when he hissed at her, "Stay here," it took her yet another moment to realize exactly what was happening.

Cutter. Guarding. The barking. A warning.

Adam grabbed up her father's Colt from the nightstand and was gone.

Chapter 31

For a moment Mandy stood frozen. The jolt from the delicious time they'd spent together—discovering that the spark between them went all the way to the bone, and from the perfect warmth of waking with him beside her—to this was more than she could process quickly. She thought it sourly, remembering how her father had always bragged about how quick and smart she was.

Not tonight, Dad.

But finally she moved, scrambling into her own clothes. She could hear sounds from outside, along the side of the house. Mostly Cutter's ferocious snarls. But Adam was out there and he had admitted himself he was somewhat limited with a handgun. She supposed with a rifle the angle his arm could take worked, but it was harder to aim a pistol accurately.

Her brain finally kicked into gear and she dashed into the living room to grab the small revolver that had been her father's off duty weapon. She wasn't in the habit, was probably very rusty, but he'd taught her to shoot with this weapon. Had told her never to hesitate if she needed to defend herself, and they'd deal with any fallout after she was safe. She would do the same for Adam. As he had done now, without hesitation, for her.

She ran to the back door. Pulled it open. The motion lights had come on, but they were out of its range and she couldn't see what she could hear. But then she saw Cutter, darting into the semicircle of light and then plunging back into the shadows, that terrifying snarl seeming to echo from the walls of the house.

She heard the sound of a blow, a human grunt. Adam? Or the shadow he was wrestling with? How could he fight hand to hand with his arm like that? She knew now— oh how sweetly she knew—just how strong he was, how well he'd adapted, but sex, even as energetically as they'd done it last night, was a very different thing. He was dealing with someone who probably wouldn't hesitate to kill him if he had to.

To get to me.

She stepped outside. Heard the thump of a body against the ground. The pavers of the far end of the driveway, she judged from the direction and distance. He'd never actually made it even close to the yard, let alone the house. Thanks to Cutter's early warning.

She heard another blow. Heard Adam swear. She adjusted her grip on the pistol as her dad had taught her, and crept that way.

A sharp, loud crack shattered the night. She froze. No mistaking that for anything other than a shot.

Not Adam, not Adam, not Adam…

Another shot, and a red-hot poker seared against her upper left arm. She heard a scream, a split second later realized it was hers. Her flesh sizzled, burned, and she had the oddly disconnected thought she should be able to smell it, like a burned steak. Then she stumbled backward as the pain radiated through her. She hit the steps up to the deck with the back of her legs and collapsed onto them. Barely managed to keep from curling up into a ball. She couldn't seem to catch her breath. Even Cutter's snarls seemed to fade as the ringing in her ears grew louder.

She wasn't sure of the exact moment when she became aware of the change. It hadn't stopped, but had at least stopped getting worse. She sucked in a much-needed breath, and then another. And another. Finally, the ringing subsided a little. Just in time for her to hear a rough voice saying, "Cutter, guard!"

And then that voice, in an entirely different tone, was yelling her name as Adam ran toward her.

He dropped to his knees beside her. "Were you hit? He was firing wild, and I heard you—"

He stopped, swore harshly and reached for her arm. She bit back a cry as he touched it, but he was incredibly gentle as he lifted her sleeve.

He didn't chastise her for not staying inside, which worried her for a moment. Was she dying, was that why he was being so kind and tender when she'd ignored his order? Was that why—

"Thank God," he muttered. "It's not bad, it'll be fine."

Not bad? It felt as if her arm was on fire. A sudden understanding hit her, hard and deep, of just how much worse Adam's injury had been. A hundred times worse. And the idea of withstanding a hundred times this pain and still being able to function enough to even think about getting to his weapon with his other hand…

Dear God, no apology could ever be enough. She was a stupid, stupid fool and—

A sudden bark from Cutter made him look that way. The dog was standing just inches away from the downed man—she still couldn't see him in the shadows outside the circle of light—who was cowering away from the dog's clearly bared fangs.

"Right," Adam said, set down the weapon he'd apparently never fired and pulled the Foxworth phone out of his pocket. But before he could hit the red button Liam materialized out of the darkness. Belatedly, she realized that was the cause for the bark.

The cavalry had arrived.

Adam was more than happy to leave the detritus to the Foxworth man. He wanted nothing more than to focus on Mandy. He knew as soon as the police arrived he was going to be tangled in statements and paperwork for who knows how long. Even with the Foxworth name and the weight it seemed to carry, he was still the primary witness and they'd need a blow-by-blow from him.

On that thought he felt another twinge from his ribs, where the guy had landed a couple of fairly solid blows. But then Cutter had latched onto his wrist and the man had freaked. There was something about a dog with his jaws clamped on you that reduced most people to terrified lumps. He'd seen it often with police K-9s, and while Cutter might be fluffier, his snarl was just as scary and his teeth were just as impressive.

In fact, the dog had reacted exactly as a trained one would. For which Adam was beyond grateful, because if he hadn't the guy might have been able to actually aim those shots at Mandy, instead of having them go wild.

Mandy, who shouldn't have been out there at all.

She was calmer now, now that the paramedics Liam had called had seen to her arm. It had actually been more of a gouge than a graze, but he hadn't wanted her to panic. She'd withstood the cleaning and bandaging stoically, had politely refused to go to the emergency room, but she'd been watching him all the time, with a rather odd expression on her face.

He waited until the medics were done with her, and had gone to fill out all the paperwork required after treating a gunshot wound of any sort, then went over to sit beside her. Liam was still outside, talking to the officers who had responded.

He hadn't meant to do it, but it came out anyway, "God, Mandy, why did you come outside?"

He sensed as much as saw her spine stiffen. And when she spoke, her voice was just as stiff. "My father didn't raise me to be a bystander."

"I know that, but you're the one he was after. And you still came out. And headed toward him."

"What was I supposed to do? Just wait inside like some helpless female?"

He nearly laughed. "Helpless? You?"

"All right, then."

He shook his head slowly, starting to smile now. "You are your father's daughter."

She met his gaze then, the stiffness vanished. "Thank you. There's no better compliment you could give me."

"I know," he said softly.

"And now I know firsthand."

He blinked. "Know what?"

"How utterly amazing it was that you were on your feet at all that night, let alone able to function enough to help Quinn."

He was saved from having to answer that by Liam stepping inside.

"You okay?" he asked Mandy. He was frowning.

She nodded. "I'll be fine."

Still frowning, Liam said, "You're sure?"

"I am." She managed to smile. "You don't need to look like you're at a funeral."

"I may well be," Liam said glumly. "My own, when Quinn finds out."

"Finds out what?" she asked.

"That I let you get hurt."

"It wasn't your fault," she said instantly.

"And I should have buzzed you first," Adam put in.

"Besides, I'm the one who went outside, when Adam told me to stay put," Mandy added.

"Armed, I see," Liam said, gesturing toward the un-fired .38 on the table beside her.

"Never had the chance to use it," she said ruefully.

"Still, took some nerve."

"It runs in the family," Adam said.

Liam looked at him. "So I gather. They're going to want to talk to you again," he added with a nod toward outside.

"I figured."

It was much later, the sky lightening with the dawn, before they were alone again. Well, almost; Liam was in his truck, now parked in her driveway. Mandy had tried to get him to come inside where it was warm, but he'd politely refused and told them to get some sleep. Adam guessed he'd probably be right there until his boss arrived. He hoped the intimidating Quinn Foxworth wouldn't chew on him too hard.

"Liam's right, you should try to get some rest," he told Mandy.

She shook her head. "I'm still too wound up."

He let out a breath, but nodded in understanding. "I get that."

She gave him a sideways look. "I can think of a way to unwind, though."

Despite everything, a sudden streak of heat rippled through him. "Can you?"

She leaned over and whispered into his ear exactly what she'd like to do. To him. His breath left him in a rush. "Liam's in the driveway."

"So?"

He gave her a look that matched the building sizzle. "You do that, and there's no way I can stay quiet."

"Oh, but it will be such fun to watch you try," she said.

"You've got a cruel streak," he teased. For a moment her expression darkened, and he knew she was thinking of…before. "I didn't mean it that way," he said quickly.

"But I was cruel."

"No. You don't have it in you, any more than your father did. You were just…angry."

"And you thought you deserved it."

"I'm still not sure I don't," he admitted.

"I am," she said, nodding toward her bandaged arm. "Even when I realized it had been much worse than I thought, I still had no idea now incapacitating it must have been. So please, Adam, can we put it behind us? For good?"

He wasn't sure he could put the guilt behind him, but he was more than glad to put her anger there. It was worth more than he could say that she no longer hated him. That she even might—

Easy there, don't make this more than it is.

His father's advice, given often to whoever needed it at the time, echoed in his head. And Adam told himself not to read too much into these precious hours with her.

But Mandy wasn't a woman to take sleeping with a guy lightly. Nor was she the type to do it out of revenge;

lure him in and then slam him down. In fact, it seemed like—if her request just now was anything to go by— she pretty much liked him. Maybe more.

And he refused to let the size of that *maybe* bother him as he swept her up in his arms and carried her gently to her bed.

Chapter 32

Quinn Foxworth didn't even blink when they came out of her bedroom together when he arrived the next morning. Oddly, he just looked at Cutter, who looked...well, smug.

"You'll be at an even dozen before long," Quinn said to the dog, who wagged his tail happily.

Mandy had no idea what that meant, but she was sure Quinn wasn't surprised.

That makes one of us.

She almost smiled at her own thought, despite the throbbing in her arm. Funny to realize now it still hurt. Adam had made love to her with such exquisite care that her body had been swamped with so much pleasure she had hardly felt her arm at all.

But barely two weeks ago, she could never have imagined she could feel that way. At all, let alone about him. Or the way she felt now, with him sitting protectively beside her on her couch as they faced a grim-looking Quinn. And she knew by the look Adam had worn when they'd awakened wrapped in each other's arms after some much-needed sleep, that he was still having trouble believing it.

She understood. She was reeling a bit herself, both with the newness of it and her own self-recriminations, and she guessed the feeling was a lot stronger for him. No wonder he'd been so doubtful.

She would just have to see to it that those doubts were wiped away. And she was wrapped up in thinking about just how many ways she could think of to do that when Quinn's voice penetrated the pleasurable fog.

"—wanted to stay down South a bit longer," Quinn was saying. "Something about fixing up a surprise for them for when they get back from their honeymoon. Knowing her, I can only imagine."

She realized he was explaining where Hayley was and pulled herself back to the moment. "It must be nice for her, her brother marrying her best friend."

Quinn nodded. "Walker's a good man. One of the best. And I think they'll work well together," he said practically, making Mandy smile.

"Speaking of working," Adam said, "you didn't chew on Liam too hard, did you?"

Quinn lifted a brow at him. "All Foxworth ever asks is that you learn and correct."

"It happened so fast he'd have had to be in the driveway to get to the guy before Cutter did," Adam said.

"And before you," Mandy said, liking the way Adam stood up for the young Foxworth operative.

"So I heard," Quinn said, looking at Adam approvingly.

"It was Cutter's warning," Adam said, as if loath—

or unable—to take any credit for himself. Something else to work on.

"What he's here for," Quinn said, reaching to scratch behind the right ear of the dog now sitting at his feet. "Among other things." The intimidating man looked as if he were on the verge of a smile.

"Other things?" Mandy asked, feeling compelled by that almost smile.

"He's…quite the matchmaker."

She blinked. Glanced at Adam, who was suddenly studying the dog as if he'd never seen him before.

"You're serious," Mandy said to Quinn.

"Afraid so," Quinn said, sounding a bit rueful.

Mandy laughed. "I know Hayley said he got you and her together."

"For which he earned carrots for life. But that was just the beginning."

"Get Hayley's brother together with her best friend?" Adam said, his tone clearly joking.

"Yes." There wasn't a trace of laughter in Quinn's tone. "And a string of others, including Liam and his lady."

As if he'd heard, Liam stepped into the house. He didn't look as if he were missing anything crucial, or even particularly downcast, so Mandy guessed Quinn had meant what he'd said about not chewing on him. She had the feeling he usually meant exactly what he said.

"What have you got on our latest visitor?" Quinn asked.

"For hire," Liam said. "Dunbar says he's been held on suspicion at least three times on the other side, but they've never been able to get proof that would hold up in court."

"And not talking, I assume," Adam said sourly.

"Not a word. He lawyered up—some creepy lowlife from the city—instantly. So he knows the drill."

"Weapon of choice?" Quinn asked.

"What he used. He didn't have a knife on him," Liam said, and Mandy realized Quinn had been wondering if he'd been the same man as the other night, just using a different weapon this time.

This time.

And belatedly it swept over her again, that knowledge that someone was seriously trying to kill her. A shudder went through her. Instantly, Adam's arm was around her.

"Wish Rafe was here," Liam muttered.

"But he's not," Quinn said levelly. "So we deal."

Mandy wondered about this Rafe she'd heard about, and why his presence would make such a difference. But before she could ask, Quinn went on briskly.

"Way I see it, we're down to two options. First, and preferable, a safe house. Far enough away they won't find you. And, hopefully, out of their zone of influence, where they won't know any…hired help like your recent visitors."

"You mean run," Mandy said, calmly enough considering everything in her was rebelling against the idea.

"I prefer to think of it as living to fight another day," Quinn said mildly.

"And living to find out who's really behind it all," Adam added.

"That, too," Quinn agreed.

She considered this. Held Quinn's gaze. "Is this a protect the helpless female thing, or would you tell a man the same thing?"

"In your position, yes I would tell a man the same," Quinn said, so levelly she couldn't doubt him. "And I have. First choice is always keep the client safe."

"Why do I get the feeling there's a however attached to that?" Adam asked, sounding none too happy about it.

"The however is the second option. Which," Quinn added rather pointedly as he looked at Mandy, "I'm only considering because of who you both are. A trained officer—" he waved off Adam's apparently instinctive protest. Yes, that was something that definitely needed a lot of work. "And," Quinn continued, "a far from help-less female."

Adam sighed at the brush-off, but nodded at the lat-ter, adding, "And the daughter of a brave cop who taught her a lot."

"That, too," Quinn agreed.

Mandy shifted her gaze to Adam. He seemed glum but resigned. His eyes met hers, and she realized with a jolt of certainty that he hated the idea of her risking herself, and was fighting his own innate instincts to let her make her own choice. As for why he hated the idea, over and above what any sane person would, she had her hopes, but this wasn't the time. For now, it was enough that he wasn't demanding she stand down.

Mollified, she looked back at Quinn.

"Go ahead. What's the second option?"

Quinn grimaced slightly. "The one you suggested a while back."

Her eyes widened. "Let them think I'm alone? Un-protected?"

"Change your mind, I hope?" Adam asked. His tone told her how deep that hope was.

"I… No, I just… Will they buy that? Whoever it is?"

"They might," Adam said. "After we took down this last guy. Whoever's behind it might believe we—or you—are deluded into thinking you're safe now that he's in custody."

Slowly, she nodded. "Enough to let down my guard, so to speak?"

"Exactly," Quinn said.

"I'm not leaving her," Adam said firmly.

Quinn lifted a brow at him. "I assumed. So we'll make a show of packing up and leaving."

"But how do we do that and not really leave her unprotected?"

"Working on it," Quinn said. "Liam, we'll need the night gear and long guns."

The young Texan nodded as if this was the kind of order he got every day, and left.

"Sounds like you have an arsenal," she said.

"We've got a selection," Quinn said.

"Surprising, on this side of the mountains," Adam said.

Quinn's mouth quirked. "Maybe less than you think. But it also helps that the government pretty much lets us alone."

Mandy laughed. "I would think so, after you took down the governor."

Adam blinked, his gaze shifting to Quinn. "That was you guys?"

"Brett Dunbar, mainly. We just helped, and handled the fallout." He smiled then. "Well, still handling some of it, but yes, it did earn us a bit of 'leave them alone' status in a place where they normally can't help themselves."

Mandy couldn't help smiling, so often had her father said something similar. She glanced at Adam, and he, too, was smiling wryly. "Talk about keeping a low profile," he said.

"We can work best when the world doesn't know who we are."

"And you have no urge for glory," Mandy said, letting all the respect she felt into her voice.

"Not a whit," Quinn said cheerfully. He looked at Adam. "I'll take Cutter, openly, but I'll send him back to you the back way."

She looked at the dog, then back to Quinn. "He'll do that?"

"And if anyone's watching they'll never see him. He can move like a wolf when he needs to, and he understands the word *stealth*." Quinn looked at Adam then. "My guess is it will take whoever a bit to regroup, so you're probably good until at least tonight. But we'll be in place before then."

Adam only nodded. But Mandy frowned. "But won't they think I'm still under guard if Adam's here?"

She felt Adam stiffen slightly beside her, but before she could say any more Quinn just grinned at Adam.

"You just keep looking at her with that love-struck expression, and everyone will make their own assumptions," he said.

Adam lowered his gaze suddenly, but he didn't deny it. And that made her feel…well, she wasn't sure what the name for it was, since she'd never been here before.

With a great show of packing up—which consisted mainly of rearranging stuff in the back of his SUV since he'd never really unpacked—and loading up Cutter, who didn't appear happy at all about the situation, Quinn left to help Liam. Likely, Adam said, to get night vision gear to go with the rifles they'd be switching to.

"They are certainly equipped," she said.

Adam nodded. "We may not have their sniper, but I'm guessing those two are pretty good."

Mandy blinked. "Sniper? They have a sniper?"

"I'm guessing it's the missing Rafe."

"The one Hayley said was after a mole?"

He nodded. Mandy looked in the direction Quinn had gone. "Wow."

"Exactly."

She turned back to look at him. He was watching her, intently, as if memorizing her.

"I've been thinking," she said.

She saw the flicker of humor she'd hoped for flash in his eyes. "Uh-oh."

She smiled, wide enough to confirm he was allowed her father's response. Right now, she'd allow this man just about anything.

"We should probably work on that image we're presenting," she said, her smile teasing now.

"Oh?"

"Yes," she said, and leaned in to kiss him.

His response was everything she could have hoped for. His arms came around her, warm, solid, strong. His injury didn't matter here, he was still able to hold her close against him, which was exactly where she wanted to be. He deepened the kiss, which made her forget all about putting on an image for anybody who might be watching. She thought only of him, the heat of him, the feel of him and the way her body responded to him so swiftly and fiercely.

And when the sound of a vehicle passing—her neighbor down the street—broke them apart, she needed that strong support because she was a bit wobbly. And nosy Mr. Inskip would have the entire neighborhood talking within five minutes, she was sure.

She didn't care. Welcomed it, in fact. Adam was hers, and she wanted the world to know it.

They'd lingered so long outside that it was only a moment after they went back in that they heard a polite scratch at the back door. Adam went, and sure enough it was Cutter, clearly happy to be back on duty.

Mandy had never taken up his food and water bowls, so she simply checked them. And smiled, both happily and wistfully at how the house seemed complete again.

As if she and Adam and Cutter were a family.

Chapter 33

Adam was torn. On one level, he liked—more than liked—the feeling it gave him to be here with her, alone except for Cutter. Cutter who, if Quinn was to be believed, and there was certainly no reason not to, had planned, plotted and pushed this. He and Mandy. Together.

But the reason they were both here hovered inexorably, and cast a shadow over the pleasant idea. Trying to ignore it, at least for the short time of peace Quinn thought they would have, he watched as Mandy began to ponder something to fix for dinner later. She said she wanted to, which surprised him. Although the feeling he got at the casual way she'd tossed out "I like the idea of cooking for us," with the emphasis on that "us," made his throat tighten.

After she tossed out a couple of ideas that earned her merely a "fine" and a shrug, she closed a cupboard door and turned to look at him.

"You don't need to cook," he said.

"But I need to eat," she pointed out. "And so do you."

"I'd say let's order in pizza, except I'd be afraid we'd be setting up some poor delivery person to be hurt so they could replace him," Adam muttered.

Her eyes widened, and he instantly regretted having spoken the crazy thought aloud.

"I'm sorry," she said before he could voice the same words.

He blinked. "What are you sorry about?"

"Foolishly thinking we could pretend things were normal. Just grab some time out of this nightmare to just... be. Together."

Did that mean it was over? The together part? "Amanda—"

"Mandy." She visibly took in a breath. "For you, it's Mandy. Don't go backward."

For a long, silent moment he could only stare at her. He hadn't even realized that at her words his mind had already put such distance between them that he'd gone back without thinking to the more formal name.

When she spoke again her voice was a gentle, quiet thing. "I was so wrong, and—" He started shaking his head but she stopped him with a sharp, "No. Stop it, Adam. You have to stop blaming yourself."

"But—"

"No buts. Was it my fault I couldn't dodge that car that hit me?"

"Of course not, but—"

"Do you blame me for not coming to help you after that wild shot caught me?"

"That's...different."

"Why? And if you dare say because I'm female I can't guarantee I won't hurt you."

He smiled, ruefully. And gave her some truth. "You," he said quietly, "have more power to hurt me than anybody right now."

"Why? Because you won't fight back?"

"No." Although he wouldn't. "Because of…this last weekend. I never thought…imagined…" He stopped, afraid he'd make things worse, stumbling around what he really wanted to say, which he was afraid she didn't want to hear. Even after this weekend together.

"I did," she said rather bluntly. "I imagined a lot. And you…are everything I hoped you were the first time I saw you and spent a long time wondering how I was going to get past my father's objections to me dating his new partner."

He blinked. "You…what?"

"Do you really think this would have happened so fast if the core of it hadn't already been there?" She lowered her gaze and her voice, and added in a thicker, more aching voice, "Do you think I would have been so blindly angry with you if I hadn't cared about you? If there weren't already strong emotions in place?"

"You had every right—"

Her head came up sharply. "I mean it, Adam. Stop it. You've got to stop it. Not only is it not true, it's…damaging."

"Damaging?"

"Us."

That word again. That beautiful, wonderful, unattainable word. But was it unattainable? He swallowed, hard, and said, "That first day, when I first saw you and forgot to breathe, and then realized who you were… I don't think I've ever silently sworn so much in my life. Because I knew your father wouldn't want you with a cop. He'd said so."

"And now you're not one, so no problem."

He drew back slightly. She'd said it so lightly, like someone who'd had a major impediment removed. It had never once occurred to him that losing the career he'd worked for could have a bright side. He added that to the list of things he needed to think about, when he had time.

He belatedly became aware of something that had been going on for a while now, as they'd been talking; Cutter, making his guard duty rounds, circling the living room, pausing near the windows, then walking to the back door and pausing again, then going down the hallway to the bedrooms and office, but then coming back to watch them for a few minutes before starting again. This time Cutter just looked at them both, head tilted in a funny, quizzical way, looking decidedly self-satisfied.

"He really does look smug," Mandy said.

"Yes."

"Think it's that matchmaker thing Quinn talked about?"

"Yes."

She glanced at him then. He couldn't get another word out. She looked back at Cutter.

"A matchmaking guard dog." The dog sat and grinned at her. There was no other word for it. She turned back to look at him. And something in her gaze made him reach for her. She moved in the same moment he did, sliding her arms around him in a fierce hug. "Did he succeed?"

He knew what she meant. Knew what he had to, if not forget, at least let go of for this to work. But it would be like excising the last five years out of his life, and he wasn't sure he could do it. Wasn't sure he could overcome that swamping sense of guilt that buried him every time he thought of her father. He would have thought knowing she no longer blamed him would have done it, but he was beginning to realize that the real barrier was him blaming himself.

Cutter got to his feet again and began the same circuit. And that brought Adam back to the immediate reality, which had to take precedence over a potential future. A future he was afraid to even hope for.

"Let's get through this first," he said, watching the dog listening at the back door.

"All right." His brow furrowed as she agreed easily. Too easily. And the moment she spoke again he knew he'd been right. "As long as we take advantage of this bit of peace we should have until tonight."

That quickly his breath slammed out of him. It took all of his nerve to turn and look at her. When he did, the way she was looking at him made him wonder if he would ever breathe normally again. Because there was such heat in her gaze, such softness in her mouth as she looked back at him, lips parted, that he couldn't seem to remember how.

And then she bit her lower lip, in the exact spot where he had lightly nipped her during that first sweet night. As if she was remembering. As if she was wanting it again. Fire rocketed through him, and his body responded so swiftly and fiercely it nearly put him on his knees.

"Can we forget about it, just for a few minutes?" she asked in a whisper that was so husky, so wanting that it blasted all his hesitation to bits.

"A few minutes," he said, his own voice nearly hoarse, "isn't going to be nearly enough."

Mandy was fairly certain she had screamed this time. She was certain she'd clawed at him as her body had clenched so fiercely she simply had to pull him as close as she could get him. She knew, somewhere down deep, that she would never, ever get enough of the feel of him, driving into her, stroking her to that incredible explosion unlike anything she'd ever felt. Only with him had she become fully aware of the glory of this, and it made her shiver inside to think of how close she'd come to never knowing.

She drew in a deep breath before saying, slowly, "Sometimes I wonder if I might have…let go of my anger sooner if I hadn't chosen to do what I do."

Adam propped himself up on one elbow to look at her. He had slid to her right side after collapsing atop her—with a shout of her name that seemed ripped from deep within him and made her own pleasure peak again—so it was his left elbow. The one that worked properly. She didn't look at the other, now resting against his rib cage. She didn't need to. That road map of scars, many of them the straighter lines of surgery amid the twisting ones of the original injury, was all too emblazoned in her memory.

"I thought…you liked your work."

"I do," she said. "And it's…necessary, sadly. It's hard enough to wend your way through the system without trying to do it when your world has been shattered. People need somebody who knows the way it works."

"Obviously, Foxworth agrees."

"I wouldn't have been able to do this without their help and funding," she said. "But still, it's hard to be in the middle of it all the time, and remembering why…" She let out a long sigh. "Maybe I should have taken that job Ms. Harris offered me."

Adam's brow furrowed. "What?"

"She offered me a job on her staff, after it happened."

"Katrina Harris?" he asked. "On the city council?"

"Is there another one by that name?" she said teasingly.

"But…why?" She raised an eyebrow at him. He shook his head. "I mean I know how smart you are, and that you'd be a great addition anywhere, you're so good with people, but—"

She cut him off with a laugh. "You don't need to flatter me."

"I wasn't."

She leaned over and kissed him for that. And that led to a need she didn't even try to deny, to run her hands over him, feeling the taut muscle, the lean lines of him. She was suddenly swamped with the need to give him a kind of pleasure she thought he'd probably had little of in his life lately, a pleasure where he was the focus and the reason. And so she followed the paths she'd traced with her hands with her lips, her mouth, kissing, licking, tasting. And when she paused near that part of him that had responded most visibly, she felt him go very still. He would never push her, probably never even ask her, so she knew it was up to her. She delayed just a bit longer, so that when she finally moved to take him in her mouth a harsh groan of her name ripped out of his throat.

And she knew how deeply she'd come to feel about him when giving him pleasure gave her a joy that went down to the bone.

When this was over, they would… She wasn't sure what they would do, only that she didn't want to be without him. She'd wasted enough time already in her blindness. And who knew better than she that tomorrow wasn't guaranteed? And she wanted tomorrow. She wanted a whole string of tomorrows.

With Adam.

Chapter 34

It was much later when, lying in her bed in the fading light of day, that he brought up what they'd been talking about again. Mandy was snuggled against him, more determined than ever that no matter what happened, they would not lose what they'd found together.

Of course, she had no idea—yet—if he felt the same.

"The councilwoman," he said slowly, "did she say why she offered you a position on her staff?"

"I assumed she was trying to be kind after Dad's death, uncharacteristic as that seemed."

"Very uncharacteristic. I remember her, and she's never been particularly helpful to law enforcement. The opposite, in fact."

"I know. That's why I was so surprised I didn't know what to say, at first. Dad used to have some choice words about her."

"But she still offered you a job."

"Which I turned down, obviously. I was never even tempted, although the salary was rather astounding. I had no idea a staff position paid that much. Made me wonder if people had any idea."

"It would take more than money, for you."

She was pleased by his words. "And it would have been a betrayal of my father to go to work for the opposition, as it were."

"Yes."

She waited, but he didn't say anything more. She studied him, watched those stormy gray eyes, but his focus was clearly inward. He was thinking, turning something over in his mind.

"Adam?" she finally asked.

"I just… It's just strange. I mean she's the one who wanted cops punished or fired for any use of force, even if justified."

"Maybe that's why," she said, sourly now. "Dad didn't actually use force, Quinn did." When something flickered in his eyes she held up a hand. "Don't even," she warned, afraid he was going to slide back into that morass of guilt.

"Actually, I wasn't going to. It's just really strange that she would do that, unless…"

Belatedly, far too belatedly, it hit her. She jolted upright in bed, heedless of her nudity, and stared down at him.

"Unless she had reason to want to…keep me close?"

He let out an audible breath and nodded. "And maybe…maybe that wasn't the normal staff salary."

She scrambled out of bed and started yanking on her clothes. "Come on, cowboy. We've got work to do."

"It's a good thing her meetings are a matter of public record." Mandy was hunched over her laptop as she made a list of dates from the city councilwoman's calendar.

"If they weren't, I have a feeling Foxworth could probably find out anyway," Adam said, feeling that buzz he'd always felt when they'd been closing in on a suspect. This was far too tenuous to say that now, but the feeling was there nevertheless.

"Probably," she agreed. "But I want them to have solid reason to look."

"Agreed," Adam said.

It was a strange feeling, to be back on the law enforcement websites he had once frequented regularly. There were a lot of screen names on the comment boards and forums he didn't recognize, but many he did, and several he knew wore the same shoulder patch he once had.

The search of their quarry's name yielded the usual public gripes and complaints, which hadn't changed much since he'd been among them.

"None of this is news," he muttered. "We all knew she hated us."

"That bad?" she asked, straightening up and looking up from her screen for the first time in a while.

"Worse. But there's nothing new here, just the same complaints about her I remember from before."

"That's a public forum, isn't it?" she asked, leaning over to look.

"Yes. So I'm guessing any serious or specific complaining goes on privately, in email or on a locked, monitored site." She gave him a curious look and he gestured at the screen, glad now he'd brought the small laptop with him at the last minute. "There are some mentions that she or someone on her staff—" he gave her a sideways glance and she grimaced "—found this site and started monitoring the complaints. Because all of a sudden some of the most vocal people were being disciplined on the job for some very petty things. Shoes not shined enough, crooked name tags and the like."

Mandy's brow furrowed. "But…wouldn't that mean someone on the department, someone with juice, was helping her?"

"Not standing up to her, at least."

"What kind of cop could ever…agree with her?"

"A politically minded one, maybe."

She made a face that reminded him so much of her father that he felt a little jolt. And the question that had been swirling in his mind slapped at him. How would Greg feel, if he knew about them? He remembered the day when, after about six months of partnering, he'd managed to de-escalate a domestic situation that was on the verge of becoming very ugly. Sitting in their patrol car afterward, Greg had gruffly approved, in his inimitable way.

You'll do, Kirk. You'll do.

From Greg Bonner, that was tantamount to a medal, and Adam had never been prouder than he was at that moment, to have earned this man's approval, his respect. Even if he did tease him that if he ever made captain he'd be Captain Kirk, and then laugh at his own pop-culture joke.

But that had been on the job. Mandy was his daughter. His treasured, much beloved pride and joy. That was a very different kettle of clams, as Greg had been wont to say.

He went back to the forums. Made himself focus on the details, not emotions, and made notes as he went. There were mentions of meetings and odd decisions that had amazed the rank and file, and not in a good way. Come down hard on this group or business, cut this one some slack. This person was to be watched, this person given great latitude. Beyond some hints, no one on the public boards had put it all together and theorized, or if they had it had been deleted, perhaps taken private.

"Let's compare all this," Mandy said. "Do you have Dad's file?"

He nodded and called it up. Stared at that annoying "Pix" again. He tried to think of some way that name could stand for Katrina Harris, but couldn't.

"Let's start with his earliest entry. Read it off to me and I'll check it against what I have."

They started, and while there was some overlap, it was far from conclusive. It took them some time to get through her whole list.

"Nothing you wouldn't expect," Adam said, leaning back in his chair. "Typical politician schedule of meetings with locals. And only a couple match with dates Greg listed."

Mandy sighed. "Well, this is her public schedule. Who knows what she was doing in private or after hours."

"Still more meetings, nearly 24/7 if you ask her ex," Adam said.

"Her ex?"

He nodded. "Your dad and I ran into him once, at court, after we'd testified on a case. He's a lawyer. Anyway, he said she was always going out at odd hours to meet with someone."

"Cheating on him?"

Adam gave her a wry smile. "Not something he'd tell us. He was only a little more pleasant to us than she would have been. We just overheard him saying that to someone else."

"I wonder where she was going all the time?"

"Who knows? Meetings of the Heterochromia Society, maybe."

She blinked. "The what?"

"Sorry, bad joke."

"Heterochromia… Isn't that when people have two different colored eyes?"

He nodded. "She's got one brown one, one hazel. It's only obvious up close. Where we sadly were a couple of times, when she came to the department to chew us out."

She was staring at him now, her eyes wide. He had no idea what he'd said that had caused the stunned reaction.

"Mandy?"

"Dad had a dog, when he was a kid."

Adam blinked. That was such a non sequitur he had no idea what to think. Or say, so he said nothing, just waited.

"A husky," she said. "She had one brown eye and one blue eye."

His brow furrowed. "That's…not that unusual with them, is it?"

"No," she said, but her eyes were still wide, and he noticed her breathing had quickened. "But, Adam…"

"What?" he asked, starting to feel concerned.

Finally, she focused on him. Swallowed visibly. And then, her voice taut, she answered him. "Her name was Pixie."

She couldn't seem to go on. But she didn't have to. He finished it for her.

"Pix," he breathed.

They had it.

Chapter 35

Quinn watched silently as they laid it all out on the meeting table on the third floor of Foxworth. They'd spent a couple of hours translating her father's secret file into calendar pages, combining the public records— including votes on various projects and proposals— with the damning information her father had gathered in nearly a year of work. Then they'd printed it so it could all be seen at once and brought it to Foxworth. It took up nearly the entire large table.

"He knew he'd have to have his ducks in a row," Adam said as Quinn stood looking at the compiled data. "There's a faction in that city who would defend her practically to the death."

"Because she sacrificed everyone else in the city to their wishes," Quinn said with a grimace.

"Speaking of ducks in a row, this is way out of my league," Mandy said warily.

"But not," Quinn said mildly, "out of ours."

She and Adam exchanged a glance as Quinn took out his phone and made two consecutive—and very short—calls. Apparently, when Quinn Foxworth called, there weren't a lot of questions asked. Nor was he required to identify himself. If this man had you on his speed dial, you knew his voice.

"We need to send all of this to Ty," he said. "He'll access whatever camera footage there might be to confirm her presence in any of these instances. We only need one to get things started."

"Uh..." Adam began hesitantly.

Quinn smiled at him. "I know, getting it that way won't do for court, but one instance, plus the presence of a friend of ours, should be enough to get the official parties looking for the rest. We'll let them worry about the legalities of evidence. We just want this over and Amanda safe."

"Amen."

Adam said it rather fervently, and Mandy couldn't help feeling a twinge that he wanted this over with as soon as possible. So he could go home? Even as she thought it she knew how silly it was; people were trying to kill her and she was worried about how he meant wanting this over with? Whether he would vanish back over the mountains to his beloved Palouse...leaving her behind?

Self-centered much? This is more important. You know it is.

It was a surprisingly short time later that Cutter announced someone's arrival with a bark. Then he headed downstairs toward the door. Since they knew Ty was at Foxworth headquarters in St. Louis, this was obviously the other person he'd called.

"That'll be Gavin," Quinn said, but he didn't follow the dog. At their exchanged glances, Quinn smiled. "Cutter'll show him where we are."

"At this point, if you told me he'd open the door for him I'd believe it," Mandy said, managing a smile.

"He could, if necessary. And if he deemed it appropriate for the new arrival to be allowed in."

Adam laughed, but quickly added, "And I believe that. I've watched him working for a couple of weeks now. If you told me he could fly, I'd only wonder how, not if."

Mandy's smile steadied at that, and Adam gave her a look that made her earlier worry seem foolish. Because no man who looked at a woman like that could be in a hurry to get away from her. But this wasn't his home. Not anymore. His home was that ranch, which she'd never even seen.

Or been invited to see.

Her self-pitying thoughts ended when the new arrival stepped into the room, Cutter beside him. He was a very striking man, and after she caught her breath Mandy's brow furrowed. He seemed familiar somehow, although she was sure she'd never met him before. Those dark eyes that did nothing to mask a razor-sharp intelligence behind them, that casual grace, the way a couple of strands of dark hair kicked forward over his forehead, that immense presence, were not something she would have forgotten.

"Adam, Amanda, this is that friend I mentioned who can more than take this on. Meet the Foxworth consulting attorney, Gavin de Marco."

She gaped at the man, while Adam let out a long low whistle. "No wonder you seemed familiar," Mandy said as he greeted them both. How could he not be, when not so long ago he was a front-page name at practically every news outlet in the known world?

"I was in the academy when the Keppler trial was

going on," Adam said as they shook hands. "We were glued to it. Afterward they used your summation as training, to show us why we had to be exacting about probable cause and evidence protocol. Because it would have to stand up to people like you."

"Somehow I think they probably used a stronger description of me," the man said with an easy smile.

Adam grinned at him. "Yeah. Unrepeatable in polite company." Then, more seriously, he said, "Always wondered why you dropped out."

She had wondered as well, when the household name had vanished from public view.

"Let's just say I saw the light," Gavin said. Then he looked at Mandy, and with an amazing gentleness for the firebrand she knew he had been, he said, "And I saw too many cases like your father's, good, brave men cut down. I'm sorry you—and we—lost him."

He'd lost none of his eloquence, or his knack of projecting an empathy that had had juries eating out of his hand. Her eyes stung a little as she thanked him, because unlike many who said they were sorry because they didn't know what else to say, she sensed on a deep level that this man meant it.

"So now he's on the side of the angels," Quinn said, with a crooked smile at the man.

"A motley crew though they are," Gavin agreed, smiling as he reached down to Cutter, to scratch that favored spot behind his right ear. Then, straightening, he asked briskly, "What do we have?"

Quinn summed it up concisely, and Gavin turned to look at what was spread out on the table. "Some interesting names here."

Adam nodded. "Some weren't surprising. These days

you half expect the clandestine meetings with interest groups buying influence."

Quinn nodded at that. "The proverbial pay to play."

"It's the others," Mandy said. Adam had told her he'd known some of those names, of even more unsavory characters, from other investigations and wanted bulletins.

"These two," Adam said, pointing to two dates a couple of months apart. "From Greg's file, he saw those meetings himself."

"Right before…" Mandy began, but couldn't make herself finish.

"Exactly," Adam said grimly. "And I know both of them have felony records, with more that couldn't be proved. Including murder."

"So," an unruffled Gavin said with a glance at Mandy, "she knew your father had been onto her, and the job offer was to keep an eye on you, make sure you didn't know what your father had found out?"

He'd gotten there so quickly Mandy felt a little burst of relief. If someone the likes of Gavin de Marco immediately saw it, they had to be right. She'd known in her gut they were, but validation on that level made it seem more solid.

"And when Amanda called a couple of her father's friends still at the department for help translating his secret file, it got back to her," Quinn said.

"So she has someone on the force," Gavin mused aloud. Adam let out a compressed, disgusted breath. The attorney looked at him. "Feels like a betrayal, doesn't it."

It wasn't a question, but Adam nodded.

"So then she decides I need to be dealt with," Mandy said slowly. Slowly, because even as she knew it was true, it seemed impossible.

"On a permanent basis," Quinn said grimly.

"But…why would she risk it? I mean, I get that it's a big deal, being on the council of a big city, and she wouldn't want to lose that, but all this—" Mandy waved at the spread of documentation "—seems a bit extreme."

"Not if the city council is just the first step of your plan," Gavin said. "She may well have much bigger things in her sights."

"And will do whatever it takes to get there?" Adam asked.

Quinn nodded, his expression severe.

"But…committing murder seems a bit extreme," Mandy said.

"That's because," Gavin said, looking up and giving her a slight smile, "you don't have the kind of need for power that drives people to things like this. To the kind of person she clearly is, nothing's too extreme."

Mandy heard a small sound from where Adam was standing. He'd been leaning over the pages, his left hand bracing him against the table, his less functional right arm at his side. Only now that hand was clenched, into a fist so tight his knuckles were white. And when she looked at his face, it was nearly as white.

"Adam?" she said, suddenly concerned.

"And it's easier," he said, his voice barely above a whisper, "if you've done it before."

Mandy frowned. Noticed Gavin was giving Adam a look that was both approving and grim at the same time.

"What are you—"

She broke off as it hit her, what should have been obvious. A chill rippled down her spine, then spread, until she was amazed she wasn't shivering. Her mind shot back to that awful time. Remembering it had always been awful, but now, in this moment, it was horrific. Because the knot in her stomach, the tightening of every muscle including her heart, told her it was true.

It hadn't been a random shot, or even a robber caught in the act shooting a cop to escape that had shattered her world that night.

It had been a hit.

Chapter 36

Adam wasn't really aware of how long it had been. He was aware that Quinn was making calls, and Quinn and Gavin—Gavin freaking de Marco!—had spent some time on a video conference with Ty Hewitt in St. Louis. Then Gavin started making calls, and if Adam had been paying attention, if he'd even been able to pay attention, he would have been certain, but as it was he was fairly sure he heard the governor's name dropped somewhere amid the discussion.

The governor who had taken over after Foxworth had taken down the previous one.

When he found himself seizing on the age-old question of whether there were more than a handful of decent, honest politicians, or if the word *politician* and anything good were oxymorons, he knew he was out of control.

In fact, the only thing anchoring him at all was the feel of Mandy at his side, her feet curled up on the couch in the Foxworth downstairs room, her head resting on his shoulder. Her warmth was the only thing that countered the ice that wanted to take over. And only knowing she had to be feeling even worse than he did kept him from… He wasn't sure what he'd be doing, but something stupid and useless like throwing things or screaming.

It had never been a secret that the store was in Greg Bonner's beat, not the way Greg had been a cop, knowing his community, and them knowing they could turn to him.

Which explained why the guy had been in that unexpected place where he couldn't really be a lookout. Because the robbery hadn't been his goal.

Murder had been.

A hit. An assassination.

It played over and over in his head, interspersed with the too vivid memories of that night, until he was reeling internally. But he tried to focus on Mandy; it was she who mattered, she who he had to protect, as he hadn't protected her father.

When the initial shock had hit, the tears had won out and she'd simply stood there with them streaming down her cheeks. It had jolted him out of his own sickening feeling enough to go to her and pull her into his arms. But the tears had given way to a fierce anger that echoed his own.

Her father, the one man he'd admired and respected above all other men except his own father, had been assassinated. Cold-bloodedly and with evil calculation, by a person who valued personal power above all else. It didn't even matter to him what she would use that power for, although he had a pretty good idea what her aims were. Nothing mattered beyond the simple fact that she'd killed a good and honorable man because he'd discovered the truth about her. He didn't care that she hadn't pulled the trigger herself; the man sitting in prison had only been her proxy.

A loyal proxy, if he hasn't talked in all this time. I wonder what she had to pay him? Or his family, maybe?

Cutter, who had been stationed at—or rather on—their feet, as if he wanted to make sure they didn't leave, was suddenly on his feet. As had become habit, Adam looked at the dog to assess, saw the wagging tail and knew whoever was incoming was welcome. A short, sharp, two-part bark told him who had arrived.

"Liam," he said quietly. Mandy managed a faint smile.

"I come with sustenance," the young Texan called out as he came in, and even in this weird state Adam couldn't miss the scent of hot, fresh pizza.

"Excellent," Quinn said. "I'll distribute, you grab yours and hit that scary computer station you and Ty put together upstairs. We need to know more about Malachi, and why he's willing to sit in prison for the rest of his life without rolling over on who paid him. And how he was paid, while you're at it."

"Got it, boss."

"You two," Quinn said, shifting his gaze to them, and speaking in a voice of command. "Eat. I know you won't taste it and it's the last thing you feel like doing but we need you functional, and for that you need fuel."

"He's right," Adam said to Mandy.

"I know."

"And," Quinn added with a knowing look, "let loose some of that anger. It'll keep you going as much as the food."

"That it will," Adam said, feeling the roiling fire of it inside, and stifled the instinct to quash it.

They'd each managed a couple of slices when Gavin came back downstairs. "Governor's read in. He'll stay out of it, of course, unless he can't. It's the city's mess to clean up."

Adam blinked. Even knowing who this man was, and his reputation, he was still a little jarred by the fact that he could simply put in a call to the governor and get put through immediately. He sat down across from them, grabbed a slice of pizza and took a bite as Quinn paced.

"What about the mayor?" Adam asked.

Quinn shook his head. "Too close. Can't be sure he didn't know."

He heard Mandy make a small sound. When he looked at her she just shook her head. "He came to Dad's funeral. I started to say he seemed sincere, but…"

"It's part of his job to seem sincere," Adam said sourly.

"Exactly."

"I'll need you both on a conference call as soon as Liam or Ty finds what we need."

He blinked. "Me?"

"To the chief."

Adam's eyes widened; Quinn didn't have to explain what chief. "Why? Me, I mean?"

Quinn held his gaze evenly. "I think you still underestimate your standing with the department."

"Hear, hear," Mandy said.

He looked at her, saw the warmth and support in her eyes. And dared to believe that she felt what he was feeling. Had felt—and suppressed—for years.

"I would imagine the chief is not going to be happy to find out the death of one of his top officers was murder with full intent," Quinn said flatly.

"And paid for by someone on the council of the city he serves? No, I don't think he'll take that well."

"Have I mentioned I'm starting to hate that place?" Mandy said, her voice a combination of anger and loathing that Adam thought would blister if it was aimed at you. Hell, he knew it would blister, because it had been aimed at him and he'd felt the fierceness of it all the way to the bone.

But no more. She didn't hate him anymore. That alone was worth everything they'd gone through since that harsh anniversary. To him anyway. He wasn't sure she'd rate it the same.

They sat in silence while the searching went on above them. Quinn finally sat down. "We'll find it," he said. He nodded upward. "Best way to guarantee it is to pit Liam and Ty against each other. They go the extra mile anyway, but head-to-head in an online search? It's…" He shook his head as if he had no words for it.

"Productive," Gavin said.

"It is that," Quinn agreed with a half smile, all that seemed warranted under the solemn circumstances.

"This is going to be big news," Gavin said, as if stating a given. But then, as the man at the top of more nationally and even internationally known cases not so long ago, he would know.

"Yes," Quinn agreed.

Gavin's gaze went from…his boss? Adam guessed so, although the idea of this man even having a boss seemed absurd. Then again, it was Quinn Foxworth, who had led men into combat. But he looked from Quinn to them, and said quietly, "You three are going to be the centerpieces when this breaks."

Adam could tell he was assessing them. The man clearly knew Quinn could handle whatever came his way, but he and Mandy were unknowns to him beyond the basics of the situation.

"I'll shield you as best I can," he went on, "if that's your wish. But it's going to be a bit rough."

Mandy's head came up. And she met and held the man's gaze. "You don't need to shield me. I've been through the worst, and now I know it wasn't just a by-product of a robbery gone bad. It was intentional. My father was murdered, and I'll do whatever it takes to see that…vermin taken down."

Adam looked at her as she spoke, saw the straightness of her spine, the set of her delicate jaw. And a warm feeling billowed through him: pride. Pride in her, for she was indeed her father's daughter.

"He would be proud," he said softly.

Mandy's head turned sharply and she met his look. For an instant, a small smile curved her mouth.

"Yes," she said, then adding very pointedly as she held his gaze, "he would be proud."

He knew what she meant. That Greg would be proud of him, too. He let himself bask in the thought, but even more that it was coming from her.

He wasn't sure how much time had passed—he was so busy processing all that had changed in the last few hours he'd lost track—but suddenly there was a triumphant shout from upstairs, followed closely by the clatter of Liam on the stairs.

"We got it!" He skipped the last four steps and jumped to the floor, his industrial-looking laptop in one hand. He handed it off to Quinn and gave an exultant look to Adam and Mandy. "This'll do it," he assured them.

"Digest version?" Gavin asked.

"It's buried under some shell corporations and other masks, but the bottom line is that Malachi's family is living in a fancy house in an expensive neighborhood—for Walla Walla anyway—and the rent is paid by a supposed charity group, founded and funded mostly by one of those shells within shells that tracks back to Katrina Harris. His mother also has a well-paying—too well-paying, when compared to the standard rate—job with that 'charity,' on paper at least. No indication she actually does anything there, since she's over there and it's in the city. And the topper is that they moved in during the trial."

"Proof to Malachi of Harris holding up her end of the deal," Gavin said softly.

"Exactly. And," Liam added, "the charity itself was funded the day after the shoot-out at the convenience store."

"Once the job was done," Adam said, his voice harsh even to his own ears.

"Exactly," Quinn agreed. He looked at Gavin. "Is it enough?"

"With you three coming at them? The orphaned child of a dead hero, and two more heroes? Enough to trigger a full investigation," Gavin said with stark satisfaction. "Because they'll know the alternative."

Which would likely be Gavin de Marco using the full power of his name and reputation to blast this to the world.

Quinn directed Liam to continue, and suggested they find out who had paid Malachi's lawyer, but that had been countered by Gavin, who said it would be better to leave the official investigation a few things to find, to make sure they were fully invested.

Mandy had lapsed into silence as they talked, but now she said in a voice that made Adam ache inside, "He never had a chance."

"No," Adam said grimly, "he didn't."

And then she turned, to look at him head-on. In a movement that startled him, she reached out to cup his cheek.

"And neither did you ever have a chance at stopping it."

It hit him like a pile driver to the gut. He hadn't taken that last step, seen that last bit of it, until she handed it to him.

He'd never had a chance to save him. Greg had been a target, and if he'd been right beside him it would have changed nothing. Even if he hadn't been shot, it would have made no difference. Even if they had changed roles, as he'd so often imagined, if Greg had been the one to head into the store, he still would have been the target and cut down before he ever got there.

For a minute he thought he was dizzy, because it felt as if his head was about to start spinning. Or the room. Which would make it vertigo. Which was a ridiculous thing to be thinking about…now. Now, when the last domino had finally fallen, and the truth was there in front of him.

Greg had never had a chance, and he had never had a chance of stopping it.

In that instant of understanding, the only thing anchoring him to this moment was Mandy's touch. He looked at her, saw tears glistening in her eyes. Or maybe they were his own tears, because she was a little blurry. Right now it didn't matter. Nothing mattered except that the burden had lifted. And he finally understood what he was feeling was lightness, the absence of the soul-crushing weight he had carried for five years.

And hope.

Chapter 37

They spent two days mostly at Foxworth in intensive research and planning and verifying, until even the man known worldwide for having those ducks in a row, Gavin de Marco, was satisfied they had what they needed. But he still insisted they wait another day. Mandy could sense Adam didn't like the idea, but he didn't say anything.

Gavin apparently sensed it, too. The man didn't miss much, which wasn't surprising. You didn't build the kind of reputation he had by not being able to read people. But when he explained why he wanted to wait until Thursday, it was clear Adam not only understood, but approved.

It was amazing how much lighter her world seemed. They went back to her place, to enjoy a day dropped out of time, it seemed. As if in appreciation it dawned bright and sunny, in that severe clear way that made living here worth all the clouds and rain the rest of the time. The mountains were out, all of them, from Rainier to Baker to the Brothers, and all of them wore a fresh coat of snow, so bright white it almost didn't look real.

But part of that lightness came from the change in Adam. She had seen the moment when he had finally realized there truly hadn't been anything he could have done that night to prevent what happened. And when he had looked at her, for the first time with open, pure hope in his eyes, her heart had soared.

He's going to be all right, Dad.

The moment she had the thought, she felt a burst of warmth that felt so much like approval that it had her wondering about messages from beyond.

They spent the gift of the day talking, sharing and, since Quinn had said he'd rather they didn't go for the long walk Mandy was itching for, not until this was over for good, they stayed close. He left Cutter with them for insurance, which said more than anything that he was not yet counting this over with. But it seemed a different Cutter, no longer the wary guardian but just a happy, silly dog who never ran out of energy to play. She had no doubt he could shift on a dime if necessary, but he had them both laughing so much it was sometimes hard to remember the fierce protector he could be.

And he seemed content to snooze in his chosen spot on the couch as she and Adam spent most of the afternoon after the clouds moved back in snuggled up together in bed, exploring and learning each other as if it were all new. It felt new, so freed did she--and obviously Adam— feel.

By the time a different kind of hunger drove them to the kitchen, she was so sure of the rightness of it, of them, that she knew with utter certainty what had to come next.

"Can you forgive me?" she asked over now empty

plates that had held piles of scrambled eggs with anything that sounded good added in.

"I never blamed you."

"You should have."

He shook his head. "No. I couldn't."

"Why? Because you so believed it was your fault?" She asked it quietly, knowing the answer would tell her a great deal, and hoping he wouldn't dodge it.

He didn't. It took him a moment, and a sip of the wine she'd poured—wine and eggs didn't even seem odd in the crazy world she'd been in the past two weeks—but he answered.

"Not just that, but…because this," he said with a nod at her, "was always there, from the first time I ever saw you."

Joy burst through her. "Yes. It was. I truly believe now that half the reason I was so angry was because I…had hopes from the moment I laid eyes on you."

He reached across the table, put a hand over hers. She turned hers in his grasp and entwined their fingers. "Can we…build on this, Mandy?"

"We can't just build," she said, letting everything show in her eyes, "we can build something glorious."

He smiled, although it looked a little embarrassed at her word choice. "I'll settle for strong and solid."

"No. You don't settle. And no blaming yourself. Not anymore. Ever." His smile was genuine then. "And when you're ready," she added, reaching up to lay a hand on his arm below his right elbow, "we'll take care of this."

He looked startled at first, but after a silent moment he drew in a deep breath and nodded. "It still may not be normal," he said cautiously.

"But we'll know we did all we could. Which is what all of this has been about, isn't it?" Another deep breath, and she realized that while she was feeling lighter than she had in five years, he was feeling decidedly off balance. "Amazing how much guilt weighs, isn't it?"

When he laughed at that she felt a renewed burst of pleasure, and vowed she would see to that as well, that Adam Kirk did a lot of laughing from here on out.

Adam could hear Gavin clearly, and realized the man had intentionally left the door to the office open a fraction.

"It's a great pleasure to meet someone of your standing, Mr. de Marco," came the unctuous voice of Councilwoman Harris.

"I'm sure," Gavin said, his tone so dry Harris had to have realized it.

"I must admit I'm curious why you wanted to see me," she said, clearly having decided to ignore the way he'd said it.

"I've heard that you make things happen in this city."

Adam could practically see the woman preening. "Why, yes. I'm very proud of what I've accomplished."

"Are you?"

"Of course."

"Nothing you're not proud of?"

There was a moment's pause, as if she were hesitating to answer. *As well you should.*

"I'm not sure what you mean," she finally said, and there was an undertone in her voice that Adam knew was wariness. "Just why are you here, Mr. de Marco?"

"I'm here about something you made happen, Ms. Harris," he said, and this time his voice had the snap of a whip. It was also their cue.

Quinn stepped in first. Adam was right behind him, so he saw the woman's brow furrow. Then her gaze shifted to him, and her eyes widened slightly. As planned, he and Quinn moved shoulder to shoulder, masking Mandy until they were in front of the woman, who had clearly stepped around her desk to greet her famous guest.

And then they each stepped sideways, revealing Mandy, who stared at the woman coldly. Katrina Harris went pale.

"What is this?" she asked, a tremor in her voice.

"You know what it is," Gavin said coldly. "It's over, Madam Councilwoman. Kiss your office and your reputation goodbye, because your goose, as they say, is cooked."

"I don't know what you think—"

"What I think," Mandy said, her voice even icier than her expression, "is that you are finally going to pay for what you did. My father was a brave, honorable man, and you aren't fit to even speak his name."

"You were right about one thing," Adam said, letting every bit of the anger he was feeling over what had been done to Greg and the five years he himself had lived in hell echo in his voice. "He had you. Dead to rights."

"And we are here," Quinn said, with as much command presence as Adam had ever seen, "to finish what he started."

"Get out," she blustered. But there was fear in her eyes.

"We'll do that, if you really want that," Gavin said with deadly calm. "But it means we'll be back tonight, with the chief of police himself, who is more than ready to cart you off in cuffs personally. In fact, he expressed a decided preference for dragging you out of the council meeting tonight, on camera, with the media in full attendance. It took some convincing to allow it to happen here and now."

She went even paler as Gavin's reason for waiting until now became clear. "He wouldn't dare—"

"Oh, but he would," Quinn said. "He's on his way right now. You're responsible for the death of one of his finest, attempts to murder that man's daughter and the forced retirement of a man who would have become the same kind of officer."

Adam felt a shot of warmth beneath the cold anger. There was still a novelty to it, allowing himself to hear and believe the praise.

"And by the way," Gavin added, "he'll also be dealing with Captain Manning."

The woman's eyes widened as he mentioned the man they were fairly certain had been the one to pass along the word of Mandy's inquiries. *Gotcha.*

"You can't prove anything," Harris said stubbornly.

"The last gambit of the guilty," Adam said coldly.

"Indeed," Gavin said, but his eyes never left the quarry. "Tell me, Katrina," he said, using her first name rather derisively now, pounding home the point that her title was gone, "have you ever heard of an instance where I went into court without everything I needed to prove my case? I can answer that for you. You have not."

The door behind them was pulled open. A man in uniform with four stars on his collar stood there.

"Normally I'd knock, but some people don't deserve the courtesy," the chief said.

Adam never took his eyes off the councilwoman. Saw the moment of realization dawn. Savored it. He glanced at Mandy, who was also watching the woman who had destroyed her life. Saw the same feeling of satisfaction in her expression.

It was over.

Chapter 38

"That's Foxworth," Liam said cheerfully. "Fighting corruption one crooked politician at a time."

"Not," Quinn said dryly, "what the intention was."

"When you fight evil, you have to go where it is," Adam said.

Quinn turned to look at them. Mandy was holding on to Adam's arm, and feeling better than she had ever thought she would feel again in her life. Cutter sat at their feet, looking up at them with that expression she could only describe as smug.

"Yeah," Hayley, who had arrived back this morning, said to the dog, "you did it."

"Again," muttered Quinn, but his mouth was quirked upward.

Hayley straightened from scratching the dog's favored spot and looked at them both.

"They're saying it's going to start snowing in the

passes again Saturday night. You two will have to beat it to get home in time for Christmas."

Adam blinked. Swallowed visibly. "I…haven't worked up to asking her that yet."

"Ask," Mandy said.

He looked at her. Took a breath. "Will you?"

"Of course. I think it's time I met your parents, don't you?" He looked so relieved she couldn't help smiling.

"Yes. Yes, it is."

"We'll need you back here when the trial starts," Quinn reminded them.

"We know," Adam said. He looked at Mandy as he added, "We'll see it through."

"Together," she said. "And then we put this behind us for good."

"You're sure?" Adam asked as he watched Mandy zip up her suitcase. "Hayley kind of put you on the spot there."

"Of course I'm sure."

"I…don't have much to offer you. It's a quiet life, where nature's the only enemy."

"Sounds like heaven to me." Finished with the case she turned to face him. "I'm going exactly where I want to. I want to learn this place that holds such a large piece of your heart."

"Not so much anymore," he said, and kissed her. "I love you, Mandy."

"And I'm going because I love you," she repeated. "And I'll stay, because that place is home for you."

A future he'd never dared think about, let alone hope for, rolled out in his mind. He still couldn't quite believe it, and said what he thought he had to.

"But this is home for you. Your father's house."

"Not anymore." She met his gaze. "Believe me, he'd understand."

He sucked in a deep breath. "I hope so."

"Besides, I have to go where you go. Otherwise I'll be alone forever, because no one else could measure up to you."

His heart might just have burst at that, had he not already given it to her. He kissed her again, because he had to. And if they hadn't had to beat that weather, it would have gone a lot further, so quick was the heat to spark.

Still, when they were on the road he took a detour. When Mandy realized where they were headed, she reached out and took his hand.

"Do you mind?" he asked quietly.

"It's exactly what I wanted," she said, just as quietly. "I just wasn't sure you would."

"I want to…tell him. I know that sounds—"

"Perfect. Just perfect."

The cemetery was quiet, mostly deserted. They made the trek together, in silent respect for those who lay there. And when they stood by that stone once more, his throat was so tight he didn't think he could speak.

But Greg Bonner's daughter could.

"We did it, Dad," she whispered. "We finished it. And found each other. Please be at peace."

"I wish I could…ask him. For you, I mean," Adam managed to say. He smiled a little tightly. "Although I can imagine what he'd say."

Mandy went still, an odd look on her face, and she lifted her gaze from her father's gravestone to his face. "You don't have to imagine," she said. "He told me."

Adam blinked. "What?"

"Back when I asked him how the first week with his new partner had gone. He said 'He's a good, solid young man, the kind any father would be proud of. The kind any father of a daughter would be glad to have her bring home.'"

For a moment Adam couldn't breathe. "He...said that?"

"He did. So you see, in a way, he already gave us his blessing."

He had no words for what he was feeling. He could only grab Mandy and hold on, making a silent vow to her father that he would never betray the faith that had inspired those words.

I'll see to her, sir. I swear it to you.

It was when they were back in his truck, and the Cascade Mountains looming ahead of them, that she said, "Do you think we could find a dog like Cutter?"

He laughed. "Are you sure you've got that much energy?"

"Good point," she said.

"We'll just have to come back and visit him. But we'll find you a good horse, if you want."

"Now that I would like. I've always wanted to learn. And I want to see those places you love."

"Consider it done, then."

"Good," she said. And reached out once more to take his hand, careful not to pull it farther than it could go. "Then let's go."

To a new life.

He squeezed her hand, and they headed for home.

* * * * *

**WE HOPE YOU ENJOYED
THIS BOOK FROM**

**HARLEQUIN
ROMANTIC
SUSPENSE**

Danger. Passion. Drama.

These heart-racing page-turners will keep you guessing to the very end. Experience the thrill of unexpected plot twists and irresistible chemistry.

4 NEW BOOKS AVAILABLE EVERY MONTH!

#2091 HUNTING THE COLTON FUGITIVE
The Coltons of Mustang Valley
by Colleen Thompson

Sparks—and bullets—fly when Sierra Madden, a bounty hunter with loan sharks on her tail, and framed fugitive Ace Colton team up to find out who really shot his father. The Colton family holds tremendous power, which puts them in mortal danger...

#2092 COLTON'S LAST STAND
The Coltons of Mustang Valley • by Karen Whiddon

FBI agent Fiona Evans has been sent undercover to investigate a cult. When the cult leader's supposed son, rancher Jake Anderson, appears on the scene, they both have a hard time focusing on stopping his mother's machinations as their attraction burns brighter.

#2093 DANGEROUS REUNION
by Marilyn Pappano

A family goes missing, throwing Cedar Creek in turmoil. Former ADA Yashi Baker destroyed Detective Ben Little Bear and their relationship with one cross-examination on the witness stand years ago. But the kidnapping draws them together, forcing them to revisit a love lost.

#2094 SHIELDED IN THE SHADOWS
Where Secrets are Safe • by Tara Taylor Quinn

A probation officer and a prosecutor team up to protect a woman in danger from an unknown abuser. As they work through a treacherous case, love never enters the equation... until their attraction becomes too hard—and lethal—to ignore.

HRSCNM0520